'This story gives the reader a fascinating in
history. It has clearly been well-researched
and encompassing knowledge of and love for his subject.'

Mark Ezra - *Film writer, director (Savage Hearts, 1995),*
producer (Waking Ned, 1998), actor and children's author.

'This is a pleasing blend of fact and fiction, set many hundreds of years
ago in a rarely written-about period of history. The reader journeys with
a wide range of fascinating characters, who pause to share their own
personal stories and to reflect, discuss and consider subjects of deep
importance to them, as they travel together through this fast-moving
and absorbing wider story.'

Susan Hardwick - *Author of 'How to Be a Great Godparent'*
and other titles.

'This is a vivid and well-constructed tale, a pacey blend of history and
invention. The author holds the reins lightly with no trace of self-
importance, treating weighty matters with seriousness and humour.
I loved the pace... the way the characters become vivid, in sometimes
humorous ways - Denua's pinpoint accuracy with the bow, the delight
in 'Greek fire', the matches between players which feel like Austen, a
Shakespearean comedy or Sheridan. The 'blind' brother, the veritable
circus of unusual abilities that are finally exploited en masse, and
Deogol whose sentence construction gives Yoda a run for his money!

It does some subtle things very well, in just a few paragraphs.
Denua's love for her two husbands is well handled. The pain of
bereavement, and pragmatism about that and the sense of exile/ new
home. The over-egging of the warm baths, the coincidences and
disguises. The shifting of alliances, betrayals, wise counsel.

The bonds of community [and faith] - the leader surrounded by a
rising body-count of living believers is funny but utterly convincing. The
elements of farce, and sudden ring of truth. The time spent in telling

stories is true to life, but a great literary device. I'm impressed. I love the gradual change-over of names, and the weight of prophecy. Patrick is hilarious! There's an amazing sentence about the way stories build up around him which is perhaps my favourite in the book. Well done.'

Andy Raine - *Holy Island, Author of "Celtic Illustrations."*

DENUA

WARRIOR QUEEN

Philip Gregge

PHILIP GREGGE

Copyright © 2021 Philip Gregge

First published in Great Britain in 2021

10 9 8 7 6 5 4 3 2 1

British Library Cataloging in Publication Data.
A record of this book is available from the British Library.

ISBN 978-1-9996397-0-9

Printed and bound in Great Britain
Published by Seabridge Publishing

All paper used is certified by PEFC
(Programme for the Endorsement of Forest Certification Schemes)
and FSC® (Forest Stewardship Council®).

Initial cover design by Anji Gregge

Cartography by Dr Alison Farnell

Branding, design, print and publishing support by Simplicate (www.simplicate.org)
The Simplicate logo is a trademark of Simplicate Ltd.

To contact the author regarding book-related events,
please email: phil@philgregg.com

For more information, visit philipgregge.com

Dedicated to

My wife, Anji, for unfailing support and belief.

All my friends who read the early versions and
gave me great feedback.

My back surgeon, after whose general anaesthetic I awoke
with my brain reset and a germ of a plot in my head.

El Elyon, the Ever Faithful One, for constant,
gentle inspiration.

Information

Please don't try to study the contents of this first part; I have put this information here for you to turn back to as you read.

The names in **bold** are historical figures. Other names reflect actual names in each culture at the time.

Name listing is in the following format:

> Name,
> (Pr.) Pronunciation hint if needed,
> (*m*) Male, (*f*) Female -
> Meaning (if any),
> Character details,
> Relations (if any).
> Name Origin:
>> AS - Anglo-Saxon (Ingwi-Seaxe)
>> B - British
>> Bg - Burgundian
>> F - Frankish
>> G - Gaulish
>> R - Roman

'=' signifies that the following name has been simplified for readability.
Note: Many of the 'k' sounds were actually like guttural 'ch', as in loch. These are indicated using 'kh' in the pronunciation hints.
Please see notes in the Appendix for more detail.

Names

Aegid (Pr. Ee-jid) (*m*) =**Aegidius** - *Retired Roman officer, living in Frankish lands*, R

Aia (*f*) [*A feminine name on an inscription; (m) would be Aios*] - *Daughter of Rodor*, B

Annis (*f*) - *Unity, sister of Claennis*, AS

Ardith (*f*) - *Good war, high-born Angle, sister of Beorn, physician*, AS

Aredius (*m*) - *Advisor of Gisel*, R

Aurelian (*m*) - *Roman pseudonym adopted by* **Clovis** *for* **Clotilde's** *rescue mission*, R

Basina (*f*) - *Wife of* **Childric**, *mother of* **Clovis**, F

Beorn (*m*) - *Warrior, high-born Angle, husband/cousin of Cwen, brother of Ardith, father of Claennis*, AS

Brecc (*m*) - *King's name, first son of Lufian and Claennis, AS*

Brennos (*m*) - *Raven, plausible thief, R*

Bricius (Pr. Bris-ius) (*m*) - *King of the Parisii in Lutetia, first husband of Denua, G*

Cadman (*m*) - *Warrior, Chief guard of **Wyrtgeorn**, B*

Caratena (Pr. Car-a-ten-a) (*f*) - *Wife of **Chilperic**, mother of **Clotilde**, R*

Caric =**Chararic** (Pr. Khar-a-ric) (*m*) - *Eastern Frankish ruler, F*

Catigeorn (Pr. Cat-ig-yorn) (*m*) - *Younger son of **Wyrtgeorn**, B*

Catuvalos (Pr. Cat-u-val-os) (*m*) - *Lord of battle, chief warrior of **Gisel**, R*

Childric =**Childeric** (Pr. "Khilde-rik") (*m*) - *Powerful in Battle, father of **Clovis**, son of **Marvig**, king of the Franks, F*

Chilperic (Pr. "Khilfe-rik" [Gaulish]) (*m*) - *Powerful helper, father of **Clotilde**, king of Lugdunum (Lyons), son of **Gondioc**, Bg*

Chlodomer (Pr. Khlod-o-ma) (*m*) - *Second son of **Clovis** and **Clotilde**, ruled the Orleans Franks, F*

Claennis (Pr. Clenn-is) (*f*) - *Purity, daughter of Cwen and Beorn, cousin of Lufian, AS*

Clotilde/Clotilda (Pr. Clot-il-da) (*f*) - *Famous in battle, daughter of **Chilperic**, wife of **Clovis**, Bg*

Clovis (*m*) - *King of the Franks, F*

Corbus (*m*) - ***Clovis's** Chief of Command, F*

Cwen (*f*) - *Queen, high-born Angle, sister of **Hengest** and **Kursa**, wife of Beorn, mother of **Rowena** and Claennis, AS*

Deogol (Pr. Day-o-gol) (*m*) - *Secret, one-time chief of Bricius's men, warrior attendant of Denua, AS*

Denua (*f*) - *Alluring, slender, sister of **Wyrtgeorn (Vortigern)**, widow of Bricius, widow of **Kursa**, mother of Lufian, B*

Dormian =**Dormitianus** (Pr. Dor-mit-i-arn-us) (*m*) - *Bishop of Geneva, R*

Edgard (*m*) - *Lucky spearman, one of **Hengest's** men, AS*

Elico (*m*) - *Advisor to **Chilperic** and **Clovis**, Bg*

Firman (*m*) - *Traveller, second son of Lufian and Claennis, AS*

Flavius (*m*) - *Bishop of Autricum =Chartres, R*

Galba (*m*) - *Brother of Rodor, B*

Gisel =**Godegisel** (Pr. Go-de-gees-el) (*m*) - *King of Geneva, son of* **Gondioc**, *Bg*

Godomar (*m*) - *King of Vesontio (Besançon), son of* **Gondioc**, *Bg*

Gondioc (*m*) - *Previous king of all Burgundy, father of* **Gundobaud**, **Chilperic**, **Godomar** *and* **Gisel**, *Bg*

Gundobaud (*m*) - *King of Vienne, son of* **Gondioc**, *Bg*

Gundric (*m*) - *Historically accepted short form of* **Gundobaud**, *Bg*

Guorthemir (Pr. Goo-orth-a-mir) (*m*) - *Elder son of* **Wyrtgeorn**, *B*

Gwrangon (*m*) - *Civilian Governor of Ceint, B*

Hengest (*m*) - *Stallion.* '**Hengist**' - *Angle warrior. With his brother* **Kursa**, *he fought back the Picts on behalf of* **Wyrtgeorn** (**Vortigern**), *AS*

Ingomer (*m*) - *First son of* **Clovis** *and* **Clotilde**, *died soon after birth, F*

Kursa (Pr. Khoor-sa) (*m*) =**Horsa** - *Angle warrior, brother of* **Hengest**, *second husband of Denua, AS*

Licnos (*m*) - *Younger brother of Bricius, G*

Lufian (Pr. Loof-yan) (*m*) - *Love, son of Denua and* **Kursa**, *cousin of Claennis, AS*

Maewyn Sochet (Pr. May-win Sokh-et) (*m*) - *Devoted friend/warlike, St Patrick's original name, B*

Magan (*m*) - *Competent, Ardith's first betrothed, AS*

Martinus (*m*) - *Warlike / of "Mars", Godly teacher from Turonensis (Tours), in central Gaul,* "*Martin of Tours", G*

Marvig =**Merovech** (Pr. Mer-o-vekh) (*m*) - *Famous ruler, First king of the Salian Franks. Latin -* **Meroveus**, *F*

Octha (*m*) - *Son of* **Hengest**, *AS*

Orvyn (*m*) - *Brave friend, Cwen's first husband, died in battle, AS*

Patrick/Patricius/Patertius/Padraig (*m*) - *Father,* **Maewyn Sochet's** *adopted name, R*

Ragnar =**Ragnachar** (Pr. Rag-nakh-ar) (*m*) - *Northern Frankish ruler, F*

Rodor (*m*) - *Sky, Pottery trader in Sulis (Pontivy), B*

Roveca (*f*) - *Wife of Rodor, B*

Rowena (*f*) - *White-haired, daughter of Cwen, AS*

Scur (*m*) - *Storm, one of* **Kursa's** *men, AS*

Senaculos (Pr. Sen-ak-oo-los) (*m*) - *'Senos' means 'old' in Gaulish*, **Chilperic's** *advisor*, G

Sigebert (Pr. Sig-e-bert) (*m*) - *Cousin of* **Clovis**, *king of the Franks east of the Rhenus*, F

Syagrius (*m*) - *Son of* **Aegid**, R

Tredan (*m*) - *Tramples, one of* **Hengest's** *patrol leaders*, AS

Trymian (Pr. Trimm-ian) (*m*) - *Encourages, Parisii commander*, G

Vortigern - *corruption of* **Wyrtgeorn** (*m*) - *British king of Rhegin, brother of Denua*, B

Vortrix (*m*) - *Retired Parisii soldier, living at the southeastern edge of Parisii lands*, G

Wictgils (*m*) - *Father of* **Hengest**, **Kursa**, *and Cwen, Prince of the Ingwi, uncle of Beorn*, AS

Wulfgar (*m*) - *Wolf spear, father of Beorn, brother of* **Wictgils**, AS

Wyrtgeorn (Pr. Wert-gyorn) - *See* **Vortigern**, B

Places

(With pronunciation hint if needed)

Alsiodorum =Autissiodorum - *Auxerre*

Armorica - *Brittany*

Augustonemetum - *Clermont Ferrant*

Aurelianum (Pr. Au-ray-lee-arn-um) - *Orleans*

Autricum (Pr. Or-tri-cum) - *Chartres*

Camulodunum - *Colchester*

Cantwarabyrig =Durovernum Cantiacorum - *Canterbury*

Ceint (Kent) - *Kent, Cantiaci - Kentish people*

Danuvius (Pr. Dan-oo-vi-us) - *Danube river*

Durovernum - *see Cantwarabyrig*

Dyrrachium - *Durrës, Albania*

Éire =Ireland =Ynys Ériu

Geneva - *itself*

Isala - *Ijssel river*

Lugdunum - *Lyons*

Lutetia (Pr. Loo-tee-sha) - *Paris*

Noviodunum =Augusta Suessionum - *Soissons*

Noviomagus (Pr. Nov-i-o-mag-us) - *Chichester*

Rhegin (Pr. Reg-in) - *British Kingdom on the central south coast*

Rhenus (Pr. Ren-us) - *Rhine river*

Rodanus (Pr. Row-darn-us) - *Rhône river*

Sulis - *Pontivy*

Tamesis - *Thames river*

Tolbiac - *Zülpich*

Toxandria =Turnacum - *Tournai*

Turonensis (Pr. Too-ro-nen-sis) - *Tours*

Vesontio (Pr. Ves-on-tee-o) - *Besançon*

Vienne - *itself, Vienne, south of Lyons*

Ynys Ériu (Pr. In-is Er-yoo) - *Ireland*

Ynys Tanatus (Pr. In-is Tan-at-us) - *Isle of Thanet*

Family Tree

Bold Names probably historical

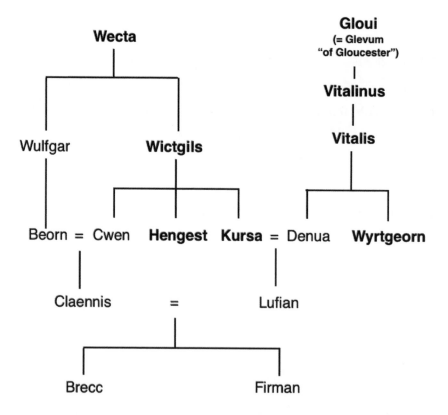

Regional Map

Contents

Part One:

The Tale of the King's Sister

Chapter One

Prologue

(Late in the year of AD 432)

*B*eorn surveyed the scene. Bodies lay in every direction, in every pose, every manner of death. He sighed. They had won the battle, but they had lost Orvyn, who had recently married Beorn's cousin Cwen, who was expecting their first child. Magan also lay dead on the field. He was betrothed to Beorn's sister Ardith.

Gone. The sun shone on friends who would see it no more. There would be weeping in the camp when they returned.

He looked down at the face of Orvyn. His friend's death grimace was fixed on his face from the moment the spear had gone through him. From the length of spear still showing, it must have penetrated an arm's length into the ground. Beorn guessed it was stuck so fast that the owner was unable to retrieve it.

He was surprised, as he mused, that he did not feel angry. Indeed, after a battle such as this he didn't feel - anything. But at least their enemy had come off worse. For the two Ingwi who lay on the field, he reckoned there must be twenty Juti. The Ingwi had been attacked very suddenly, but their training had paid off. Battle ready in seconds, they went on the attack - and only then found out how many Juti there were.

The Tribe of the Ingwi were caught between the Juti to the north and the Seaxe to the south. The Seaxe had become more friendly over the last few years because they themselves had been raided by the Frisians to their south and had called on the Ingwi to help. Together, the two tribes had been successful in war, and also in love, as some intermarriage had occurred. The phrase Ingwi-Seaxe was being heard more among the surrounding tribes.

But there was scarcely a month, at least in the summer, when the Juti would not try out a raid. The only consolation was that the Juti were weak men, and could only succeed by trying to overwhelm by weight of numbers.

Beorn's patrol had been sent out by Hengest, their battle-captain, because of reports of Juti raids on the northern villages.

Hengest and his younger brother Kursa had been combining their warriors to fight the threat from the Juti.

Beorn reached over the body of his friend to the spear and effortlessly slid it from the ground. Juti! Weaklings!

Chapter Two

The Old Woman

*I*t was a beautiful room; the woven hangings - so many colours! - and the thick woollen drapes gave both loveliness and warmth. We had eaten so well from our wooden platters of meat, bread and honey, that my belly was feeling fuller than it had for years. We sat on seats which were padded with hair and wool - a rare privilege for me.

The old woman relaxed in her chair. I say old; her thick chestnut hair, once breathtaking, was showing a few streaks of grey, and her skin was no longer quite as smooth as I remembered it, but her manner was as strong and powerful as ever I knew, and her body, to me, seemed to have lost none of its vigour. In particular, that familiar, piercing gaze which she turned on me was just as disarming, yet compelling, as it ever was.

'Are you ready?'

We both knew, of course, what we must do, but it was one of those moments when going ahead with our task would break the spell of our sweet rest and quietness after our repast.

Gathering myself, I put down my jar of mead and prepared to write. It was warm. We were comfortable. She started to speak.

Chapter Three

The Start of the Sister's Story

I am sister to the King.

I am old now, and enjoy telling the stories which I have gathered during my long life. Listen and write, for of all the stories I have - and I have many - this is my own story. Most I have seen with my own eyes; the rest has been told to me.

My eyes are dim with age, but I still retain the power to see again in my own mind what I saw then.

The King, my brother, we called Wyrtgeorn. We laugh when the Ingwi say 'Vortigeorn', as if their ears cannot hear. He is two years older than I. He ruled from Noviomagus, the greatest city of Rhegin, west of the land of the Cantiaci.

I say without shame, I was good to the eye of a man, though you see me wrinkled and fat now. My appearance was the stuff of common talk even before my breasts were grown. My father had kept me secluded when I was a small child, but as I grew, I found ways around his restrictions. I watched the men train with sword, bow and spear. I listened to their tales of war, and wars gone by.

Most of all, I loved the tales of Boudicca. Father said she was our ancestor, that was why we were high-born. He also used to say that the Romans came to Britain despite her battles, yet they had departed in our day; so in a strange way, we shared in a victory she fought for but did not see.

How I wished to be like her! How I wished to learn to fight with sword, bow and spear! Though I knew I was slight in frame, and could probably not prevail with sword yet I felt that fighting with a bow should be mine to do if I wished.

So from my earliest years, I pestered my father to let me learn the bow. He was a good man, though he would kill if displeased, and eventually, he said, 'Very well, little one, because you have persisted, you may learn.'

I suppose I was about ten years of age at that time.

I love the bow. I have done so all my life. I could not get the range the men get, even when I was grown, but range is not everything. El Elyon has allowed me accuracy as my gift.

What is the purpose of shooting as far as the eye can see if you cannot hit your man? Far better to wait till he is a little nearer - but not so near that he can hit you - then fix him with an accurate shot.

So, I saw my share of war, though the men insisted I stay back and just use my bow. Many, at the battle's end, would come and pledge me their thanks, as they had seen their attacker suddenly transfixed with one of my arrows. They knew my arrows from their shortness.

I suppose, looking back, it was surprising that I lived. Were I to be the sister of a lesser warrior than Wyrtgeorn... who knows what battles we might have lost?

The day finally came that my father decided that I was enough grown and was now useful for the making of alliances by marriage.

He had long heard of the tribe called Parisii, who live in a land towards the sunrise, and about one day's journey across the narrowest part of the sea.

The Romans still ruled in that land, though they had left ours, but they had nevertheless removed most of their men to defend their own land. The Parisii tribe (that is the Roman way of naming them) centred on a great Roman town called Lutetia, and, because the bulk of Romans had left, they were wealthy, had room and to spare, and were unthreatened.

As my two younger sisters did not care for war, they had already been married off to the heads of British clans, to weld the alliances for which our people is famous. As with all our family, they were also attractive to the eyes of men, though not quite as I was.

So my father told me that my warring days were over, and he must marry me to a chief of the Parisii, to form an alliance across the sea.

It was spring, about twenty years since the Romans had left Britain, when we set off to the east on horseback through the land of the Cantiaci towards the coast.

For many months before that, my father's servants had travelled back and forth - how many times I do not know - but eventually they had reported that there was 'a' Lord, then eventually they said, 'No, THE Lord', of the Parisii - and I was to be his wife. I was to marry the king!

I do not mind saying that as we rode off, the feeling in my belly was like that I felt just before a battle. You know that there will be earth-shaking events, that lives will be changed, destinies will be changed, forever, and that, no matter how well prepared, you cannot quite forecast the result as closely as you need to quell the beating of your heart.

The tears had been spilt, my mother's and my sisters', and there had been much embracing. But that was now done. It belonged to who I was, not who I would be.

We were nine in number: myself, my father, my brother Wyrtgeorn, my father's chief servant, who had negotiated the match, his interpreter (for though we could all speak Latin, it was respectful to use their strange tongue) one lady to wait on me, and three menservants to deal with the food and the horses.

It was dusk on the third day of our journey when we saw the sea. I had seen the sea before, of course; battles with invaders preferably took place near the shore, so as not to allow the destruction of inland towns.

Nevertheless, my heart leaped when I saw it, just as it did when I saw it first as a girl. I wondered, as we rode a pathway above some white cliffs, what it was about the sea which raised my heart to think on El Elyon, who was the reason I was who I was, and the reason I did what I did.

I thought on the vastness of it, like his vastness. I thought on the calmness of it, like his peace which crept slowly back into my heart in the weeks following battle. I thought upon the sweet warm caress of its waters, on a summers day, surrounding me and lapping over me, like his love which has followed me all the days of my life. Then I thought on the uncontrollable power of the sea when it was roused, and wondered on his power. I was taught that his power was not capricious, it was in perfect control, but, my teachers forcefully reminded me, it was not mine to control, but his alone. I must go where he did.

And so it was for me now. I was going where he was going. There was no going anywhere else, the power was not mine to make the decision.

Calmness descended as I thought on that.

Chapter Four

Crossing

We crossed the narrow sea two days after arriving at the harbour in the land of the Cantiaci. We had waited for the seas to settle, and on this day calm sea and a good breeze had been foretold, though how they knew that, I am still unaware.

As I said, I was familiar with the appearance of the sea, yet I had never been... how do you say that - IN a boat, ON a boat? Even after all these years I still do not know how it should be said.

Anyway, we, all nine of us, plus the three boatmen, were both on the boat and also in it. Indeed I was very far in, as I was not allowed anywhere near the side. So I climbed onto some cargo and sat in the middle and continued my marvelling at the sea. When land faded from sight - it was without beginning and without end. Just like El Elyon.

There were maybe three hours when I could see neither the land we had left, nor the land to which we went, and though the boatmen seemed sure of our direction, I had no idea how they knew. I have since discovered they use the sun by day and stars by night, but in those days I knew nothing.

They used the power of the wind in a sail rigged to a large mast in the centre of the boat. Did you hear me say 'rigged'? That is the proper word. I learnt it!

Twice, when the wind weakened for a while, they used oars with which to row, but the effort of it caused much cursing and growling. Contrariwise, the change in the boatmen when the wind sprang up was remarkable, their faces shone with delight, and you would call them the most pleasant and kindly men on earth!

It was near night when we pulled into the harbour in Gaul. There were many crowding the harbourside. I suppose that we were quite a large ship for them, and the number of us, and the richness of our dress caused much staring.

'Richness of our dress!' I was wearing my old travelling robes, and even the King was not dressed richly. But compared to those we saw around us, this was rich.

I was starting to wonder how we were to travel onwards, when two men appeared, they looked like soldiers and my father's chief servant recognised them. They led us through the staring crowd to an inn.

'We stay the night here, and they will have horses for our onward ride in the morning', said my father.

I slept well that night; I left my father and brothers carousing below and got my best night's sleep in a week.

I was woken by the sound of horses and shouting in the road. Almost at the same time my maid entered to wake and dress me.

What a change came over me at that moment!

My finest blue and gold gown with a thick gold clasp, a golden circlet in my hair, so many gold rings that my hands felt heavy!

So, my preparation finished, my maid and I went outside. I was gratified, as I walked out, to hear breath sucked through the teeth of the menfolk. Then I realised how many of them there were. No longer just the nine of us, I counted fifteen other horsemen, all armed with swords, and two with bows as well. No wonder I had been woken by the noise!

Chapter Five
Raid!

When I had mounted - I was the last to mount, for protocol's sake - we set off in a colourful procession to the southeast. The horses were decorated with pennants and bells, and one of the riders flew a large banner with, I was told, the device of their Lord emblazoned upon it.

I was placed in the centre of the troop, between two horsemen. After about an hour's riding, I asked the one on my right, in Latin, why so many men had been sent.

'There are Frankish raiding parties coming much further west than before, my Lady. We would not want any... unfortunate events.'

The words were scarcely out of his mouth when an arrow flew past me and hit him full in the chest. He toppled from his mount and fell to the ground. All the troop looked around wildly for the direction of attack, but all too soon it was obvious, as a group of roughly dressed men raced from a nearby clump of trees to our left. I reckoned there were about the same number of them as us, but they had the advantage of surprise.

It was one of those times when you know perfectly well what you should do, yet you still ask yourself if that will be a correct course of action. My head said ride away fast, but I followed my heart. I slid quickly down from my horse, on the opposite side to the attack, right where the unfortunate horseman had fallen.

For, you see, he was not just a horseman. He was one of the two bowmen! And in the blink of an eye, I had his bow and quiver.

I do not to this day know how the attackers did not spot me, though I took as much cover as I could from my horse. It seemed that all their attention was fixed on our horsemen, and none on me.

Quick as a lightning flash, I loosed off one arrow. It was longer than I was used to and the pull was much heavier. But here, this was no disadvantage, for the fighting was close, and all that was needed was what I had, quickness and accuracy.

I had already notched my second when I saw the first hit. I blazed away, I swear I had never shot so swiftly till that day.

Suddenly it was over. The remainder of the Franks melted back into the trees, and we were left counting our losses.

We had four men dead, though astonishingly, only one from our group, one of the servants.

Our Frankish enemy had lost fourteen, and ten of those to arrows.

It was then I sensed a change in the air. The horsemen were looking at me differently. I went over to my father, who was in deep conversation with the leader of the Parisii force. As soon as they saw me approaching, they broke off their conversation. My father waited for my approach, but when I stood before him, he embraced me strongly.

'My sweet child', he said, 'I must convey to you the thanks of the Parisii. They are so grateful.'

I was truly astonished and speechless. 'What for?'

'Do you not realise, my child? The other Parisii bowman was killed immediately after his first shot. Nine of the ten arrows which found their marks were yours. It is to your credit that we were not all slaughtered by the Franks!'

We remounted and rode on. The Parisii rode a little bit further away from me, and whenever I looked at them, I swear that they were looking back at me.

We made camp again that night, Every soldier was on watch as we slept.

In the morning, the soldiers looked dreadful, but I was bright and full of life. My heart felt quite unsteady, no matter how I tried to calm myself. This was the day! This was the day! This day I would meet the one to whom I had been given. My life, so far my own - though my father would think it was his - was to be given to another.

You think... don't you! You think I was like a slave in this matter! You think my destiny was shaped by others; I was carried where they wished and not allowed any say!

Well, it was not so.

I was an experienced battle warrior, though I was a woman. I was older, and wiser than my sisters. And, dare I say it, I was more beautiful than any of them (and I did not understand my beauty from what I had imagined, no, I tired of being told of it from almost all who met me).

I knew I could marry any man I wished. Yet - I loved my father, and would not willingly have displeased him.

So - you might think it happy coincidence, but I thought it a gift from El Elyon. The one to whom my father wished to give me became the one to whom I wished to give myself.

How did I know?

I made sure I heard of him, this Lord of the Parisii. I made sure accounts were given to me by those who had crossed to arrange my marriage. I made enquiries with those warriors with whom I fought, those who had travelled.

And all I heard was attractive to my heart. A man with strength, yet with kindness, with wealth, yet with a care for those with less, with power, yet with gentleness. A man who had fought in battle, yet loved peace. A man who could have his pick of any woman he wished, yet who had grown just that bit older than the usual marriage age, without finding just the one. And I presumed he had heard of me, as I had of him.

The only thing I could not imagine was his face, though they had told me that he had some sort of disfigurement. But I had not a care for such things! I had spent years with men in battle! Many of the best of them returned with changes to their countenance which were gruesome, if looked at alone. Yet they were the same men for all of that. I was blessed by El Elyon that I had no serious wound to disfigure me, though my upper left arm bears a long thin scar from a lucky sword strike.

No, though I could not picture his face in my mind, yet I felt I already knew his heart in my heart. And I sensed that El Elyon, who had already gifted me with so much, had this match also as a great gift for me.

That night, we arrived at Lutetia. I had never seen - I still have not seen - any city as big. When we had passed the edge of the city, we rode for another three hours and still had not reached the centre.

Quite suddenly, as we rode, the leader stopped. My heart slowed as I wondered whether there was to be another attack, but then the troop turned aside to great wooden gates in a wall to the right hand side of the road.

There was a shout from within the gates, and in seconds they swung open and we entered.

What a sight! The compound we entered was the richest Roman villa I had ever seen. We had entered through gates on one side of a quadrangle. Before us was a double colonnade of pillars crossing a beautiful rich green garden in the centre of the quadrangle.

Somehow, four fountains of water in the centre of the garden rose the height of a man. It was not till months later I learnt that the water was piped from a spring flowing from halfway down a nearby hill. The power of the water running down from the hillside caused the fountains to operate.

Off each side of the quadrangle opened doors to rooms - I had not any idea of their purpose. But ahead, on the far side of the quadrangle, rose the most beautiful building.

It was two floors high! It was built of small bricks, like our mud bricks, but these had the colour of red clay. It was peppered with huge windows, each the size of a man's chest!

But then... but then... for all of my amazement with the place, there was yet a greater amazement which fell upon me.

There, standing in front of the house at the end of the colonnade of pillars, was the Lord of the Parisii.

And he was... beautiful.

He had, on the side of his face, a red mark the size of two of my thumbs, but he stood tall and proud. He was dressed in a green tunic with a leather jacket over it and wore a thick gold torc at his neck.

But that was not the source of his beauty.

The source of his beauty was... his smile.

It entranced me. It was for me that he smiled. It was at me that he smiled. It was because of me that he smiled.

And his mouth was beautiful. I had heard men and women speak of the kiss of love and never found within me the desire to know it. But now! I desired that mouth more than any thing.

So it was that I found that my father's desire and mine were one. I pleased him and pleased myself at the same time.

We were welcomed into the house and found a great hall, with tables laden with food, most of which I had never seen. I sat to the right of the Lord of the Parisii - I did not yet even know his name - and my Father sat to his left. He talked to my father, and smiled, but talked little with me.

Then one of his horsemen approached him - I think he was their leader - and spoke to him privately. As they talked, the Lord of the Parisii looked round at me. When they finished speaking and the chief horseman had gone, he turned to me and said, 'I have many bowmen, but do I hear that you are a bow-woman?'

Chapter Six

Married

That night my maid and I were given a room off one side of the quadrangle. The night was chilly, but the room was warm - I knew not how this was done, but later I learnt that underneath all the rooms was a space the depth of a man's forearm into which blew hot air from a fire at the far side of the building. The Romans called it a hypocaust. I am so glad of this comfort now that I am old!

The next day we were up at dawn; my maid had been instructed in duties which would employ us both for all of the morning.

My face was whitened with fine powder, My dark hair was made to rise high on my head with a fine gold circlet upon it. My dress was the finest white linen, brushing the floor, with gold threads shot through across my breast and long flowing sleeves revealing my forearms. I wore a neck band of gold inlaid with pearls, gold bracelets on both wrists and the same heavy gold rings as the day before.

At the appointed time, my maid, who had been watching through the crack of the door, indicated that I should go into the quadrangle. I went out and was immediately met by my father. He conducted me into the colonnade of pillars and towards the house, as the night before.

There stood my husband, tall, slim, clad in purple cloth with a gold breastplate, gold helm and gold greaves on his legs.

Together we entered the house, which had been riotously decorated with colourful pennants and hangings.

We stood before a priest - I knew not of what religion - who spoke in a tongue I did not know for a short time, and then, in Latin, he asked me if I was willing to marry my Lord. I answered without hesitation.

My Lord turned to me and kissed me. I was glad he held me, for my knees buckled.

That night, after the feasting, as we became man and wife, I reflected upon my strange life. Who would have thought that, in such a strange place, with a strange bed-fellow, I would be so strangely happy?

After our love-making, we fell to talking. We only had Latin in common. Mine was reasonable (thank you, my dearest father, for ensuring that I had a good education!) and my husband spoke well, though he confessed his speech was better than his reading.

We started to share details of our lives, and laughed when we already knew the story the other was telling. We found that we had both been so well prepared that we both felt that we knew each other before we met.

There! You can tell how we were by the way I am saying 'both' so much! We were already two become one.

Nevertheless, he asked me to tell him more about my training and times as a warrior, of which he had heard only a broad outline, and the account of my part in our troop's recent skirmish had far surpassed his expectations.

So I recounted what I have already told you, my desire to be like Boudicca (he had heard her name), the way I pestered my father and got my first bow, the long hours of practice... all this provoked smiles and gasps, but what surprised him most was the same thing which surprised me when I learnt to shoot, the fine accuracy I found so natural for any target which was not too far away.

'But you have left out your shooting speed!' he interjected.

'I had never thought of that as a special ability', I replied.

'But the way you got off nine shots in just the few seconds of the battle', he went on, 'I don't think you realise the effect you had on the men of my troop. They know of only two women who use a bow, and then only for sport, but they had never seen shooting at that speed from any man. They are wondering, light-heartedly, whether I could spare you from our marriage bed to go with them on patrols!'

We both laughed - it was so good to laugh with him - then he was quiet for a while. I sat quietly with him, enjoying his nearness, his smell - not like men who have worked and sweated, but dark and rounded, with a hint of the perfume he had been anointed with for our marriage.

Suddenly he said, 'So, tell me how it is that you have this unusual ability?'

I stilled. I knew the reason, of course, but I did not know whether telling it to my new lover would please him or dismay him. I am ashamed to admit that I feared he would not like me having another Lord, besides him.

I waited so long that my husband said, 'Why so quiet my sweet love?'

I cannot tell you how my heart leaped in my breast to hear him addressing me in such a way.

Slowly, and hesitantly, I told him of the One I called El Elyon. I watched his face for a sign of displeasure, but could not see any. I explained that El Elyon was the one who had given me all things, my ability with the bow, yes, but also himself as my husband.

Again, I studied his face intently, but there was no sign of pleasure or displeasure. I waited, just looking at him. Despite my worries, I found just looking at him was a pleasure. He was not handsome, in the way that some men are, but his face had a... presence, I think is the word.

Then, just a hint of change. The corners of his mouth lifted, ever so slightly. Then he suddenly burst out into laughter. 'I knew there was something like that! My servants had the most extreme difficulty recounting this part of you. Everything else they could tell me in detail but this part they could not understand, so were unable to explain.'

'But my Lord, are you not angry?'

'Other men might be, but I am not. And now it is time to reveal something about me. Have you ever heard about a holy man from a country to the east who became a priest in Turonensis in central Gaul? In Latin, his name was Martinus.'

I confessed I had never heard of him, but desired my Lord to tell me more.

'I have only recently heard of him from one of his followers, who passes this way on occasion. Martinus himself is now dead, but the community he formed and the way he followed lives on.'

'I have lived my life worshipping no god, yet what this man had to say about the God whom Martinus obeyed has swayed me, and though I would not say I am a believer, I find myself thinking about the creator of all things. Martinus taught that this creator had a son, born in our world, who died yet lived again.'

'Yeshua!' I blurted out, unable to still my own tongue.

'I think the Gaulish pronunciation is different, but I think that is the man.'

'Yeshua is the way they said it in his own tongue.'

'And how do you know all this?' he asked.

'In the days of the Romans in Britain, our kingdom was visited by a man from the east, from the Hebrew race. He spent a year learning our tongue, but all the while he taught us in such Latin as we could understand. He spoke about El Elyon and his son who died yet lived again. This understanding was given to us, and though the Hebrew has now died, we still recount the stories. The thing we never saw was the book of which he spoke.'

'The book!' my husband almost shouted, 'I have one!'

A servant was despatched to obtain the book for me to see. He returned with a parcel wrapped tightly in cloth.

My husband took it and gently unwrapped it. 'My sweet love', he said, 'this is a great treasure.'

I had seen, but never touched, something similar before, but not one as beautiful or elaborate as this. It was, explained my husband, a codex. It consisted of many identical four-sided leaves of vellum all joined together down the left-hand edge. The front leaf was lavishly decorated with pictures in coloured inks, as were several leaves on the inside.

It would take too long to tell of how we pored over the book. The writing was Latin, which my husband could read only haltingly, so I turned back and forth, so excited to see at last the stories I had so often heard. Turning to the later pages of the book, I read out to him some accounts of Yeshua, whom the book called Iesus.

I am not ashamed to say that when my eyes tired, we fell to love-making again. I had not known anything like it, though I had heard much talk and 'good advice' from women well-wishers before I left my home. But his kisses were so sweet, his touch so light, that I felt more than once as if my belly would explode.

Two days later my father left, with my brother and the servants. My maid had elected to stay with me. We had allowed her to decide to go back to Britain if she wished, but her mind was fixed on being my maid. 'Lady's Maid to the Queen of the Parisii' was how she styled herself.

The interpreter also stayed behind. He had the task of acquainting me with the tongue of the Parisii. I found the language not too difficult, as many words, and the structure of speech, bore a resemblance to my own. I found from my interpreter that my husband's name was Bricius, which means 'speckled'. And so he was, for the red mark on his face made him so.

Chapter Seven

The Slave-Market

And so we went on, for months. Bricius (I loved using his name) occasionally had to depart for a few days to attend to matters of his Tribe, but generally he was at our villa. I was permitted to come and go as I pleased, for in our city of Lutetia, the Romans still gave some protection, though their numbers were now very low.

I listened in as he dealt with his men, and his people. Though I was still learning his language, I could make out enough to know that my understanding of his nature was not deceived. Except, perhaps, in one thing: I had not realised how deeply he felt injustice. When one was brought before him who had unjustly treated another, he came the closest I ever saw him to rage.

Spring turned to summer, and autumn went by, the weather grew cold, and I was so glad of the fire which sent hot air under our floor.

Then, quite suddenly, my maid fell ill. She developed a high fever, coughed for some days, then one morning, we found her stiff and cold.

I, who had lived with the death of men in battle, was surprised at the depth of my grief. She had been a good servant, strong and dependable, and so quickly, she was gone.

I put my head on Bricius's warm shoulder and cried till I felt I had no more tears. When I had quieted he still held me.

Two days later we laid her to rest just outside the wall of our villa, where trees gave shade and the hill started to rise.

When we returned to the villa, Bricius took me aside and said, 'Now, my love, we have an opportunity!'

I wondered at his meaning, but he went on, 'A few miles to the north of Lutetia, on the edge of my domain, there is a market. I go there whenever I can, because they sell slaves.'

My blood ran cold.

'I cannot stop the trade. It is beyond my control at the edge of our lands, but what I can, I do. I buy all the slaves I can manage, to prevent them falling into other hands and being mistreated.'
'But what do you do with them?' I asked, entirely unsuspecting of the truth.

'My love', he said, 'Where do you think all these people around you have come from? Many of my horsemen, gate-keepers, cooks, even the one who tends the fire which warms us come from that market. When I became chief of my tribe I took a vow to take slaves for servants, then treat them well. Many of my horsemen who have shown loyalty have been freed, and live as members of the Parisii.'

I looked at our villa workers with new eyes, and I fancy, started to treat them differently.

So it was that we set off, with some horsemen, to ride north. We had ridden for two hours when we approached a town, and I saw my first slave-market.

I knew such things existed, of course, though they were rare in our part of Britain, but I was still shaken when I saw the wretches tied to posts and displayed for purchase.

I rode past one sorry group, all cowed and stooping, but there were few women, and those I saw, I could not imagine handling the tasks required.

As I rode past the second small group, of three men and two women, I saw that one of the women was heavily pregnant. As I drew level with her she stood tall and looked at me insolently! There stands a woman I need to know, I thought to myself.

'Bricius. I would like to see this woman closer.'

We dismounted and I went over to her. She defiantly looked me straight in the eye. I swear if she had possessed a weapon, she would have used it there and then.

'Bricius, I would like this one.'

'My love, we must enquire with the slave master where she comes from.'

Our enquiries revealed that she was of a northern tribe, the Ingwi, who are closely linked to the Seaxe.

'My love', said my Lord, 'She is heavily pregnant, do you think we will manage the birth as well?'

'Of course!' said I, with more confidence than I had a right to.

So, we took her home. Our first problem was communicating with her, as she was unable to understand Latin. However, Bricius was fairly fluent in the Frisian language, having spent some years as a young warrior in that area. So after failing with one or two, we settled upon Frisian and found she also had some understanding of it. So began the long process of incorporating this new person into our home.

Immediately we arranged for her to share my classes in the Parisii language, and soon she had outstripped me.

But more surprising than her abilities in speech was what she told us of her background.

So I think it is time for me to tell you her story...

Chapter Eight
Cwen's Story

(Early AD 433)

*A*rdith and Cwen walked quietly southwards along the shore in the bright sunlight. Both grieved the loss of their men, four months before.

Cwen had been born to Wictgils and his wife, the younger sister to Hengest and Kursa. The Ingwi, unusually for the surrounding tribes, kept the detail of their ancestry in memory. The three children recited:

'Wictgils,
Son of Witta,
Son of Wecta,
Son of Woden,
Son of Frealof,
Son of Fredulf,
Son of Finn,
Son of Foleguald,
Son of Geta'.

Woden was not of course, the god Woden, who was more usually called Odin, but Geta was said to be son of a god.

And as such, Cwen was a royal princess. She had married Orvyn, one of the high-born of the Ingwi tribe, but he had died in a skirmish with Jutes just as Cwen found she was pregnant.

Ardith and her warrior brother Beorn were high-born cousins of Hengest, Kursa and Cwen.

Ardith and Cwen were so deep in conversation that, as it will, time slipped by. Cwen noticed that the light was fading. 'We had better go back. I didn't mean for us to come this far away from home.'

They started to make their way over the dunes towards the path. Some of the dunes were quite a climb. 'Race you to the path', shouted Cwen, and soon she was well ahead of Ardith.

As Cwen came over the last dune, five men suddenly stood in front of her. They looked as surprised as Cwen, but they quickly seized her arms.

Her scream alerted Ardith, who dropped down out of sight. Cwen struggled and hit out at her captor, but was rewarded with a heavy blow from the back of his hand which knocked her to the floor. Immediately she was seized and dragged to her feet again. The men started to talk in a tongue which she did not recognise, though she was adept at several local tongues.

'Let me go!' she shouted, with no result. She tried again in Jutish, then Frisian.

One of her captors seemed to understand when she spoke in the Frisian tongue. He replied in very poor Frisian, 'Oh, no, my pretty one, you and your whelp will fetch good money!'

Ardith watched, petrified, from behind the dune as Cwen was dragged to horses on the pathway. 'If you don't let me go, my brother will follow you and kill you!' shouted Cwen in Frisian.

There followed translation into the unknown tongue, followed by much laughter.

'And who might your brother be? Hengest?'

At this, Cwen could bear no more and started to scream for help, but this brought only another heavy blow across her face which swayed her.

Ardith watched, transfixed, as the dreadful drama unfolded before her. She had understood some of the speech between the men and recognised their Frankish language.

There was more talk between Cwen's captors, and eventually she was pulled, despite her struggles, onto a horse, and rode out of Ardith's sight.

Ardith raced back home as fast as she could. Beorn was not there, so she sought him out at the home of Hengest. She entered and threw herself upon him shouting 'Cwen, Cwen! She has been taken by Franks!'

The whole room started to move, Beorn jumped up and raced out to order horses. Hengest quickly questioned Ardith about where it had happened, then raced out to his horse, shouting for men to follow as they could, despite the oncoming dusk.

It was about four hours later when they returned, dejected. The night was too dark to allow pursuit, they would have to resume at dawn.

No-one slept well. Dawn broke, and the troop set off again, but returned in the early evening without having caught up with the Franks. Heads hung low, they broke the news to Ardith.

Cwen was put on a horse, but her hands were kept tied and a rope was tied around one leg.

They travelled all night. Cwen was so exhausted that she thought she would fall off at any moment. At dawn they stopped and Cwen was pulled down and taken to a wooded grove, where she was allowed to lie down. While some of her captors slept, others watched.

She slept the sleep of the exhausted, waking late in the day, when water and some stale bread were thrust on her. That night they rode again, stopping at dawn in a small wood. But that day, the two horsemen on watch suddenly shouted and ran out of the wood. Two of the others followed and all soon returned dragging a man bound with rope. As Cwen had done, he started to shout, but he also was rewarded with blows till he stopped. Again they travelled at night, and stopped by day, but this was the last time they did so. This stop lasted all day and all the next night. Cwen was so thankful for the rest, and started to feel as if she was recovering her strength.

Her fellow-captive was thrust against her that night (so that only one man was needed to watch them, thought Cwen). She had determined to stay awake if she could, and was rewarded with the sight of the watchman's head nodding onto his chest.

She dug her elbow into her fellow captive, 'Speak to me', she whispered in Seaxe. No response. She tried again in Frisian. This time the man's head came up and he looked at her. 'I am Frisian', he said.

'Where are we? Who are these people? Where are they taking us?' Cwen had so many questions, but the man seemed to realise what she wanted to know.

'The men are Franks', he whispered. 'They send out raiding parties to get gold by stealing or slave-trading. We are right on the edge of my tribe's land, the Belgae are south of us. I am not sure where we are going, but my guess would be Lutetia, far to the south. The Franks do not rule there, in fact they keep attacking it, but so far they have been beaten back by the Romans and the Parisii, the local Gaulish tribe there. Nevertheless, that is the biggest slave market.'

Cwen shuddered at the thought of being sold as a slave.

'My guess is that they will sell us to some of the Parisii at the edge of their land, and they will take us to Lutetia, or at least near it, for I hear that the new chief of the Parisii thinks ill of the trade in human flesh.'

And on they travelled, day after day. The Frankish raiding band stole more horses, and by two months after Cwen's kidnap they had three men and another woman tied and walking behind. All were well aware that if they gave any trouble, they could expect severe pain and no food.

One day they came to a large hamlet with a mead-hall. At their approach, people came out from the hall and greeted their captors. Obviously, this was either their home, or a regular stopping place, thought Cwen.

Then three rough-looking men came out. The sorry band of captives was dragged to meet them. Cwen was pulled off her horse and made to stand with the others. The three men looked all of them over carefully, inspecting their arms, legs, teeth and eyes. Cwen's condition met with raised eyebrows, but satisfied nods.

Earnest conversation went on between their captors and the three men. Eventually bags were handed over from which their captors poured coins. They counted the money carefully, but seemed satisfied.

To Cwen's dismay, she was made to go back on her horse. They set off immediately heading, she estimated, due south, taking the stolen horses which were ridden by their new guards.

These new guards were no kinder than the old ones, but Cwen noticed they were not Franks, for she had picked up a little Frankish from her original captors, and now she heard a different language.

It was two days later when they started to meet more traffic on the road, animals being driven, some of which were carrying loads, carts, people walking to and fro; this was busier than any place Cwen had ever seen. Houses and huts lined the road; sometimes they seemed to stretch back in rows behind the road.

They passed a market, and the noise and the bustle were incredible to Cwen. How could people live like this, she thought to herself. They passed another market. Every kind of commodity appeared to be available, animals, foods of every kind, weapons, building materials... then Cwen saw something which made her blood run cold. Men and women stood in a row on a small raised area, tied with ropes. This was a slave market! She had tried not to think about this time, but now it seemed obvious what was going to happen.

Without a pause, their little convoy made its way to the front of the market and again, Cwen was forced from her horse.

The crowd pressed about her. Hands came out and felt her skin, looked at her hair, checked her belly. Her guards swatted away the interest of most, but there were some who seemed to be offering to pay. Very quickly, one of the men was taken by his new owner. Then Cwen became aware of two people on horseback. They were dressed very richly, and the woman was looking fixedly at her!

Cwen did not easily anger, but this was too much! How dare these people look at me as if I'm a chattel!

She stood up tall, and met the woman's gaze with a defiant glare. She saw the woman turn and speak with the man, then they approached the chief of Cwen's guards. She saw gold change hands. Then her rope was untied from its post and the mounted couple led her away, walking behind their horses.

They pushed through the crowd and met a group of horsemen. Cwen's new owners detached a horse from the group and indicated that one of the men should help her to mount. Cwen saw red. She pushed the man away. Tied or not, she would mount on her own!

Once mounted, they rode for about two hours, before reaching huge gates, set into a wall.

Cwen heard shouts from inside, and the gates swung open.

Chapter Nine

The Old Woman

The old woman stood and stretched. 'More mead?' she said. I held out my jar for her.

'You have been writing for many hours. It is well if we stop and resume another time.'

'Can I come tomorrow morning? I want to hear what happened next to you and Cwen.'

The old woman's face saddened for a moment, but then she breathed deep. 'And so you shall.'

Chapter Ten

The Clouds

So, I found out that the slave I had taken as my servant, was, in fact, a princess!

High-born of her tribe, she was brought up with servants of her own. She was captured by Franks and sold as a slave - to me!

I gave thanks to El Elyon that he had arranged this incredible gift - not just to me, but also to my new servant. Whatever happened to her in service to me, it had to be better than the slavery she may have endured.

Cwen gave birth to a healthy girl who she named Rowena as she had a mop of fair hair. Bricius called upon one of the women servants to help Cwen with her care so that she had time to serve me.

And she became an exemplary maid to me. She knew exactly what was needed from her previous life, so she was able to do just what I needed to make me the Queen of the Parisii - a task which I found very daunting.

The next spring neared. One whole year since I had been taken as Bricius's wife! We had not lost anything of pleasure with each other, quite the opposite. As we grew to know each other better, our pleasure had increased.

But after our love-making, our next pleasure was to dig into Bricius's Book. His Latin was getting better and he was starting to read for himself the accounts of El Elyon in the book.

One day, after Cwen attended to me in our rooms and Bricius had left, she enquired of me, 'What are you reading about in your book?'

So I told her the story about the man in the book, four hundred years before. At first, she was disbelieving, especially about the way he came back to life. But when I explained to her how many people had seen him alive again, talked to him, even eaten with him, she was quiet.

'I feel, inside me, that I must think about this.'

She paused, as if she had more to say.

'But I would like to hear more about this man. Somehow, hearing of him excites me.'

Two years slid by. I settled into my new role as Queen of the Parisii, I even enjoyed it somewhat.

There were only two dark clouds on the horizon. One was that I had been Bricius's wife for a long time, but I had not yet had the joy of becoming a mother.

The other was Bricius's younger brother. Licnos had been a tearaway from his youth, raging round the countryside, stealing from villagers, even burning the houses of the peasant people.

More than once, Bricius's men had brought him back after a drunken spree, with requests for judgment against him from his poor victims.

Bricius had spent much silver on repairs and restitutions for his wild rampages, but he was completely unable to think of a way of stopping him, short of chaining him up.

Once, he breezed straight into our rooms to demand money, as he had debts over which he was being threatened.

'Licnos! How dare you walk in unannounced!' I shouted. I was entirely unafraid of him, knowing he was powerless to threaten us.

He looked at me in the way that defiant children look at their parents.

'I must speak with your King.' He was trying to intimidate me by suggesting that I was lesser than the Parisii high-borns.

'I am as royal as you are, you upstart!' I had completely lost my temper with him.

Thankfully, at that moment, Bricius entered. 'Licnos! What are you doing in here?'

'Dear brother', (Licnos was always so obsequious when he wanted something!), 'Could I have a word with you,' he looked sideways at me, 'in private.'

They departed to a back room to talk, and soon a pleased-looking Licnos slid back out past me, giving me a triumphant glance. I glared back.

'Bricius, why are you so kind to him when he acts so badly?'

'My sweet love - Licnos, for good or ill, is my brother. Our father, when he died, put upon me the duty of making sure he did not get into too much trouble. I do not want him to be attacked by those he has aggrieved.'

'Pah! He would not have the same regard for you - or me!'

'No, my love, yet it is for us to act correctly even if he will not.'

How I loved to be led in righteousness by this man!

Chapter Eleven
Maewyn's Story

*B*ricius had become even more benevolent since he started learning about El Elyon from his book. His Latin reading improved, and he could now read for himself.

Then we heard that a famed holy man was due to pass through Lutetia. His name was Maewyn Sochet and he was a disciple of Martinus from Turonensis. He had been living in the land to the west of Britain, the land of Ynys Ériu, but he was visiting Gaul because of connections with Martinus, and also the town of Alsiodorum, where lived his old tutor, Germanus.

Many people gathered to hear him speak in the city. It was said that he had a voice like honey and spoke about El Elyon as if he were in love with him.

Bricius did not hesitate to send a messenger to ask Maewyn to visit us and discuss with us about the man in the book.

So, Maewyn arrived at our villa. We welcomed him with every hospitality, though he seemed to be embarrassed by so much, saying he was used to simpler fare.

When we had eaten with him, Bricius asked him to tell us firstly something about himself, then something about the God he served.

Maewyn had seemed quiet during our meal, but at Bricius's request, his face brightened, and he spoke.

I will try to speak briefly about myself. I was born on the west coast of Britain, north of the city of Mancunium. My father was Calpurnius, who was a governor under the Romans and my mother was Concessa, the niece of Martinus of Turonensis, in whose steps I follow.

Through my early years I took no thought of my creator. But at the age of sixteen years I was kidnapped by men from Ynys Ériu, which the Romans called Hibernia. I was sold as a slave to Milliuc Maccu Boin, a violent godless man, who ill-treated me for six years. My duty was to tend the swine of my master. I would take them to the foot of a nearby hill known as Slemish.

In despair I cast myself upon my mother's God. Slowly, I learned to know his presence. I found it sweetened my tribulations to speak to him and listen to his voice. So I spent all my days, working or resting, in conversation with him. I would get up in the night and ascend the hill of Slemish where I spent many peaceful hours with him.

After six years of captivity an angel appeared to me who announced that my captivity was at an end, and that I should immediately leave. I went that night, journeying overland in a direction which I knew would lead me to the southeast angle of the island of Ynys Ériu.

There I found a boat bound for Armorica in Gaul. I had no payment, but eventually persuaded the master to take me. From Gaul I found my way back to my home in Britain, where I was reunited with my parents.

During my captivity a deep desire had grown within me to serve the one I had come to know, so I informed my parents that I wished to visit Turonensis, where Martinus, my mother's uncle, had established a believing community. I was shocked that my parents were strongly opposed to my calling, but as I was equally strongly given over to it, I prevailed and they reluctantly bade me God speed.

I visited the community at Turonensis, but then was advised to seek out Germanus, a holy man in Alsiodorum. He became my tutor and taught me to read the holy book and understand the things of God.

I was eventually sent back to Ynys Ériu, the land in which I was enslaved, to tell them the good news of the love of the Most High for them. I was given the name Patricius as I was sent to become a father to those I spoke to. The people of Ynys Ériu call me Padraig.

I have had many adventures and seen many miracles but now I must not continue to talk about myself, for you have asked me also to talk about the one I serve.

Here is what I have to say: in the Book which speaks of him, the Son of the Creator said, 'No-one can come to know Father God except through me.'

Here Maewyn, or Patricius, stopped speaking. We wondered what had come over him. But it seemed he had finished what he had to say.

'Is that all?' demanded Bricius, in a tone which shouted disappointment.

'That is all that the one I serve has given to me for you', said Maewyn, quietly. 'And if those words are all I am given, then those words are the most important words which you will ever hear.'

Maewyn thanked us for our hospitality and asked to be excused, and within moments, he was gone.

Bricius was puzzled, thoughtful and angry by turns. He seemed severely discomfited by being given so little when he had expected so much.

'Why could he not have been more plain?' he asked. 'I gave him my best hospitality and he rewards me with just one sentence.'

'It may be', I said, 'that you also need to remember what that sentence was. And that he said that his words were given by God for you, and were important.'

For some time, Bricius seemed particularly affected and thoughtful.

Some hours later, he came to me. 'My sweet love, I hear the stories of this man in my head, but he seems to have your heart. How does that happen?'

So I explained to him. I reminded him that the book says the man who died came back to life again.

'So', I said, 'if he came back to life, and there is no record of him dying again, he must still be alive.'

'Ye-e-s.'

'So if he is still alive, we should be able to know him as we know each other.'

'Ye-e-s. But - .'

'But?'

'But how does that happen? How do I get to know someone I can't see?'

'My love, close your eyes and sit away from me for a moment. Now. How do you know I am here?'

'I can hear your voice.'

'And how can you let me know what you are thinking?'

'Well, I just talk to you, I suppose.'

'And I hear what you say, and you can listen to me.'

'Yes, I suppose.'

'You do the same with this man. You really can talk to him. He really can hear you, and speak to you, if you listen.'

'I think I am beginning to understand.' His brow, which had been furrowed with the difficulty of understanding, started to smooth and his eyes began to brighten.

'So, when I speak to this man, tell me what I must say.'

'You need to say very little. Tell me, my love, when you buy a slave, then you set him free to be one of your warrior troop, how do you know that he will be loyal to you?'

'First I need word from him that he wishes to serve me, and live under my authority. Then I watch to see if he means what he says.'

Bricius was very still, then his eyes widened, his head lifted ever so slightly and he drew a deep breath. 'Oh, of course! Now I see!'

'So, best of husbands, shall we talk to him together and tell him what he needs to hear?'

Like little children, we talked and listened, and Bricius said what he needed to.

From that moment, he was a different man. Somehow more settled within himself, more unafraid of the future, more prone to break out into his entrancing smile.

He sent word to Maewyn of what he had done, and seemed pleased that he had publicly acknowledged the change within him.

One day, not long later, I came upon Bricius and Cwen in deep conversation. I am ashamed to say that I suddenly wondered what was happening, but Bricius looked up at me and smiled, and said, 'My sweet love, Cwen has been asking about what has happened to me. She sees I have changed and does not understand, though she knows it has something to do with the book.'

I smiled and sat with them. Together, we both explained to Cwen what had changed Bricius. We continually interrupted each other, me with information, he with enthusiasm, till we both fell about laughing.

That was enough for Cwen. She wanted no more talk from us, but rather talk with the man in the book.

So that was what we did. And the same change overtook her as had overtaken Bricius (and myself too, though that was many years since).

I had never seen Cwen smile so much. Previously, her only joy had seemed to be her girl-child, but now she seemed to have a deeper joy which remained with her and gave her, so she said, a peace that did not leave her.

Chapter Twelve

Bricius

The years went by. My only sorrow was that I had not, possibly could not, have any children. Bricius tried to hide his disappointment from me, but I could tell that he was worried that his brother Licnos might get his grubby hands on our little kingdom.

It was the winter of my sixteenth happy year as queen of the Parisii. The weather had been cold and snowy but we were snug and warm in our villa, thanks to the hypocaust.

Bricius had to visit a village to the north where there had been a dispute between two people who both claimed ownership of the same cow, and both were causing trouble. He had taken a small troop of men with him, as the Franks had been making more frequent raids. Bricius thought that they were annoyed at being repulsed by the Romans, and therefore tried all the more to make incursions into our land.

I was not particularly worried when he did not return that night. He would often stay with the local people if there had been a particularly difficult dispute.

By the next afternoon, however, I was worried. He had not gone very far, only about two hours' ride, and he would normally have sent word of delay by now.

Then the dreadful event happened which has left a scar on my life which will never leave me.

Just at dusk, there was a shout. I ran to the window, my fears lifting. Horses came through the gate. There were men walking with them. I peered into the dusk, but could not see. I raced out into the courtyard. They were men of Bricius's troop, and one of the horses had a body draped over it. I screamed that it must not be him and ran to it, but, of course, it was Bricius.

I threw myself upon him, pleading with him to be alive, angry with him, even to hitting with my fists, for being dead.

Gently, his men pulled me away as they took his body from the horse and laid him down. He had been run through with a sword and died within moments, said his men.

When I had quietened from my screaming, they recounted what had happened. They had been attacked on their way back from a very successful visit to administer justice. Bricius had delivered a judgement which had astonished the whole village with its wisdom.

I will recount this story now. If I wait until I have told the next events, that would lessen its significance.

There were only two families in the village, two men, two wives, and their children. Each man had a good milking cow, and the two cows had grazed together on land outside the village. One cow died. Then both men claimed the remaining cow, each man testifying against the other to Bricius.

Bricius simply followed one of the stories we had read in his book, though slightly adjusting it to this situation. 'The solution is simple', he announced, then called to his horsemen, 'Bring the cow, divide it into two parts and we will all eat it tonight!'

One of the men stood forward, 'My Lord, that will break the hearts of my wife and children! Our cow is like one of our family to us. Do not kill it, I pray, rather give it to this other family. At least it will remain in our village.'

The other man said nothing.

'Aha', said Bricius, 'Now I see the truth.' He turned to the man who had spoken forth, 'The cow is truly yours. You may take it and keep it. But I have two small duties to place upon you, if you desire to mend the relationship with your neighbour.'

'The first is to accommodate one of my best bulls which will arrive at this village within a week. Any male calves which issue you may keep as your own, to eat, or grow for mating. The first female calf to be birthed will be given to your neighbour. My bull will stay here until there is at least one female calf.'

'The second duty is that, until that calf gives milk, you shall sell milk to your neighbour, up to one third of the yield of the cow, at one half of the usual price, so that his family will live.'

The whole village had praised the wisdom of this solution, which was gladly accepted by the true owner of the beast, and sullenly accepted by the other man.

Bricius and his small band of men left the village just after nightfall. After only a short time, as they passed through a forest area, they were set upon by a band of Franks. It was only later they realised they must have been trailed. Two of the Franks were on horseback, and one, spotting Bricius, galloped out of the darkness with sword extended. It was an unlikely strategy, but this time, it succeeded.

Deogol quickly turned his horse and struck the killer. The rest of Bricius's men chased down the others, despatching about four of them. The others melted back into the forest.

I spent the rest of the night weeping for my husband, but by the time dawn broke, I found that two tasks had formed in my mind. They were both urgent, for within me I knew what was to come, and I dreaded it. The first was to bury my beautiful husband that very day. The second task was to ensure that his order about the bull was followed. I gave that order in the morning, and we gathered at mid-day to bury Bricius. Every person in our compound was present, but no others, as we had deliberately withheld the news from surrounding households.

Bricius had loved a great spreading elm at the south of our land. It had been planted by the Romans, who favoured elms to provide support for viticulture.

The men dug a grave near the tree and there we laid Bricius, bound with a shroud. Before the grave was filled, I asked all to be silent.

'Deogol, please bring the book and open it at the first place I asked.'

Tears were streaming down my face.

'You all know that Bricius and I revere a holy man, whose story is found in this book. His teachings are such as to change lives. He is renowned for his miraculous works, and many attest that he returned to life three days after Roman crucifixion. His followers find that they can speak to him, and hear his voice in their hearts. I will read some of his words.'"

My voice was cracking as I read to them,

'I am the resurrection and the life. Anyone who believes in me will live, even if they die; those who live by believing in me will never die.'

'Do not allow your hearts to be troubled. Believe in God; believe also in me. There are many dwelling places in my Father's house. I have told you that I am going there to prepare a place for you. Would I have said that if it were not true? And since I go to prepare that place for you, I will come and I will take you to be with me. '

Then I spoke to them as friends, not as servants. 'You have all been as a family to Bricius and me. Our dearest wish was always that you should find this holy man, real in your own lives. Many of you have.

He tells us that we should not fear death as an end, but we should know it is the start of a new life with him and his heavenly Father. By returning to life, he showed that he had power over death. And not just his own death. He died for us all.

So we should know that though Bricius's body is here with us, he lives on in the home of his Creator. All who choose to follow the holy man will meet Bricius again one day.'

I nodded to Deogol and the grave was filled. Some great stones had been gathered that morning, and they were piled as a cairn over the top.

I turned, then was arrested by the voice of Deogol. 'My Lady, one moment if I may?'

One of Deogol's men came forward with some pieces of wood, fashioned into the likeness of a Roman cross. He rooted it into some stones at the head of the grave.

Deogol cleared his throat, 'My Lady aware are we that this symbol is becoming the custom in Lutetia, to denote those who have followed the holy man of whom you speak. We hope that angry you will not be, but we wish that others will recognise the resting place of this holy man, Bricius, King of the Parisii.'

That afternoon, I began to prepare myself, and Cwen, for what was to come.

'Cwen, my dear companion', - for she was more than just a maid to me - 'our time here has come to an end, and I must shortly depart. You are already free. I will give you gold, and you may take a horse and some men to protect you and Rowena, and you may return to your people.'

I watched in surprise as her face fell. 'Denua', (in private I had asked her to call me Denua, for in her way she was just as royal as I), 'must I depart from you? You have been more than a sister to me. I have been away from my people for many years, and if I return, I do so as a widow. I do not even know if my family live. May I not continue to enjoy serving you? I will go with you wherever you go.'

I was so moved that tears sprang again to my eyes. 'My dearest Cwen, of course you may go with me. But the way may be dangerous and long. I intend to return to my own tribe in Britain, but we may have to travel as two women alone.'

Chapter Thirteen

Departure

*J*knew what would happen, but I did not know exactly when, though I suspected it would not be long. So, while I had authority as queen, I made preparation.

I called the chief of Bricius's men to me.

'Deogol', (he had a northern name, as he was brought from that area as a slave, as Cwen had been), 'I want you to ready me my horse, and keep it ready, and two good horses for Cwen and Rowena by its side. Put my best bow - you know the one?' He nodded. 'Sling it securely on the left of the saddle, and a good quantity of my short arrows in my own quiver on the right. And Deogol.'

'Yes, my Lady?'

'This bag, Deogol. It contains some precious items. It must come with us and not be lost.' Though I did not say, in the leather bag were the book, and all the gold coin Bricius had in the villa - a fortune.

Deogol, who was never known for the quantity of his speech, looked at me.

'I see, my Lady, that you are allowing wisdom to rule your actions.' He spoke with a thick Ingwi accent, rather like Cwen's, but much more difficult to understand, and he had a rather odd way of ordering his words.

'May I be so bold, my Lady, as to enquire whether you and Lady Cwen intend on your own to travel?'

I was not sure how to reply, but as I hesitated, he continued. 'For if you intend to Britain to go, there are some among Bricius's men who with you would wish to travel.'

'Deogol! How do you know that?'

'My Lady, already have we discussed this very circumstance.'

'Deogol, I am utterly humbled by your loyalty and kindness. Very well then, mark out the ones who will wish to accompany us and tell them to be ready to leave at a moment's notice.'

'Yes, my Lady. One other thing there is, my Lady.'

I waited, not wishing to impede yet further the slowness of his speech.

'My Lady... ', he hesitated so long I thought he had forgotten what he wanted to say, '... I think it would be good if you, Lady Cwen and little Rowena, sleep in the same room, with a guard - until - it happens.'

So it was that, two nights later, as Cwen and Rowena slept and I spent another night in weeping for my beloved husband, there was a fearsome row in the courtyard, and a drunken Licnos barged into the villa.

Without pausing, he stumbled into our quarters, and came right over to my bed. 'Now, my sweet Queen! Now we shall see who is an upstart! Now we shall see who is royal! Now we shall see who reigns on the throne of the Parisii!'

He pushed his drink sodden face right against mine and slid his hand under the covers. Then his eyes widened and his head jerked back as he was grabbed by the neck from behind by Deogol.

'My Lord, is it now that you have come? Regret we that stay we cannot your hospitality to enjoy.'

Somehow Licnos dropped down and twisted sideways, slipping momentarily out of Deogol's grasp. He turned upon Deogol and grabbed him by the throat. 'I'll kill you!'

I had prepared for a moment like this. I had a stout cudgel beneath my bedclothes and I gave Licnos a hearty whack on the back of his head. He fell to the floor.

'I have not killed him, I hope, Deogol?'

Deogol checked Licnos, 'No, my Lady he lives, though sure I am not whether a good thing that is.'

'Let us leave.'

'Yes, My Lady.'

Deogol put his fingers to his mouth and gave a piercing whistle. Within moments, there was the sound of horses in the courtyard. We put on cloaks against the night air and hurried out. Cwen and Rowena mounted ahead of me, I mounted my horse, noting there my weapon with odd pleasure, considering the circumstances.

It cannot have been more than fifty breaths from the time I hit Licnos to the time the gates opened and we rode out.

'When Licnos recovers, what is to stop him sending men out after us?' I breathlessly asked Deogol, as we rode.

'The men remaining, my Lady, have decided on the route they will from the villa take to search for us. The same route that we take it will not be.'

'But will he not realise that there is a plot by the small number of men remaining?'

'The men he knows none of, my Lady. Never interested in us he was. He will be told that only you, Cwen and I left have. He has not intelligence enough to know that lost half his men he has.'

Our troop of about thirty men rode out through the night, thankfully not too brightly moonlit, but enough to see our track.

We stopped at dawn by a stream for water. I wondered about food, but Deogol's men had brought a feast!

We rested only for about three hours, then remounted and rode on, moving the horses as quickly as we dared.

It was nightfall when we reached the harbour, the same through which I had entered this land, it seemed a lifetime ago.

Deogol and I went to the same inn where I had stayed before. When the innkeeper saw us, tired and disheveled, he looked down his nose, but as soon as I showed him a gold coin, he changed his tune.

'We will need to see the horse-trader in the town at first light.' I told him. It was a regular thing that those who travelled over the sea sold their horses on one side and bought new on the other. Though they did not get the best price either way, there was no place in a boat for a horse, so it had to be done.

Cwen, Rowena and I stayed in one room in the inn, with a guard allocated by Deogol at the door of our room. The men were just as happy staying with the horses on the straw in the warmth of the stables. I spent another night trying to weep quietly for my Bricius, so as not to disturb Cwen and Rowena's sleep.

Next day, we got a poor price for our horses, but what did I care? Bricius was gone. What did I have to live for?

We paid the captain of the largest ship in the harbour to take all of us across. The men were so excited to be crossing the sea, as I had been when I came. They were also apprehensive about going to a different land, but their camaraderie together reassured them.

The sea was, thankfully, calm, and soon we saw white cliffs ahead of us. 'There!' I almost shouted to Cwen and Deogol, 'There! Those white cliffs! That is my land! We are safe!'

Chapter Fourteen

Home

(AD 449)

We pulled into the Cantiaci harbour and disembarked. I went with Deogol to the horse-trader and asked to buy horses. The trader looked at me very strangely, then I realised I had spoken to him in the language of the Parisii! Kicking myself for a fool, I repeated my request in my native Brittonic.

While we were waiting for the horses to be brought, I made conversation with the trader, enquiring as to the state of the nation and Wyrtgeorn, though, of course, I did not say who I was.

The trader told me that Wyrtgeorn's wife had died four years before and he had not remarried. I also learnt that our father had died. I had long known that it could well be so, but my heart sank within me, though I did not show it.

However, Wyrtgeorn was well, and still ruled the land, though the peace had been shattered of recent years by Picts, who had been raiding the villages. The latest news, he confided, was that Wyrtgeorn had invited warriors from another land to help to repel the Picts. Which land, he knew not.

The horses obtained, our troop set off into my own country, along roads which made me weep with relief and the pleasure of home-coming.

We stayed at inns along the way, the men sleeping in the stables, which they seemed to prefer. The number of men caused alarm occasionally, but regularly I called out loudly in Brittonic that we posed no threat, but were travelling to see Wyrtgeorn.

By the third day, we were entering my home villages. I started to see people I knew, and when I said that I was Denua, we had not a few joyful reunions along the way.

As we neared Noviomagus, my home city, we noticed many men in roadside camps, the type of camp warriors make. As we passed one camp, Cwen suddenly cried out in her own language, and to my astonishment, received replies from the men.

'Denua! These are my Ingwi people!' she said.

We had to stop. Cwen and Deogol dismounted, and were soon chattering away in their own tongue. I called a rest break for the men, who dismounted and sat on the grass. Soon Cwen and Deogol were no longer to be seen, having been invited to this tent, then that.

It was about an hour later when they returned, apologising for delaying us so long, but they were both so obviously delighted to have met their own people that it was impossible to be even slightly annoyed.

'Denua! We have found that most of the Ingwi warriors are here, and they are led by my two brothers, Hengest and Kursa!'

'That is astonishing news', I said, 'Have you met your brothers?'

'No, they are being entertained at the home of your brother!'

'Well, as that is where we are going, we had better make all speed!'

We remounted and were at Wyrtgeorn's home - which used to be my home - within an hour. As we came close we saw men and horses; Cwen was squeaking with delight.

I had not thought, however, of the effect of a whole troop of foreign warriors arriving at Wyrtgeorn's gate. The effect on my brother's guards was stunning. There were shouts, men started running to and fro and forming into companies, with their arms, to repel us.

I shouted as loudly as I could, 'My name is Denua. I am sister to King Wyrtgeorn. These are my men, we come in peace to greet my brother.'

We faced a row of pikes and spears. I thought I recognised the chief guard, but he looked so much older that I could not be sure.

'You will all stay there!' he roared.

At last I recognised the voice. 'Cadman!' I shouted, 'It is Denua!'

Chapter Fifteen
Reunion

Cadman stared. 'Denua?' He stood forward and peered at me. 'Is that you?'

Cadman and I had fought many battles together. Once, one of my shots picked off a man who was about to slice off his head with a long sword.

He seemed delighted to see me, but his men did not drop their weapons.

'I'm sorry, Denua', he said, 'although I do not doubt you, only Wyrtgeorn can give authority for your men to enter. I have sent a man to ask him to come to us.'

'Denua! Denua!' It was Wyrtgeorn's voice. He came running, although he slowed slightly when he saw how many men I had with me.

'Denua, it is good to see you, but what are all these men?'

I dismounted and went over to embrace him. 'It is a very long story, my brother, but know that these men are loyal to me even to the cost of their lives.'

Suddenly there was a loud commotion, and shouting in another language. Cwen was also shouting. I looked to where she pointed, and saw two burly men pushing through the crowd. These must be her brothers!

It took an hour before the hugging ended, my men were accommodated, and Cwen, Rowena and I, with Deogol, were invited to join the royal party in Wyrtgeorn's home.

We all, eventually, sat in Wyrtgeorn's great hall.

I was introduced to the leaders of the Ingwi-Seaxe, for those were the tribes which my brother had invited to help him to deal with the Pictish raiders. In return he had promised a monthly allowance of gold for them and their men.

The leaders were indeed the two burly men I had seen earlier, Cwen's brothers. The elder was Hengest, whose name means 'stallion'. The younger, who was not quite as heavily built, was Kursa. The Ingwi pronounce the first letter at the back of the throat, but the nearest many get to the sound is 'Horsa'. His name means fast, speedy, so it has been adopted as the name of our steeds.

I liked both men immediately. They looked as if they were capable of hard fighting if needed, but they had an easy manner and a ready laugh. However, as we sat together, I had this strange sensation that, while Hengest's attention was on my brother the King and the arrangements they had made, Kursa kept looking towards me.

Cwen, meanwhile, proudly introduced her daughter to her brothers. I suddenly, and for the first time, noticed that Rowena suddenly looked very grown up, at the age of nearly seventeen years. Cwen chattered away to the two men as if she knew not how to stop.

Wyrtgeorn's sons, Guorthemir and Catigeorn, sat apart from us, not attempting to hide the scowls on their faces.

'My brother', I said, 'when I left Rhegin to be married, your sons were not unpleasant. I had hoped they would grow into good-hearted young men...'

He interrupted me. 'They have been unhappy about many aspects of my reign over this land, which do not resemble the ways they would have ruled. They are hard-minded men, who give no quarter and do not attempt to see any other view than their own. I think they would rather be rid of me and rule as tyrants in Rhegin, though Catigeorn desires to head west and make a name for himself as a ruler there. But now, dear sister, enough of my sons, tell me about what has happened to you.'

I sat with him and told the whole sad story, just as you have heard it. I wept as I recounted Bricius death, and he gave me a brotherly embrace and allowed me to cry onto his shoulder.

Chapter Sixteen

The Allies

The next day, Wyrtgeorn came to see me early in the morning. After yet another time of greeting, he became more serious.

'Denua, you may not be aware of how propitious is your arrival. We are beset by Picts who have moved from the north in droves. Whole armies of them seem to be coming into our land. If they were peaceful, we might find some way to deal with them, but they seem to wish to destroy our villages and our people to give them room.

As you know, I have invited the Ingwi-Seaxe to help us to repel them. Hengest and Kursa are good men, but know nothing of the land. I was going to detail Cadman to guide one of them, but I confess I was uncertain who I could ask to guide the other. Now you have arrived. Who better to ask than my warrior sister?'

So, he decided that he wished Cadman to guide Hengest's men, and he wanted me to guide Kursa and his men, with my troop assisting me.

He had already sent out scouts throughout the land, in pairs. If they spotted a Pictish raiding party, one man would ride back, and Hengest and his men would ride out. If a second pair spotted another, Kursa would go out, and for the third, Wyrtgeorn and his men would go.

'So, dear sister, the problem is that we do not know when we shall be called upon. It could be any moment, and I am so aware that you have only just arrived from an arduous journey. If the need were not so great... '; he tailed off.

'My dear brother, I am not so tired from the journey, we had restful stops. It may be that El Elyon has brought me back just at this time.'

'El Elyon? Do you still care for what the old Hebrew taught us? I have not thought on it for many a year. I do not think El Elyon brings any benefit to me, or my people. If you want gods, why do you not choose some British ones?'

'Dear brother, it is not I that has chosen El Elyon, but he who has chosen me. I can no more step away from him than fly.'

'Indeed, my dear sister, I will leave you to follow your El Elyon as you wish. However, I will need to bring you and Kursa's men together, so that they may know who is guiding them.'

An hour later, I sat on my horse while Kursa and his men were summoned. As they assembled, a few glances were cast in my direction, but when Wyrtgeorn introduced me as their guide, there was a commotion.

Kursa pulled forward, red-faced, 'This is a jest, surely, my Lord!'

From behind him, several of his men started to jeer. 'Do you wish to get us all killed, sending a woman with us?' sneered one, who, I noted with pleasure, was wearing a woollen cap and standing in front of a tree.

I had done this before. In one fluid movement, I leant to my left, caught my bow in my left hand, leant right, caught my arrow and sent it swishing towards the man. He had not even time to twitch before his cap was off and pinned to the tree.

'Who is next?' I called. 'I am a warrior with a bow and I hit whatever I will!'

The commotion stilled, then, as always happens, one near the back said in a low voice, 'Lucky strike!'

Though he was far back, I was high on my horse, and I saw well who it was. 'You! Do you have a purse? Hold it up!'

The man said nothing, but leant his head down as if he would not be seen.

'Scur, you vermin!' This was Kursa. 'The lady asked you to hold up your purse!'

As Scur was raising his purse, my arrow took it from him.

'I do not have lucky strikes! My arrow may save your life, be glad of it!'

I was satisfied to see Kursa's face as he turned back to his men. I am willing to swear he had never seen the like, but he had enjoyed what he saw.

'My lady', he said, after the troop had been introduced to me, 'would you do me the honour of riding back to our quarters with me?'

'Certainly, Kursa', I said, still glowing with a warrior's victory.

As we rode, he asked where I had learned my accuracy. 'In these fields around you, my Lord', I replied.

His curiosity did not let him stop there. 'But you must have had an excellent teacher.'

'Oh I did; his name is El Elyon.'

'I have not heard of this man, but I would be glad of his instruction for some of my men.'

How I laughed! When I recovered my breath, I said, 'My dear Kursa, El Elyon is a title in an Eastern language. I would be glad to introduce him to you and your men whenever you wish.'

'My lady, you puzzle me. What does this title mean and who does it belong to?'

'It means "The Most High God" ', I said. 'It is a title I learned from an Eastern man who had much knowledge of that One God who created all things from the beginning.'

'One? Do you have only one God?'

I will say this, I noted that he was persistent in holding me in conversation. I wondered whether he was really so interested in a divine being, or whether he had another reason for keeping me talking.

'Kursa, do you really want to know about my God?'

He smiled, quite a winning smile, and winked one eye at me, 'Well, one day I would like to know more about him, my lady, but for now I just wanted to keep you in conversation.'

Chapter Seventeen
Fighting

Two days later, a rider came in from the northwest with the news that a village, only an hour's ride away, had seen a Pictish band approaching. Cadman and Hengest raced off with their men, but hardly had they left when another rider came in from due north with the same story.

'They have planned to attack at several different places!' shouted Kursa to Wyrtgeorn as we left. 'Send the scouts back to the villages. Tell them to meet us at our position with further reports, then we can move swiftly from battle to battle!'

I realised that this excellent strategy came from dealing with the attacks of the tribes around the Ingwi-Seaxe lands, the Juti and the Frisians.

I led Kursa, his men and my troop to the village we were to deal with. It was surrounded by forest. Kursa sent half his men left, half his men right, and motioned for my troop to go straight in.

As we approached, we were set upon by about forty Picts, shouting and yelling to scare us. They wore hardly any garments. They carried spears and a few had swords.

I had my bow out in less than the blink of an eye, but as I shot my first, I heard a crashing in the forest, and Kursa's two bands of men had caught the Picts in a three way trap.

In a way it was sad. They did not have a chance to fight us. If I had not known that they were set to destroy the villages and kill the people, I could have reasoned with myself to hold back.

But it was not so, and we all did what we had to. I followed my usual practice and stayed back so that I could see who was where, and could place my shots exactly as needed.

The sun had hardly moved in the sky and it was finished. We had lost no-one. The Picts were all dead. The villagers, who had hidden in the forest, came out and threw themselves upon us in thanks.

We had started to help them to clear up the mess and the bodies, when we heard hoofbeats. We all picked up our arms in readiness, but it was a rider from another village, with the same story.

'I knew this was happening!' yelled Kursa as we rode. He shouted to the scout to ride to a further village, then return to us again.

The same events repeated at the next village. We used the same tactics, trapping the Picts between us and finishing them.

That day, we dealt with four villages before the scout returned to say that there were no more attacks.

We returned to Wyrtgeorn's hall to find that Hengest's men had done the same as us, with the same result. He had split his men into three parts, as we had. They had dispatched five Pictish raiding bands with no loss among his own men.

Wyrtgeorn was not so fortunate. He had not developed the tactics the Ingwi-Seaxe had used, and had lost five men, but still had saved two villages.

He relieved his scouts and sent out fresh men to ensure that the immediate threat was over, but as we waited, no-one returned. We returned to Noviomagus and went to our beds tired, but satisfied we had finished the task, at least for now.

It took six weeks for the Picts to try more attacks, but we used the same tactics, and my brother had by this time learnt what he must do.

We lost no men and as far as we could tell, we killed all the attackers. Wyrtgeorn at last lost his worried frown.

Chapter Eighteen

The Old Woman

The old woman looked at the fading light. 'I think it is time again for us to be taking our rest. When do you wish to return?'

'I will return in the morning if I may, as I did today.'

'Very well. I think we may reach the end of my story tomorrow.'

'I have liked it thus far. I think I will miss listening to you when it is finished.'

Chapter Nineteen

Love Blossoms

One day, after we had been out to train with the men, Kursa and I arrived back at Wyrtgeorn's hall to find that we were the only ones to have returned. We ordered meat from the kitchens, and sat and ate and talked.

It was the first time I had had an ordinary conversation with a man since Bricius had died. It felt so odd to be talking to a man in this way, I had to keep reminding myself that Bricius was gone, and I lived on.

We talked in Latin, which he knew well, for though I had picked up enough Ingwi-Seaxe from Cwen and Deogol to deal with the men outside, I had not enough words for more personal matters.

I told him, as I had told Wyrtgeorn, and as I have told you, of what had passed while I was a British princess, then Queen of the Parisii. I was gratified to note that he had heard of that tribe, and our city Lutetia, though as I thought on it, I realised my heart ached for Bricius.

He told me of his life as one of the Ingwi-Seaxe kings. I said it was strange, and he agreed, to have two kings in one tribe, but he and his brother had such a bond that for them, it worked.

We talked of Cwen, and how she had been lost, and now found by her people. As we talked of her, she returned, with Rowena, Deogol and some of her people. I recognised Beorn, who I had learnt was Cwen's cousin, and Hengest's chief warrior.

And so we settled. We remained on full alert, ready to move at a moment's notice, but the days went past slowly and peacefully. I expected

Pictish attacks at any moment, but for reasons I still know not, the peaceful days turned into weeks. It was about three months later when we had another very minor attack on two villages, which we repulsed as we had all the others.

There is something about being ready to die. It brings you to the place where only the important things matter. And the important things for our little band, Wyrtgeorn's guests, were each other.

Rowena blossomed into a very beautiful young lady. One day, as Kursa and I were alone in the eating hall, I mentioned her beauty. His eyes crinkled. 'Do you know what is happening there?' he asked.

I confessed I did not.

'It seems that an - understanding - has developed between her and Wyrtgeorn.' He gave a broad smile. I like it when men smile.

'But he is more than twenty years older!' I confess I was shocked.

'That is true, but firstly Rowena is a very mature young lady.'

'And second?'

'They are both very much in love. We have been seeing it for weeks.'

And so it was, that when the others returned, I watched more carefully what Rowena did, and found it was true! My brother, who had never taken much notice of women, was all eyes for Rowena and she for him! How had I not noticed this?

Having entirely missed Wyrtgeorn and Rowena, I began to take more notice of who spent time with whom, and was rewarded with the realisation that Cwen was spending an inordinate amount of time talking to Beorn.

But, as always, my own ignorance crept up on me. After many peaceful days - more than I thought we would have - Wyrtgeorn took me aside. 'My dear sister, do I see that a certain - friendship - is growing?'

I had no idea what he meant, but searched my mind, 'Do you mean Cwen and Beorn, or do you mean you and the beautiful Rowena?'

'Neither, my sweet blind sister', he laughed, 'I mean you and Kursa.'

I was aghast!

Had I led Kursa to think that I - I - ?

Well, yes I suppose I had. I thought on what had passed, and admitted to myself that I had enjoyed having the attention of a man again, but my grief was so recent that I had denied it.

Yet it was nonsense to let past events spoil the present. Tomorrow I might die. That moment I decided to let the past be past, and live for the present and the future.

So when Kursa asked me to sit with him at the next meal, we went and sat apart from the others in Wyrtgeorn's great hall.

The only difficult times we encountered were when Wyrtgeorn's sons, Guorthemir and Catigeorn, came. They showed no hesitation in expressing their opposition to Wyrtgeorn's relationship with Rowena. More than once there were raised voices, followed by crashing departures.

I tried to ask my brother about it, but he was so obviously distressed that I did not press him.

Chapter Twenty

Weddings

I suppose it was only to be expected. Wyrtgeorn came up to me one day and said, 'My dear sister, you know that Cwen and Beorn desire to marry?' I didn't, but I was not surprised.

'And Rowena and I also...?' I still was not surprised.

'And while the trouble with the Picts is abated, we are fetching in a holy man of your religion to marry us', I was pleased, but not surprised.

'And Kursa has asked me if I will allow him to marry you.'

Now I was surprised.

But as I thought on Kursa, I realised I could love him. He was not the same man as Bricius, of course, but he would make a good husband. He loved me, this I knew, and the more I dwelt on my feelings for him, the more I was swayed.

When next I met him, I pretended to be angry with him for talking to my brother about marriage before he talked to me. I could tell he was worried, then I burst out laughing, and we clung to one another as if we had never embraced in our lives.

The next day, I notified Wyrtgeorn that there would be a third marriage. He was delighted, and went off to send notification to the holy man.

We were all married two days later, when the holy man came. He used Greek and Latin names for El Elyon, but I suppose he knew what he was doing.

He determined that each couple was free to marry, and that each pair desired to marry the other, he supervised the giving of rings, then he pronounced us all men and wives!

I thought, as Kursa took me to his bed that night, of my first time with Bricius, how little I knew then, and how much I knew now. So, though Kursa was a very different man, much stronger and smelling like a warrior, I gave myself to pleasing him, and I found as much enjoyment in our love-making as I had in our conversation.

It may be that this is strange, but at that time I thought on Bricius, and how my heart stopped when he called me his sweet love. Would - could - the same be true of Kursa?

'Kursa.'

'Yes?'

'We don't know each other well, but I want you to know that I am glad to be your wife.'

'Denua, it may be that I know you better than you know me.'

'How can that be?'

'Aha!' He laughed. 'You forget who is my sister.'

'Cwen? What has she been saying?'

'She has been telling me about you. What a remarkable woman you are, how your beauty is matched by your understanding and kindnesses to her and by your ability as a warrior.'

'Cwen! When I see her I shall scold her!'

Kursa laughed till he shook. 'No, my beautiful British wife, you shall not scold her, for she only answered as I asked her. I loved you when I saw you shoot the cap and the purse. I would not let Cwen rest till she told me all she knew of you.'

I raised myself on my elbow and leant over him, my lips finding his. Compared to Bricius, Kursa was unpolished, even a little primitive, but I found I liked primitive!

The next morning, we went together to break our fast, and found Cwen and Beorn, and Wyrtgeorn and Rowena, all looking slightly sheepish.

I bounced in and asked if everyone had had a good night, and was met with blushes and smiles. It was enough.

It was two months later that I was sick early one morning. When I had recovered a little I joined the others and found a white-faced Cwen. 'Whatever is the matter with you, are you sick?' I asked.

'Do you not know, O observant woman?' said Cwen in a voice I had come to recognise as joking, 'And I might ask the same question of you!'

I am quick with arrows, but immensely slow of understanding of the ways of people. At Cwen's words, at last the light dawned. Of course! There was a reason we were both sick in the mornings!

I was stunned and sat for some time with my thoughts in turmoil. All those years with Bricius, with our sweet love-making. Now, suddenly, I spend a few nights with Kursa and...

Our bellies grew large together. Cwen knew what was happening, but as I did not, she was a great help in telling me what I must expect.

There was only one more Pictish raid that year, about three months later, again on only two villages. We dealt with it in the same way, but now my belly was getting rather large for battle. I was thankful that

Wyrtgeorn said that for the time being I was no longer needed, as the Ingwi-Seaxe could now find their way around the land well enough.

Cwen and I were delivered of two healthy babies only three days apart. She had a daughter, who she called Claennis, and I had a son, Lufian. It means love. I settled on the name because I had found love again, when I thought it had gone forever.

Chapter Twenty-One
Cracks in the Unity

month passed, then, quite unexpectedly, Wyrtgeorn called me to his rooms, 'Sister, dear, we have a problem with the Ingwi-Seaxe, and as you know them well, I seek your advice.'

'If I can help, my brother, I will, but what is this trouble you speak of?'

Then he explained what had been going on, unknown to me.

The very successful Ingwi-Seaxe tactics had quickly made the Pictish threat subside, but there were two consequences.

One was that the Ingwi-Seaxe warriors had started bringing over their wives and children, as they had found the land so hospitable. Hengest had written back to his home tribes to tell them of the pleasant land, with few inhabitants because many British had fled under the Pictish invasion, some to the western lands, some south across the sea to Gaul.

Then the British who remained had become angry with Wyrtgeorn, for inviting the Ingwi-Seaxe in the first place. Some British lords had even formed an opposition which wanted to get rid of the Ingwi-Seaxe.

The second consequence was that Wyrtgeorn, who had promised the Ingwi-Seaxe a monthly payment of gold while the Picts were attacking, was regretting his promise now that the threat had lifted.

And not only this, but the harvest for the previous year had been bad, and this year was worse. So lords and farmers who should have been rich enough to pay taxes to Wyrtgeorn were finding the expense of Hengest's force was just too much. In fact many had stopped paying altogether. Rebellion against the King's rule was simmering.

Then Wyrtgeorn made a bad mistake. He replied by sending Ingwi-Seaxe forces into the local estates to restore order, but of course this rebounded on him by causing even more ill-feeling among the British.

I was in a difficult position. Married to Kursa, I had some loyalty to the Ingwi-Seaxe, but I also understood that Wyrtgeorn had a serious problem with our own British people.

'My dear brother, I think you must call Hengest and Kursa and lay out this situation before them. I understand that the threat from the Picts has now come to an end, yet you have made promises to the Ingwi-Seaxe which still hold you. You must ask them to release you from this obligation. Perhaps if you promise them land, it will be enough.'

Wyrtgeorn called a meeting with Hengest and Kursa to find some way through the problems which now were besetting them.

He told them of those who wished him ill because of the arrival of the Ingwi-Seaxe, and that he now wished to cancel their agreement for their hire and for his payments, now that the threat from the Picts had gone.

I understand that some heated discussion followed, ending with Wyrtgeorn issuing an ultimatum that he would give the Ingwi-Seaxe the land of Ynys Tanatus in the east, where they had landed at first. They should now go back and live there.

Kursa stumped back in. 'Your brother has broken our bond!'

'My love, do you not think he is in a difficult position?'

'He may well be, but it is of his making, not ours!'

'So what shall we do?'

'We shall move to Ynys Tanatus. There is no way round his demand short of war, and as you are my wife, we cannot go to that.'

I called Deogol, my faithful warrior, who still served me in person, with his Parisii guard. I had been using the gold I had brought from Lutetia to ensure that he and his men remained well paid.

'Deogol. Our time here is now at an end, and we must move east to the island of Ynys Tanatus. It is time for me to repeat my offer which I made in Lutetia. If you wish it, you are released from your obligation to me, and you may return to your own people. I will cover the expense.'

'My Lady.' I knew his words before he said them. 'My men and I desire no more than you to serve wherever you wish to live, to the end of our days. You still are our Queen and to you our loyalty is.'

Tears came to my eyes, though I tried hard not to show them.

So, about a week later, the whole of the Ingwi-Seaxe army broke camp and started to move east.

Chapter Twenty-Two

Cantiaci

Cwen, Beorn, Kursa and I rode with my men, with Kursa's men following, then Hengest's men at the rear. Claennis and Lufian were only a few weeks old. Cwen and I bound them to our backs. We moved into Ceint, the land of the Cantiaci, the tribe to the east of Rhegin. The Cantiaci are a mixed tribe. For as long as has been known, a trickle of Juti and Seaxe have been coming across the water, settling and intermarrying with the Britons. They made a peaceful, tolerant people.

But things were different when the huge army of Ingwi-Seaxe swept east towards Ynys Tanatus. Villagers poured out of their homes and shouted at us, though we were only passing through their land.

It was fortunate that Ynys Tanatus was rather separate from the main part of Ceint, because the Ingwi-Seaxe were like locusts on the land.

Kursa was rather surprised when I told him of the size of home I desired, with quarters for my men, but I had been careful to spy out the land. I had sent my men into the Roman city which they called Durovernum, on the western edge of Ynys Tanatus.

My men had found, in the centre of the city, a fine Roman house, with walls panelled with exquisite Roman mosaics and a mosaic pavement in the centre of the house. But the beauty of the house was not the main object of my desire. No! I had found my desire! The house had a hypocaust!

The house was occupied by the governor of the Cantiaci, by the name of Gwrangon, but when I showed him the colour of my gold, I soon had possession.

'Kursa, my love', I said as I arrived back at the camp after acquiring the house. 'I wonder if you would like to come and live with me?'

Kursa looked at me quizzically, a look I have learnt to love well. 'What new surprise do you have for me now, you woman of surprises?'

'Come and see.'

It took months, but gradually the Ingwi-Seaxe camps faded as we built homes and settled. My city was now being called Cantwarabyrig, as the Ingwi-Seaxe were now taking on the name of Ceint and calling themselves the Cantware.

Cwen and Beorn moved into our house with us. It was easily big enough for all of us. Kursa vowed that he had never lived in such luxury, in fact he vowed it every day! We were the envy of all. My men repaired adjacent dwellings and we soon had a thriving Ingwi-Seaxe enclave.

Hengest had become the ruler of Ceint without a struggle, as Gwrangon had wisely decided to make himself scarce. He did well, however, as he moved to Londinium, which was becoming a popular town and growing fast.

Despite the initial response of the Cantiaci tribe to our arrival, Hengest soon became popular as governor of Ceint, because he kept good order, and decided wisely when disputes were brought to him. Kursa took responsibility for the warriors, providing security against attack.

We watched the children grow, walk, talk. I delighted in having a son. Cwen and I devoted much time to teaching them to read and write. I made sure they understood Brittonic, and Cwen Ingwi-Seaxe. We both shared our understanding of El Elyon.

We lived comfortably for five years in our luxurious house. I had gradually fallen more and more in love with Kursa. He was a gentle giant when he was with me, though a formidable foe on the battlefield. Deogol and my Parisii guard found wives, homes and land to work.

And then the attack came.

Chapter Twenty-Three
Attack

A messenger for Cwen came on a heavily lathered horse. Hengest was there as the messenger arrived, asking for Lady Cwen, and we all gathered to hear what he had to say.

'My Lady Cwen, I bring urgent news from your daughter, Lady Rowena. Wyrtgeorn's sons Guorthemir and Catigeorn have fomented a rebellion within the army. Many of Wyrtgeorn's loyal men have been killed at a banquet when they were set upon by rebels posing as guests. Wyrtgeorn has been deposed, though he has escaped and fled west with Rowena.'

'But, my Lady, Lords, there is graver news. Guorthemir has put it about that the evil massacre was your work, the work of the Ingwi-Seaxe. He is even showing copies of invitations to the feast to prove you and your men were there. This has caused much ill feeling against you, so that many British have joined their army, determined to see the land cleansed of Ingwi-Seaxe.'

Hengest spoke, 'This is distressing news indeed. Have you knowledge of when they might be here?'

'When I encountered them, Guorthemir was just south of Londinium, but his army were sweeping east into Ceint, intent on meeting your forces on Ynys Tanatus. They are traveling slowly with foot soldiers, so I estimate it will be another two days before they arrive.'

Hengest and Kursa convened a council with Beorn. I was invited to attend with Deogol, as it was thought that my small Parisii troop could play a useful part.

'The first thing', said Hengest, 'Is that I do not wish to engage in a battle in Ynys Tanatus. We will battle away from our homes, then return for succour. We will be much better fed and watered than they.'

'We will also attack them when they are not yet ready for battle. We will depart immediately and march west at Roman pace. We will send out scouts to find their position, then we will select our own battle site, wait there and surprise them.'

'Denua. Your men will act as the fly to the spider. You will draw them out, making them think there are only thirty men. My men and Kursa's men will attack from hidden positions on each side. We have done this before, I think?'

His eye had a merry twinkle, despite our serious situation. I thought to myself that he and Kursa seemed to be more alive when a battle was in prospect.

'When we have made them look to the sides, you will then attack hard from the front, yes?'

I looked at Deogol, who nodded.

'You can still shoot faster than any bowman I have ever seen?'

I blushed.

'Just ensure that your men surround you so that your safety is not at risk, then shoot as fast and as accurately as you can.'

I called Deogol and my Parisii guard together. They seemed to arrive only just after the call went out. I had the distinct impression that they too were excited to be going into battle again, after so long at peace.

We started to travel west. Our men were fresh and travelled fast. Although I rode, some of the foot soldiers almost kept pace. Our scouts were about two hours ahead of us.

We had travelled for about four hours when a scout returned to say he had seen the Rhegin army pitching camp for the night about one day's travel away.

'They have come faster than we thought', said Kursa, 'But now we have our chance!'

Hengest, Kursa, Deogol and I went ahead on our horses. After an hour we found a valley which lay in the path of the Rhegninses.

'Here is our place', said Hengest. 'Denua and Deogol, when you are given the signal that the Rhegninses approach, you will take your men down the valley to meet them. Ensure that you make as much noise as you can, then appear frightened when you see them. Make as if to turn back, then wait for our attack from the sides. When you see them confused, push in your attack from the front. And Denua.'

'Yes, my Lord?'

'You will need to put on some disguise to prevent them recognising you, or the game will be up!'

So it was that early the next morning, my small troop of Parisii found ourselves waiting for the huge Rhegin army. I wore a hood as a disguise. Scouts had gone up either side of the valley, and when we had waited (in my case impatiently!) for over two hours, the signal came.

We saw two people waving from a position on the hill to our left, which could not be seen by the Rhegin army.

We advanced, shouting, laughing and screaming, as if returning drunken from a feast. We pretended to be unaware of them, but we saw the first rank of men stop and look to their commanders for orders.

Cautiously they started to advance, upon which we turned as if to flee. That was enough for the undisciplined horde, they came after us like madmen.

We retreated before them, then we heard shouting to either side. Hengest and Kursa had swept in behind their main force, cutting off their escape and trapping them exactly as we had done so often with the Picts.

Now! I turned my Parisii round, and we advanced on their front line, which was in disarray because of the unexpected attack from the side. Two-thirds of my men I sent on ahead to press in our attack. One third surrounded me and supported me as I started to let fly my arrows.

I shot fast and on target. The men round me cheered as each one hit. Rarely was there one which did not. I saw yet another wave of uncertainty sweep over the front lines of the Rhegin army as they started to lose men from our attack.

Hengest and Kursa's men were working their way towards each other through the Rhegninses. Now we had advanced, I could see Guorthemir and Catigeorn standing in the centre of their army.

In my mind I knew what would happen.

Hengest and Kursa rode at the head of their men into the enemy. Soon they had their horses hacked from beneath them and were swinging their heavy swords into the Rhegninses.

I shouted to my men to push forward fast, but as I was on my horse, my enthusiasm to advance carried me through their protective wall.

From my position, I could easily see what I dreaded. The attention of Hengest and Kursa was on their immediate attackers, but they did not know that they were being channelled towards Guorthemir and Catigeorn.

Hengest backed further and further towards Catigeorn. I saw Catigeorn raise his sword. He was just two paces behind Hengest. There was no way to warn him in the noise of battle. I raised my bow. I had never had range before, but this would demand it. I pulled back harder than I ever remember, and loosed an arrow for a distance I never dreamed I would need.

The arrow caught Catigeorn full in the centre of his neck. I saw blood spurt, his sword fell sideways, then he fell after it.

My men roared, but I knew we were not free of danger. I swept my view across the Rhegninses, and found Guorthemir. Like a nightmare repeating itself he was also raising his sword behind Kursa.

This was an easier shot. He was closer. I pulled and loosed. My arrow hit him full in the chest. My heart lifted within me. But then I paused, Guorthemir was still on his feet! He swung at Kursa, but due to his injury his aim was not good. His blow caught Kursa just below his right shoulder. Kursa fell! My heart was in my mouth as I watched Guorthemir then raise his sword to strike. His sword dropped.

Then another arrow caught him in the belly, and he fell on top of Kursa. I looked down at my bow. I had shot the second arrow. I did not even realise what I did.

'Not again.' I shouted at El Elyon, 'Not again! I have lost one good man to warfare, I cannot live if I lose another!'

I pushed through the battle to Kursa and rolled Guorthemir off him. His right shoulder was dreadfully injured and he had a deep wound to the stomach from Guorthemir's second strike. I shouted to my men to gather and protect me and Kursa. The battle raged about us as I tore my cloak for bandages to stem the blood.

Chapter Twenty-Four
Life or Death

*G*radually the battle subsided. The Rhegninses, though they outnumbered us by two to one, were in disarray because of the loss of their leaders. They started to flee, from the back at first, then those who fought at the front.

My men did not need to be told what to do. Some had already formed a pallet to put Kursa on, and as soon as the fighting lessened, they caught him up and headed off towards Cantwarabyrig.

On horseback, I was there before them, but not long before. They arrived exhausted with their effort. After a short time, Cwen arrived. Together we laid Kursa on a bed and started to dress his wounds. The belly wound looked serious but not immediately deadly. The right shoulder wound was much more serious, with light coloured blood flowing freely from it. We devoted ourselves to staunching the bleeding by pressure.

It was much later, after dark, when an exhausted Hengest came in. 'How does he?' he asked.

'He may die.' I could not stop the tears flowing. Hengest came and hugged me. 'Not if we can do anything. I may be able to help.'

I did not know what he meant, and he immediately left the room.

A short while later there was a timid knock on the door. In walked a small woman, about my age, but dressed in a long cloak and hood which concealed her features. She swept the hood back and Cwen gasped, 'Ardith!'

The old woman stopped, looked at me, and smiled.
Then she continued.

They hugged and danced round the room while I wondered if Kursa and I had been forgotten, but soon they stopped and Ardith came to me with a look of concern on her face.

'Denua - may I call you Denua?'

'Of course.'

'Denua, I have spent many years learning the deep secrets of the physician. I lost my betrothed many years past, and I swore I would no longer have a man, but I would have learning. As I am high-born, I was able to pursue my desire.'

'I have my bag with me, which contains things which may help to stem Kursa's bleeding, and prevent the wound fever. May I use my skills to help him?'

I watched as she carefully removed the rough dressings I had applied. She took from her bag a small pot. Lifting the lid, she took out what looked like mould with a finger and pressed it into the wound on Kursa's belly, then on his shoulder.

'The belly wound does not look deep, but it has caused some damage inside him. I will do what I can.'

Out of the bag came another small pot, filled with liquid. She lifted from it a small needle and thread. Bending over Kursa, she started to sew, first his belly, then his shoulder. She pulled apart each layer of flesh and sewed each separately. It was only then that I heard Kursa make a sound, as if he was in pain, and he jerked his shoulder.

'My love, rest easy, we are tending your wounds.'

'Well I know it. I have tried to lie still, but my shoulder gives much pain.'

'I thought you asleep.'

'Not so far, my love.' For just a moment Kursa broke into a smile.

Ardith stopped her sewing and took out a small flask from her bag. She removed the bung and held it to Kursa's mouth. 'Drink this. The pain will lessen.'

Kursa drank and swallowed. It was only moments later that his features relaxed and he closed his eyes again.

It took much of the night for Ardith to be satisfied. Eventually she said, 'There, I have done all I can for now. Keep him quiet and warm, his wounds clean, and I will come again tomorrow.'

Then, quietly, she said to me, 'His life hangs in the balance. Despite all I know, these wounds are so serious that most will die. Prepare yourself.'

Cwen and I watched him all that night. He slept fitfully, waking and groaning, then breathing more deeply. Near dawn Cwen insisted that I take some rest, and when the sun was well risen, I relieved her.

Around that time Ardith returned. She laid her hand on his forehead, gave him more of the sleeping draught, spread some more mould onto his wounds, then replaced his dressings. Then she said,

'Not long now. The wound fever sets in. You must keep him warm if he shivers and sponge him with cool water if he sweats.'

And so we did.

While I was on my watch, Kursa started to shake as if he were frozen, yet he did not wake. I lay down beside him and held him until he quietened. He lay quiet for a long time, then his face started to redden. I felt his forehead as I had seen Ardith doing. He was so hot! I brought the bowl we had put ready and sponged him till he cooled. He still did not wake.

And so we went on, day after day, tending him as he lay, not knowing whether he would live or die. Ardith came every day but could do no more.

On the eighth day, he opened his eyes and looked at me. I was so delighted to see him awake that I ran to him and embraced him, which caused him to yell with pain.

'How do you feel, my love?' I asked.

'I am in pain from my arm, but my belly seems to be better.'

'We have been so frightened for you.'

'Yes, I know it, and I have been frightened for myself, for I heard Ardith say, "His life hangs in the balance. These wounds are so serious that most will die. Prepare yourself." '

'Oh, she did not know you heard! I am so sorry that her words frightened you.'

'My love, it may sound odd, but I am somewhat glad they did.'

I looked at him quizzically.

'For I have lain here, aware that I might not survive, and my thoughts dwelt constantly on the God you serve.'

I raised my eyebrows at this, but he continued.

'Cwen had already told me much about this God and his son. I think I know, by now, all the stories that exist about him. But at that time I did not take her seriously. I felt I needed nothing.'

He stopped and took a deep breath.

'Then I heard Ardith's warning to you. I was too weak to show I heard, even to open my eyes, but in my mind I knew I faced the end of my life.'

'Oh my love!' I leant over him and embraced him.

'So, I thought if I was about to stand in his presence, it would be wise to make my peace with him. My voice failed me, so in my mind I called out.'

His face seemed to brighten.

'And, do you know? He came to me!'

His voice took on a fervent edge, and he gripped my arm till I wondered if he was in control of himself.

'It was him! The one of whom Cwen speaks. He came to me and he spoke to me!'

'Tell me what he said, my love.'

'He said, "Do not be afraid, you will not die, but when you return from the dead you will serve me!"'

He seemed so bright and agitated that I said, 'Calm yourself, my love. Now it is time to rest. We will think on these things when you are well.'

Chapter Twenty-Five
The Call

I was not sure whether Kursa would remember, when he was better, what he had said when he was unwell. But as he recovered, he spoke many times of the change which had come over his life. He said he felt 'as if my name has been called', and like a good soldier, he intended to report for duty.

I was pleased. Yet again I had witnessed this remarkable change.

But he did not recover completely. To be sure, his belly wound healed leaving a scar only as long as my thumb. But his right arm and shoulder, well, they were so damaged. The sword had cut deeply into the muscle, and despite Ardith's sewing skills, it was plain he would never swing a weapon again.

I tried to put myself into his mind, tried to wonder what it would feel like to lose the ability to fight, when fighting is all you know.

'Kursa', I tried, when he was well healed in all other ways, 'You know your right arm has been deeply wounded?'

'Yes...'

'And it may well be that it will not recover enough so that you can go into battle again?'

'Yes...'

'I wondered - just how you felt about losing an ability which has been so important to you...'

I had been looking away, dreading his response, but my hesitant speech was interrupted by loud laughter.

When I turned, Kursa was crying with laughing, 'Important? Only because it had to be; my brother had to rule and I had to support him, that is how it has "had to be" since we were only just out of boyhood! But now it "cannot be" and at last I am free of an obligation which I never asked for, and nobody is more joyful than I!'

'But...'

'At last I am free to do what I want. And at last I think I know what I want.'

I was amazed by his reaction, swept up into his joy. 'And what is it you are thinking about?'

'I need to talk to two people before I am certain: you, and Cwen, but I think I would like to see you together.'

Cwen arrived with Beorn; both faces showed they were wondering what was happening.

Kursa didn't hesitate, 'Cwen, my dearest sister, you have long been telling me stories about the one Denua calls El Elyon. I was careful to ignore you, but during my illness I realised I might meet him sooner than I thought, so I made my peace with him. As I did so, he appeared to me, whether to my eyes or in my mind I know not and it matters not. He told me I would live - and serve him. That is what I intend to do.'

Cwen and Beorn sat with eyes staring as if they had been struck, but Cwen was smiling.

'Sister dear, I have been thinking much about your story of Maewyn, the one the people of Ynys Ériu call Padraig. I need to ask my beautiful wife', he looked at me with a smile, 'whether she would be willing to come with me to Ynys Ériu to find him. I sense that the one I now serve is calling me to help in Padraig's work.'

Now I know that some would greatly dislike leaving the comfort of a grand residence to follow the footsteps of an itinerant preacher around a distant island, but something in me leapt for joy to hear Kursa's plan.

'My love, nothing would thrill me more than to go on such an adventure with such a man as you!'

We were gazing at each other, suddenly so much more in love than before, when we heard a discreet cough. Cwen!

'Cwen, my sweet friend, I am sorry, we were swept up in our plans and had lost you!' I said.

Then, unexpectedly, Beorn spoke. 'Denua and Kursa. I know that at present I do not share your knowledge of this "Elyon", but I do love Cwen. I also know that if she has given herself to serve Elyon, then that will be the best for her and it will be best for me also.'

We sat open-mouthed; none of us had ever heard Beorn say so many words together. But he was not finished.

'And I know that Cwen loves to be with Denua, and that nothing pleases me more than to serve Kursa, and that our children, Claennis and Lufian, are inseparable.'

'So, if Cwen is agreeable, we would like to come with you.'

It was four months later when we arrived on Ynys Ériu. We had paid off my Parisii guard and instructed them to put about the story that Kursa had died from his wounds. Otherwise, we knew that he was so famous that his enemies would track him down.

We had sent messengers ahead, and we arranged to meet Maewyn at a place they call Tara, where a King had become a believer.

As we approached the meeting place an old man came out to us from a small house. He looked at each of us and spoke. To me he said, 'It is good to meet again, servant of El Elyon. He has you in high regard.'

He then looked at Claennis and Lufian, 'You are destined to be Royal servants of the Most High God. From you will come one who will unite two Royal Houses. But you must remember this. Be you ever so high, higher than all you rule, yet you are still only a servant to Him. So you must keep your hearts humble, as a servant is humble. Keep this in mind when you administer justice.'

He spoke to Kursa and said, 'You have received your life and you have received a call to serve your new Lord. You have answered the summons faithfully. God will give you more success in this new life than you had in the old.'

To Cwen he said, 'You are curious to know. God will reveal much to you. It will be your task to reveal it to others.'

He turned his gaze upon Beorn, who gazed back just as intently. He was silent for some time, then said, 'You are not yet where you need to be, yet you have an honest heart, and you desire to know the one you seek. You must, for a short time, leave your friends and come with me.'

Beorn looked round at us, suddenly nervous, I laughed, 'Off you go, we will wait here for you.'

It was about an hour later when Beorn emerged. He looked as if the weight of the world had suddenly been lifted from him. He ran to Cwen and they embraced, weeping on each others' shoulders.

Padraig spent some days with us, discussing our task. We decided to come here to set up this little community. And so we did.

Chapter Twenty-Six
The Old Woman

The old woman looked at me. To my eyes she suddenly looked less aged, as if the telling had renewed her.

'So, Ardith, thank you for writing my story. I hope you have enjoyed it. I did not realise at first that your ability as a scribe would match your excellence in healing. Would you carefully keep your vellum and when Claennis and Lufian are grown, they shall have it.'

Part Two:

The Tale of Claennis and Lufian

Chapter Twenty-Seven
Prologue

*K*ursa smiled weakly at Padraig. 'Not this time', he said, quite gently, and shook his head.

'Are you sure now? Won't I be bringing you back, like before?' Padraig lifted his eyes to meet Denua's steady gaze.

Denua sat on Kursa's bed, her eyes moist. By the bed stood Lufian, a tall and handsome man in his early twenties.

Beorn, Cwen, Deogol and Ardith stood in the background.

'What was it that Paul said?' Kursa spoke quietly, but with no sign of distress in his voice. 'He would rather be away from his body and at home with the Lord? I've had many years of service to El Elyon, and many years of enjoyment of his presence and strength, of his gifts of a strong, beautiful wife, a son who is a credit to his father, and friends who cannot be matched for their faithfulness and love. But now he tells me in my spirit that he wants me home with him. Do not be sad. But a short time and we shall all meet again in the throne-room of El Elyon.'

Kursa closed his eyes. 'Hold my hands.'

Denua took his left, Padraig his right. Kursa's breathing quietened. It seemed as if he would sleep again. Then his eyes opened wide; he seemed to stare straight past them. A huge smile broke out on his face. 'Ah!' He cried out as if he had suddenly found something he had lost. Then his head, which had lifted, dropped back to the bed; his body relaxed and he breathed out for the last time.

Chapter Twenty-Eight

The Old Woman

he door opened and there she stood, unchanged from my memory of her. She had seemed to be old for so very long, yet always vigorous, as if life were thrusting through her very being. Her hair, once of vibrant chestnut, had whitened into a glorious cascade of pale brown.

She greeted me almost with a shout, 'Ardith! Come in! Thanks be to El Elyon that he has led you here at this time!'

I went in. The door opened to a square courtyard, with rooms opening off all around. In the centre was a beautiful garden, full of vegetables and herbs. Of course I had seen it before, though not for some years, but its life and fruitfulness quite made me gasp.

She led the way to one of the rooms. Though I could see my breath when we were in the open air, the room was warm and cosy with woollen drapes and thick woven hangings.

She called outside the door, and soon a young man arrived with jars of mead and wooden platters full of meats.

'Is this suitable?' she said, 'I presume you"ve been travelling in the cold for some time, you must be hungry - and do you still like mead?'

'So, what has brought you to my door after so long?'

We had eaten well, and had finished sharing our news since we had last met, and she looked at me with that piercing gaze of hers; you knew nothing could slip past it.

'I have been holding in my heart the words you wrote in your last letter. You said...'

'... I have another story which I would like to see written on your scrolls.' She finished off my sentence for me.

'Yes, but is this occasion suitable for you? I do not want to take your time from other duties, yet I would dearly love to continue my adventure into your life.'

She laughed; that high full sound which was so infectious that others found themselves smiling along, even if they did not know the cause.

'Little do you know my dear Ardith! It was only yesterday I was speaking with El Elyon and explaining to him that the busy-ness of my life had dimmed and I needed something new to give my time to. Then, today - here you stand at my door! So, have you brought all that you need?' Here, she looked at my bag, which I had loaded down with all my scriptorium apparatus.

'Of course. I have been so hopeful we could continue. But what have you decided you wish to tell me?'

'What else? The story of Claennis and Lufian. The adventure which changed a whole nation! This time I intend to be a true narrator - a story-teller! But, let me ask, are you free to stay? I have a comfortable room for you, and we are all heated by the hypocaust.'

'Deogol is on a long hunting trip with some of his old comrades from the Parisii warriors. He loves it so much, and he expects to be away for many weeks. He has said he will send a messenger to inform me when he finishes. Until then, I am free.'

I prepared to write, and she settled in her seat as she started to speak.

Chapter Twenty-Nine

Prison!

*L*ufian woke from a bad dream. Surely he had not drunk so much last night? His heart was pounding and his head was throbbing. He realised only slowly that he was not waking from a bad dream, but to one instead.

The events of the previous day filtered back into his mind. Then the regrets flooded in. If only he had been more careful. If only he had taken the safer route. If only he had watched out better. If only he had not started this foolish mission at all! If only his mother had not accepted the request of the Parisii.

He opened his eyes to the darkness of his cell. In the dim light from some sort of grating, he could just make out the heavy Roman stonework and the thick door.

The Romans knew what they were doing when they designed this one!

He listened. There was no sound at all, apart from a distant hiss of a breeze.

His left leg was hurting. He tried to move it and pain shot through him like an arrow. He nearly cried out, but realised that may not be wise. He took a deep breath and gritted his teeth till the pain subsided.

'Who's there?' The sudden sound made Lufian jump and jerked his leg. This time he did cry out, a muffled yelp.

'I said, who is there?'

Trying not to move his leg, Lufian twisted his head round to see where the voice came from. Behind him were thick wooden bars, dividing off his section of the cell. And there was a figure, staring at him.

It was difficult to make out any features, but he got the impression of a thickset man with a large beard, sitting on the floor, but leaning against the bars and staring through.

'I know there is somebody there, I heard the door shut last night and I heard you snoring and I just heard you yell! Who are you?'

'My name is Lufian.' Lufian spoke through his pain. He did not want to give any information away, he was in enough trouble already, but he also didn't want this man to keep shouting and alert any guards.

'Lufian, eh? Where from? Your speech sounds Saxon, or British.'

'Who are you?' said Lufian. His mind was still slow, but the man had been speaking Brittonic, his mother's language, though his accent was unfamiliar.

'My name is Galba.'

'Your accent is Gaulish.'

'I am from Armorica', said Galba, 'but my parents were Brittonic. They came across to Gaul when the "Saxons" invaded.' Galba said 'Saxons' as if he were spitting, and Lufian took a warning. 'Where are you from?'

'I am from Éire', Lufian said, truthfully but incompletely.

'I thought your accent had some Éireann', said Galba triumphantly, as if he had been trying to work out in his head what Lufian's voice reminded him of. 'There were some Éireanns in my home village, you sound a bit like them.'

They were suddenly interrupted by noises from outside: shouting, and something being dragged. Lufian's cell door burst open, a body was thrown in, and the door slammed shut again.

Lufian raised himself up as far as he could without hurting his leg. Whoever it was had been thrown against a far wall, and wasn't moving.

'He can't be dead', said Galba, staring through the wooden bars, 'or they wouldn't bother throwing him in here with us.'

'Can you see him any better than I can?' enquired Lufian.

'No. I see only in the light. I see nothing in dim places as others do. The physician says there is something wrong with my eyes. In here, I'm nearly blind.'

That explains why he is pressed up against the bars, staring, thought Lufian.

They were quiet for some time, then Galba said 'We used to have a holy man come through Armorica from Éire, name of Patricius. Have you come across him?'

'I have heard of him, but never met him', lied Lufian. He had decided that he was in enough trouble already, and if this man hated Saxons, he had better give away as little as possible and try to steer the conversation into questioning Galba.

'So, tell me', he said, 'what encounter have you had with him?'

'It's a long story', said Galba.

'We may have a long time', Lufian replied.

Galba began his story.

Chapter Thirty
Galba's Story

I suppose I must have been about eight when I first heard the name Patricius. The whole village was abuzz with the news. He was coming from Éire to visit the place where he had studied in central Gaul; Alsiodorum, the Romans called it. In those days you could travel from Armorica to central Gaul without any trouble, apart from the occasional thief. Those were the peaceful days before the Franks and Gauls started raiding our lands.

All the men of the village went to greet him as he came through. I asked my mother if I could go but she said no. I went to my sleeping pallet and pretended to lie down to sleep. When she went to stand outside the door, as I had thought she might, I crept out of the back of the house and joined the crowds.

And what a crowd it was! People had come from villages all around. I had thought I would easily find my father, but there were too many people. I just got swept along with the crowd, to the hill outside our village.

Patricius stood high on the hill and we all sat down. He started to talk. He talked about God, which did not surprise me, but what did surprise me was the way he seemed familiar with him. As if he knew him. Like a person would know another.

I crept closer and closer, till there was only three rows of adults in front of me. I peered round the nearest person and tried to listen to what he was saying.

Suddenly he stopped talking and looked straight at me. 'Look for the bent tree, and run past it!' he said. I had no idea what he was talking about. I looked about me and saw no sign of a bent tree.

I looked back at him, then he spoke again to me, 'Make the most of the light, but learn about the darkness.'

Here is a man who talks in riddles, I thought to myself, though if I had known then what I know now I would have paid more attention.

Patricius talked on, people in the crowd were asking questions, the sun was warm, and I didn't understand some of the things they talked about. I just got sleepy.

The next thing I know, I woke on the hillside, still in the warm afternoon sun, but nearly everyone had gone. There were a few people in the distance, but only one man near me.

He looked nasty, and smelt bad too. 'What have we here?' he said. 'A little boy! You are far from home, where are your parents?'

When I didn't answer, he suddenly grabbed my arm and started to drag me away. I shouted at him, but it made no difference. We went over a small rise, me fighting and kicking, then he hit me hard. Knocked me pretty well senseless.

As I started to recover, I saw a woman coming towards us. My hopes lifted, but then were dashed when she smiled at him, then hit me herself. 'You do as we tell you and you won't get hurt.'

We must have walked for an hour before they stopped to rest by a brook. The man said he was going to get water. The woman started to unpack food from her bag.

I realised I had no idea where I was. Even if I could have escaped I didn't know the way home. I would have stayed there because I was afraid, but as I looked towards the brook, where the man was stooping for water, I saw, beyond him, a tree, impossibly bent over, as if a great hand had come down and squashed it.

Patricius's words suddenly flared into courage in my head. The woman was bent over her bag. I jumped up and gave her a good push.

She fell with her head in the bag. I raced to the brook, up behind the man and gave him a good push too. He fell right into the water. I headed as fast as I could for the bent tree, knowing in my heart that they would recover and catch me.

I raced past the tree, looking behind me. I realised too late that the tree was bent by the wind, which had been blowing up a steep escarpment. I was running so fast I went straight off the edge.

I seemed to fall for ever. It took so long I had time to think as I went down. I was certain I would die from the fall. The only thing I could think of was the way the holy man talked about God. As if he was real.

'Help me God!' I'm sure I didn't actually say it, it probably just happened in my head. Then suddenly I hit something. I seemed to be falling through something painful, scratching me all over. I put my arms over my head and gradually I stopped.

I was astonished I was not dead. I had fallen into a thick bush at the bottom of the embankment. I was held in a small cocoon of leaves and twigs, right in the middle of the huge bush. Although I was scratched, I seemed to have no bones broken, and I was still alive.

I was so winded by the shock and the fall that I stayed quite still where I was, and it was a good thing I did. I heard shouts from the couple as they made their way down the escarpment and started to search for me.

I froze, hardly daring to breathe. They came right up to the bush I had fallen into, obviously realising I must have fallen near to it. They tried to push into the bush but it was so dense that they couldn't get in.

Then the woman said, 'He's not here, perhaps he has run off.' She sounded disappointed, and I was glad.

It seemed like an age before their voices died away, but eventually, I was sure they must have gone. I started to try to get out, but I was held so fast by the bush that the only way out was to climb up, the way I had fallen in.

I was already badly scratched, but climbing upwards through the bush made me doubly so. Eventually I reached daylight at the top and started to move down the side. As I reached the ground a hand shot out from behind me and grabbed my arm! They had hidden in wait for me!

'Aha, you little rat!' said the man. 'So, you were in that bush after all!'

I began to cry, sobbing more than I ever remember. Then I became angry, but here's the strange thing, I found myself angrier with Patricius's God than with my captors! I began to shout at him, 'Why did you not save me? Why did you let me fall then get me caught again?'

'To teach you something important!' came the reply. I jerked round, it wasn't my captors, but another voice which had spoken. I twisted as far as I could and could just see Patricius himself! He was about thirty paces away!

'You get away from us!' yelled the man. 'Leave my wife and son alone!'

'I'm not his son!' I screamed.

'Peace, Galba.' Patricius's voice had an immediate effect. 'And you two evil people, sleep!'

To my astonishment, both the man and his wife fell to the ground as if they had been slain.

Patricius turned his gaze on me. 'Remember this Galba: There will be times when your body will not be free, but God will always be there with you, and he will never fail you. Now we will leave these two to the mercies of God, or his judgments, and take you home.'

And truly I tell you, eight years later I was enslaved again for a short time, but I remembered the words of Patricius. I spoke to his God, and immediately I was given an opportunity to escape.

Chapter Thirty-One
Elico Wakes

Galba's story was interrupted by a groan.

'Hey there!' Galba called over to the newcomer, 'You awake?'

Lufian twisted round, despite the pain in his leg. He could dimly see the man, who was trying to sit up, and groaning.

His head turned towards Lufian and suddenly he flinched. 'Are you Burgundian?' he said in a voice which sounded full of fear.

Galba replied, 'No. I'm from Brittany.'

'And you?'

'No, I'm not Burgundian.' Lufian had a strange sense that it would be unwise to reveal his background.

'Ah, the Lord be praised. I asked him to give me some allies in my distress, or at least no more enemies.'

'Allies? Who are you fighting?' Lufian asked, innocently.

'Same as you I would have thought - are we not all in the same trouble?'

He was still for a moment, then looked at Lufian, 'You do know what the fighting is about, surely?'

Galba and Lufian replied at the same time:

Galba said, 'Of course!'

Lufian said, 'Not the faintest idea.'

The man looked at Lufian quizzically, but Galba came to his aid, 'He's from Éire.'

'Ah, you haven't been here long then?'

'No, I only recently came over.' It was obvious to Lufian that he was about to probe further, so he decided to change the subject. 'Tell me what all this is about so I don't get myself into more trouble.'

The man looked at Galba. 'Do you want to explain, or shall I?'

'Help yourself.' said Galba.

Before Elico could start his account, the sound of scraping came from the doors, as boards of bread were pushed under. Someone dropped a leather sack of water through the wooden bars.

They all fell upon the stale bread as if it were a feast.

My name is Elico and I am a servant of Chilperic, the King of Lugdunum in Burgundia.

Yes Galba, I hear you suck your breath between your teeth, but hear out my story.

There is a tradition in Lugdunum that once a year, the local families are permitted to select candidates to serve in the Lord of Lugdunum's court. The child must be at least ten years old and not more than one child per family.

The Lord and his advisors choose children to learn to serve at the court or as a warrior. It is a great honour for a family to have a child selected, for it gives them access to the court.

I was chosen when I was ten years old to train to be a servant to the Lord. I was trained well, and worked hard, and five years later I was attending the Lord regularly. I served his food, carried messages when he sat in judgement, I even travelled with his retinue when he rode to hold court in his villages. My favourite occupation was to write the Lord's judgments - yes I can write, I was taught by my mother from my earliest years, and she from her mother.

When the old Lord died with no successor, King Gondios, King of Burgundia, installed one of his sons, Chilperic, as Lord. The whole city was apprehensive that he would act like his father and take no notice of the views of the people, but he was a good Lord, and listened to us. As a result, he kept our much-loved traditions alive and retained all the old Lord's servants as his own.

One day we heard that King Gondios had died and his kingdom had been divided between his four sons. The third son, Chilperic, already the Lord of Lugdunum, now became the King of Lugdunum. He took a renowned wise man, Senaculos, as his advisor.

When I was eighteen years old, Senaculos called me into his rooms.

'Elico, you have attracted the attention of the king. He has noticed your loyalty to him, your diligence and careful attention to detail.'

I started to speak, 'My Lord, I was only doing... ', when Senaculos interrupted me.

'Be quiet, boy! Now is the time for you to be listening, not talking!'

I realised my error, and quickly looked down.

'Now, as I was saying. The king has noticed your abilities, and wishes to see whether you have the wit to learn to be his advisor. I am to teach you and assess you.'

I could not hold myself back, 'But my Lord, you are his advisor!'

'If you do not keep silent when I speak, you young whelp, I will see that you speak to the walls of the king's cells! Nevertheless, as you are so keen to speak, I will make you answer me a question. What is the meaning of my name?'

'Senaculos, my Lord.' I spoke timidly for fear of further reaction. 'Senos means... ', I hesitated, '... old.'

'Quite right. I have spent my whole life with this name, "Old". I was old even when I was young. But now my body is catching up with my name. In fact I am so old that I have become ill. The king's physician says I have a disease which will shortly kill me.'

I looked askance at him, shocked by his matter-of-fact delivery of this news. 'My Lord! I am sorry! But how does he know?'

'He knows this disease well. It makes me tired and thin, and my vision has gone. He asked me to make water into a drinking vessel, and pronounced that it tasted sweet. He has instructed me to stop drinking mead, in fact I am barred from anything made with honey, and I may not take much bread. He said that if I follow his instructions I will live a while longer, maybe even a small number of years.'

'When I told the king, we agreed that it would be wise to search for a replacement. We think you may be able to learn the Law from me if you give yourself to studies as well as you have given yourself in service to the king.'

So, for a while, I lived under the instruction of Senaculos. They were the most pleasant years I remember. I was free of my previous mundane duties and I found that study was a delight, though I am sure that some would consider it unappealing.

Senaculos lived longer than any had expected, and I learnt from him for nearly five years. Over the last two years of his life he became so ill that several times he asked me to attend the king for more routine legal matters.

The day came when the king called me into his presence. 'Elico, it is now time for you to leave off your studies with your master.'

He saw my face fall, and he softened his tone. 'Your master is now not long for this world. He has had more years than the physician foretold, and I am determined to allow him to have a peaceful end. So I now require you to take on all his duties, advising me on the laws of my father when I pass my judgments.'

And so I became advisor to the King of Lugdunum, though I had not even reached my twenty-fifth year. I knew that eyebrows were raised amongst the king's companions on account of my youth, but the truth was, none of them had an ounce of my legal knowledge, and most of them could not even write! As for me, because Senaculos had taught me well, my understanding was sufficient for the king's requirements. I found my duties were pleasant, and my life was peaceful.

The only jarring note in this peaceful life was hearing of the rampages of Chilperic's elder brother, Gundebaud. He was known as Gundric, for short.

Gundric had inherited Vienne, a small town about a day's journey south of Lugdunum. He had once been an important official of the Roman Empire, on the grounds of his royal connections. He was a greedy man, and greedy especially for power.

When he learned of his small inheritance, he became enraged and sought to destroy his brothers. He did not dare touch Lugdunum, as my master, Chilperic, was too strong and had taken good care to train his warriors.

One day, when I was with the King, a messenger arrived in haste. 'My Lord', he panted, 'I have grave news from the north. King Gundric and his warriors have moved north around Lugdunum and taken Vesontio!'

Vesontio was the city which had been given to Chilperic's brother Gundomar. Due to carelessness, or perhaps lack of understanding of Gundric's true intentions, the city was only lightly defended.

'And what of Gundomar himself?' Chilperic's face had paled at the news.

'My, Lord, I am sorry, your brother Gundomar is...'

'Yes? Speak man!'

'I am afraid your brother and his family are all dead, my Lord.'

Chilperic fell silent, his eyes cast down.

'And, my Lord...'

'And? And what?'

'And it is said that Gundric has claimed all Gundomar's lands.'

'That does not surprise me one whit!'

'And...'

'What more? Why can you not just speak?'

'It is said that Gundric has forced Gundomar's warriors to submit to him.'

Chilperic questioned the messenger for over an hour. Once the messenger had left us, Chilperic started to plan our response.

He called in the commanders of his warriors and told them of the situation.

'Gundric now has forces both north and south of Lugdunum. But I am determined not to allow him to conquer us as he did my brother at Vesontio.'

Then together, he and his commanders worked out plans to increase our defences against Gundric.

I listened, then I asked to speak. 'My lords, I am sure that what you are proposing to do is necessary. But there is a possible further measure. I wonder if you would consider an alliance with the Parisii?'

'Have they not got enough trouble with the Franks to their north?' said Chilperic.

'And any contact with that dreadful Licnos would be a millstone around our neck', said one of the commanders.

'My Lord', I ventured, speaking directly to Chilperic, 'I hear Licnos has recently died, and if we can find someone who can represent the Parisii, we may be able to construct a mutually advantageous alliance.'

'You mean if they help us from the north against Gundric, we could help them from the south against the Franks.'

'Yes, my Lord.'

'So we need two things. One is a suggestion of whom we could send to the Parisii to offer this treaty.'

There was a resounding silence from the whole room.

'I will gladly go, my Lord.' I was a rash youth. What did I know of caution?

'The other requirement is some idea of whom we might deal with who has authority with the Parisii.'

'Ah, there I have another observation, if I may, my Lord?'

'Please. Go ahead.' Even now I still think I saw a little smile at the corners of his mouth as he permitted me to speak further.

'It is rumoured, but it is a strong rumour, from more than one source, that following the death of Licnos, the Parisii gathered and chose to invite one who had been their queen in former years to return. She is a Briton, who had been the wife of Licnos's brother, Bricius.'

Chapter Thirty-Two

Realisation

Galba gasped, 'What?' spitting a mouthful of stale bread across the room.

'Her name is Queen Denua', said Elico. 'The Parisii felt that they needed time to choose a permanent King, following their suffering under Licnos. Choosing to invite Denua to be Queen has many advantages. She is an aged lady, so she will rule for only a few years, she was well-loved by the Parisii, and still maintains her own small force of Parisii warriors.'

'But that is who I am searching for!' shouted Galba.

Lufian, unseen in the dimness of the cell, rolled his eyes. It was always the same! 'Galba', he said, 'perhaps you would then tell us how you came to be looking for her?'

Chapter Thirty-Three
Galba's Second Story

I am from one of the leading families of my community. When Patricius returned me to my parents (Elico, we will tell you this story later), he appointed them to speak for our people.

And it was not just his wish, our whole people were confident that my family - my family! - had the ability to lead them.

Let me first admit our failures. Our people had occupied the western coastland of Gaul. We had displaced a few Gaulish families, who had moved south and east into central Gaul. They have become our most implacable enemies.

But we ourselves had been displaced from the south of Britain, Wales and Éire. With the same Celtic language, we quickly became one community.

In recent years, though we look for peace, we are being attacked by the Gauls on our southern flank and the Franks to the north.

So six months ago, my father called our people together to discuss what we might do.

Some thought we should raise two armies, one to fight the Franks, the other for the Gauls.

Then I spoke. 'My people, we could raise armies and lose men in battle, but what if we could make an alliance with the Gauls?'

There was some muttering at this, with reference to my youth, but I carried on.

'You all know that one of us, the Briton who became Queen of the Parisii, passed through our lands some weeks ago. I had the advantage of a conversation with her. She told me she had been invited to take up the leadership of the Parisii for a short period, to give them time to determine how they wished to be ruled.'

'We know this already', someone shouted from the back, 'what do you want to do about it?'

'I think we should appeal to her for a treaty to stop the Gauls invading our lands. As she is a Briton herself, I think she may be sympathetic to our cause!'

To my surprise, the whole community agreed. No-one was eager to raise an army. They agreed to send an envoy to her, and chose me.

'I can hardly believe it! It is just too amazing that both of us are searching for the same person!' said Elico.

They were all quiet for some time. Then, from Galba, came the question which Lufian was waiting for. 'So, Lufian. You have heard how we are both looking for one person. Tell us, why are you here?'

Lufian swallowed hard, 'I am her son.'

Chapter Thirty-Four

Claennis's Breakfast

Claennis opened the door and looked out over the green hills. From here you could just see the coast, a thin line with blue sea beyond. The sky was peppered with light puffy clouds. She drew in a long breath of the warm air. What a privilege to live like this!

She walked the hundred paces to the eating hall. She could already smell the freshly baked bread for her breakfast meal. As she went, she reviewed her tasks for the day. It would be a pleasant day. She could spend some time writing, then she had two groups of students to teach: one Latin, one Frankish. After eating together again, she would meet with the other community leaders to plan Padraig's next visit.

She rolled through in her mind the choices they had. He could visit their two daughter communities; obviously they would want him to spend some time teaching in their own community; but what Claennis really wanted was to take him to the three villages on the coast, about half a day's journey. She was sure they had never met him, and if they had heard of his message at all, it was sure to be a garbled version, full of rumour and outrageous speculation. People like Padraig collected fables like a floor collects dust. They just settle.

But then, she had to be mindful of his age. As long as she had known him he had looked old, but he had always lived like a man half his age, with immense energy and always ready to take on a new task. He said that was why he had never married. 'Will you be finding me a wife who can keep up with the pace I set? Her feet would never touch the ground, to be sure!'

His strange way of speaking Éireann came from being born British, but it was oddly appealing. So much so that there were some who had started to copy him, no doubt thinking that if such a great man spoke this way, then they should too. Claennis laughed to herself at the strange ways of people. It was the same in Britain, relatively few Angles and Saxons had crossed over, but as the British saw their way of life, and heard their tongue, they were starting to speak Anglo-Saxon as a mark of higher status.

She was soon sitting at her meal. What could be better than this bread? Her first thick piece she coated with delicious dripping from last night's meat, the second with the community's own local honey. She washed one down with thick creamy goat's milk and the other with cool, fresh water, brought up from the brook this morning. She looked down at herself. I'm getting fat on this wonderful food, she giggled. Fat was good. It was thin which betrayed ill health.

Her lazy breakfast was ended by the sound of shouts and horses. She was immediately alert, but the shouts sounded friendly, and the hoofbeats were slow, not galloping. She went to the door to see who had arrived and was delighted to see Annis, her little sister!

She ran to greet her and help her dismount. All the women in their family rode the same way the men did. Then their parents, Cwen and Beorn arrived, slightly out of breath. There were embraces from all and a few tears from Cwen. Annis looked at Claennis then looked skywards at the fuss.

'Greetings from all at Alsiodorum', she said as soon as she could speak. 'My studies have finished and I am home for good. My brothers and cousins all wish you the best of health and want you to know that they are in good health and their studies are progressing well. And you should know that Aunt Denua has arrived there. She sends her greetings.'

Suddenly the mood changed. 'And Lufian? What of him?' demanded Beorn.

'He had not been seen when I left', she replied, 'was he due in Alsiodorum?'

'He was not. Five months past we heard of attacks on the north of Lutetia under a new Frankish King, so he left for Lutetia, to warn Denua and be of help to her if she needed.'

Cwen's brow furrowed. She was visibly worried. 'So, Denua has left Lutetia and moved south to Alsiodorum. She is safe, but then what of Lufian?'

'I'm sure he will find what has happened and follow her', said Beorn, optimistically.

'But it has been five months!' said Cwen. 'How long ago did you leave, Annis?'

'We travelled four weeks to Armorica, then took one week on the ship to the harbour here.'

'Five weeks ago! He should have arrived in Alsiodorum before you left, surely!'

Claennis thought quickly. She was known as a hothead, but that was simply because she assessed the situation and knew what action to take before everyone else did.

'Is your ship still likely to be in the harbour?' she demanded of Annis.

'I think so, the master said it would take two days to load provision and collect cargo and passengers before they return.'

'Then I shall go and find him', Claennis said firmly. 'Annis, you are to take my lessons with my students till I return. And you will need to plan Padraig's visit.' Annis's face lit up as she realised what trust was being placed in her abilities.

'Not so fast, young Claennis!' interrupted Beorn, 'You can't just wander off to a Gaulish battlefield on your own!'

'May also I go?' came a deep voice from the back of the group. Deogol!

'And I may be of help if a physician is needed.'

'Ardith!' shouted Annis as she ran and embraced her aunt.

Claennis sighed. What she had planned in those few seconds was a knifepoint strike. It was now starting to look like a family tour. They retired to the eating hall to discuss strategy. A small piece of bread and honey was left from her breakfast. Claennis wolfed it down. It might be a long time before she would eat this well again.

They sent a messenger to the ship to enquire exactly when it was due to leave, and to arrange for the three to go.

Chapter Thirty-Five

The Hunt Starts

After ten days on a calm sea they arrived in harbour on the Armorica coast. They went to the horse trader to purchase the mounts they needed. The Brittonic spoken here was slightly different, but Claennis thought she could manage it without much trouble. Beorn and Cwen had passed her a generous amount of Denua's gold to finance the journey. If there was any problem, showing a coin usually solved it.

The horse trader was already dealing with a man as they arrived, so they waited their turn. His customer was a tall, imposing young man with a deep, clear voice. After dealing with the trader, he turned and looked at Claennis with piercing dark eyes, holding her gaze until she became embarrassed and looked down.

The trader took his payment and turned to Deogol. 'Yes, sir?' he said.

Claennis stepped in front of Deogol. 'We want three horses. We will have that one, that one and... that one.'

The trader stepped back, momentarily disconcerted by her boldness, then he remembered his trade and started to argue prices with Claennis.

At last agreement was reached. Claennis asked Deogol and Ardith to take the horse they wished, then said to the trader in an innocent voice, 'Do you remember a young man from Éire, about five months ago, passing through on his way to Lutetia?'

'Sorry, my lady, we get so many people through here, I wouldn't be able to remember any particular one.'

The tall man had stayed in the trader's yard, tending to his horse, while they were purchasing, and as Claennis led her horse to join the others, he approached her. 'My lady, I'm sorry, I couldn't help overhearing your conversation. It just happens that about five months ago, I was here, again purchasing a horse for my journey, and there was a young man from Éire doing the same. He said he was going to Lutetia, and we travelled together for a while. Do I take it he was your...'

'Cousin!' replied Claennis, excitedly.

'Yes, I did wonder because of the similarity of your appearance. His hair, was...'

'Blond, like mine!'

'Exactly so. And I think he was somewhat taller than you?'

'Yes, yes, that is Lufian! We are searching for him.'

'Lufian, yes that's the name. Well, my lady, I don't know if I can help you, but I would be happy to ride with you and try to aid your search for Lufian as much as I can.'

Claennis was overwhelmed by her stroke of luck and when she rejoined Deogol and Ardith, she burst out with her news. She was surprised to see a less than excited reaction from both of them. 'My lady, sure are you that he can help us?' said Deogol.

'Yes, he has described Lufian, and even knows his name!'

'Well, my lady, if you wish him with us to travel, let it be so.'

They all set off towards Lutetia. As they rode, the man (they had found his name was Brennos) looked in her direction and caught her eye more than once. Eventually, on a narrow section of the track, Deogol and Ardith rode ahead, and Brennos pulled back to ride with Claennis. 'I must say it is such a delight to ride with such pleasant people.'

Claennis was flattered and slightly embarrassed, looking straight ahead to avoid catching his eye again.

Brennos pulled back his horse to ride slightly slower, and gradually Deogol and Ardith went on further away from them.

'And it is a delight to find that such a lovely woman as you is also capable of such astute business dealings. Where did you learn such things?'

Claennis could feel her face reddening, 'At home, women learn the same as men.'

'Indeed. I suspected as much. That is an admirable custom, and especially so when it adds to my delight in finding you.'

Claennis found herself unable to speak, and her heart was racing. Brennos was far too impertinent. He was making rather obvious advances! She looked ahead and found Deogol and Ardith nearly out of sight. 'We had better catch up with the others', she mumbled and urged her mount on forwards.

And so it was for the next two days of travel. They stayed at inns by night, but during the day, Claennis found Brennos riding close enough to engage her in conversation. He was always deferential, always charming. She was surprised that she was enjoying his attention.

At the end of the second day, as she fell asleep, Claennis found herself thinking about all that was said between them. There was something... she was not sure what it was, but something was bothering her.

She gradually became aware that it was she who had done all the talking. Brennos had put in a compliment here, and a question there, and she had revealed much about their mission, but she still knew nothing about Brennos. She idly wondered whether this was a problem, but dismissed it from her mind, and slept.

Nevertheless, on the third day, she was more careful. She rode with Deogol or Ardith, and avoided conversation with Brennos.

Disappointingly, as that day was drawing to a close, they had not come across an inn or even a small village in which they might find lodgings.

'We shall need in the open to stay, good job it is that the night is warm', said Deogol. They had come prepared for such an eventuality, and took out blankets from their packs. Ardith found a bank of moss and they settled down for the night.

'Claennis! Claennis! Brennos has gone! There is damage to your pack!'

Claennis had been sleeping so soundly that even with Ardith's cry it took her some time to remember where she was. But then she sat up, her heart beating. Ardith was sitting up as if she, too had just woken. Claennis looked round wildly for her pack. She kept it right beside her every moment. But now it lay open a little way away; its contents scattered. She raced over to it, already aware what she would find.

'The gold! That - pig! - has our gold!'

Claennis's mind raced back over the events of the previous days. Crashingly, it dawned on her that the man had known nothing of Lufian! She had supplied all the detail he needed to feign knowledge himself and deceive them. And on the journey, she had given away all he needed to be able to guess what their packs contained, as only hers had been touched.

'And I have been a fool! ' Claennis stamped her foot in anger. On any other occasion this would appear an appealing trait, but this time it signified drastic action.

'He will not get away with this!' she fumed, grabbing at her pack and racing towards the horses.

The horses! They had been loosed!

Claennis let out a scream of anger. She could just about see one horse, by a distant clump of trees. 'Collect our things! I will get that horse, then find the others!' she shouted to Deogol and Ardith.

Chapter Thirty-Six

Recover All

*I*t took over an hour to collect the three horses, bring them back and load their belongings.

Claennis had lost her red anger, and now felt a steely determination. He thought he could steal from her without consequences! Little did he know what kind of woman she was!

'Will it be you at the head, my lady?' said Deogol, already aware of what she planned.

'Yes. Would you be so good as to bring up the rear? Both of you make ready for a little "disagreement" when we find him.'

He was about two hours ahead. For most, this would be too much, but Claennis had been trained by none other than Beorn and Kursa.

Her piercing eyes surveyed the surface of the track. 'This way!'

They rode at a pace which others would find difficult, even ignoring the need for tracking their quarry. At one or two forks in the track they stopped, circled, then Claennis would give a low whistle, and race off down one way.

Deogol marvelled. When Beorn was younger he had seen him do this, and if anything Claennis hesitated less and tracked even faster than him.

Eventually, she came to a halt, dismounted and motioned for quiet. 'We are getting closer', she said quietly, 'Look at the hoof prints, he has slowed down and is walking his horse. He thinks he is safe.'

They rode on slowly for quite some time, then Claennis stopped and put her finger to her lips. She pointed down the track, just off to one side, and dismounted.

'Ardith, please stay near the horses, but keep your sword drawn.' Ardith took a small, slender sword from its sheath in her pack and retreated behind some bushes with the horses.

Claennis looked at Deogol and swept out half a circle with her hand. He knew exactly what he should do. Despite being part of Padraig's community, they were also of warrior stock. They knew well that raiders could come in from the sea and destroy them all, so they trained hard in case of attack. Deogol moved out to the right, through a hedgerow and away from the track.

Claennis silently walked along the track. She peered through leaves. Brennos sat facing her direction, but looking down at - her gold! He was counting how much he had stolen!

She waited. Deogol must be in place by now. Then she heard a high woman's voice from beyond Brennos, 'Brennos, Brennos...' How did Deogol do that?

In a flash Brennos stood, turned towards the sound and drew his sword. Deogol drew back into the cover of the bushes. He watched and marvelled as Claennis stepped from the cover of the bushes onto the open track, took something hanging from her waist, held it high in the air, twirled it, and let go. Two short, heavy metal bars, attached by a rope, spun through the air towards Brennos's legs.

They hit around his knees, then went on spinning, wrapping themselves around his legs. He shouted as he fell. Deogol sprang from the opposite bushes, and held his sword at Brennos's throat.

Claennis walked calmly forward. 'Brennos, my would-be lover!' she said, brightly. 'Such a surprise to see you here! And I see you have been taking care of my gold for me, I am so grateful!'

She looked at Brennos's terrified face. Was it wrong to enjoy this moment so much? She put her fingers to her mouth and emitted three piercing whistles. A few moments later, Ardith emerged with their horses.

'Ardith, your knotting skills need we will', said Deogol.

Ardith produced lengths of thin rope from her pack, and while Claennis and Deogol held Brennos at sword point, she expertly tied his wrists and ankles, and added a length between his wrist bonds and Claennis's horse for good measure. Brennos shouted loudly that the bonds were too tight.

Ardith, in a rare display of anger, knelt and wrenched his head back with his hair. 'I have allowed room at wrist and ankle for movement! You are so used to deceiving people, you still think it will work even when it is obvious they know your little game!' She pushed his head away in disgust.

Now that the threat was neutralised, they started to collect their belongings. Some of their gold lay on the ground, some was in a money bag by his side, but Claennis knew there had to be more. 'Check in his packs.'

'Get your hands off my packs!' shouted Brennos as they opened them. Their eyes opened wide when they saw what the packs contained. Gold and silver coins, precious brooches and jewellery, a small silver chalice, all tumbled out.

'Oh yes? All this is yours is it?' laughed Ardith. 'Do you often wear this brooch?' she said, holding up a particularly ornate item. 'Must have been a very fine lady you stole this from. I think we will try and return it, don't you?'

Chapter Thirty-Seven

Sulis

They decided, between them, that their mission would have to be suspended while they tried to rectify some of Brennos's crimes. They trekked back to the village they had left and asked whether they had heard of women being deceived and robbed.

They were not too surprised to hear that it was a common story. They were directed south, to the small town of Sulis, which appeared prosperous by the size of the homes. As they rode in, people stopped and stared at the trussed-up Brennos.

Suddenly they heard a woman's voice, shouting, 'Mother it's him! It can't be! Yes it is!'

Now they attracted even more attention. The young woman who had called out ran across, followed by a well-dressed grey-haired woman and an older thickset man.

The older woman called, 'Aia, are you completely sure?'

'Yes, of course! It is him!' cried out the younger woman.

'Have you had valuables stolen by this man?' enquired Claennis.

'Yes, he stole four gold coins, fifteen silver and my beautiful brooch.'

'Your brooch, what did it look like?'

'It was oval, about "this" long, with a decorated edge and a green stone in the centre.'

Claennis rummaged in one of the packs. 'This one?'

Aia's eyes opened wide with delight. She took the brooch from Claennis, held it high and started to dance round and round, laughing.

The man slowly approached Claennis. 'And would there be any, er, news, about the gold and silver he took?'

Claennis had already removed their own gold, so she opened the purses the man had carried. 'Four gold pieces and fifteen silver? I think you will find a lot more than that here, you may as well take what you lost.'

She could not remember ever seeing a face so grateful as the man showed at that moment.

'Please come into our home. We will give you a meal, and - do you have a place to rest for the night?'

Aia was so delighted by the recovery of her brooch that she said she would cook the most delicious meal she knew. So within the hour, they were seated at the family's table, feasting on better fare than they had had for some time. Aia ate with them, but also dashed in and out, serving them at table.

They left Brennos outside, tied up.

It turned out that the thickset man, Rodor by name, was a trader in pottery. Brennos had befriended his daughter, and deceived her, just as he had Claennis, before making off with their money. The trader was fairly wealthy, but the stolen coins had been a huge loss and their recovery had amazed them all.

They were nearing the end of the delicious meal when, with a loud bang, the door burst open. Brennos ran in and held the tip of a sword to Claennis's throat. They were stunned.

Ardith was first to recover. 'Wha... what are you doing? How did you get free?'

'Stupid village people! They are just like - you! They will believe - anything!' Brennos made a tiny movement, jabbing his sword into Claennis's neck. She leapt back. Brennos followed her, keeping the sword at her throat. He looked sideways at the table. He snatched up the bag of coins lying there. 'Now. You. Move away from the door, or she will die!'

He kept his sword at Claennis's neck and watched them as they moved to clear the door. He drew back the sword a hand's breadth. 'And this is for you, you interfering witch!' He started his thrust into Claennis's throat, then suddenly stopped, with horror on his face. A thin blade emerged from a red patch on the front of his tunic.

Aia stepped out from the doorway, bent down and spoke into the face of the dying man, 'You really need to make sure there is no-one just behind you when you try to murder people!'

The town elders arrived and convened a meeting in the house. They soon agreed that there was nothing else which could have been done. Aia had acted appropriately for the circumstances. They had heard many rumours about Brennos, but because he moved on constantly, no-one had been able to apprehend him.

Some locals were called in to explain how he got free. Apparently, when a newcomer happened on him, he feigned injury, and quickly overpowered the man once he got close. The newcomer had been slightly wounded when Brennos had snatched his weapon to cut himself free. The newcomer was very apologetic, but the elders realised he had been stupid, not malicious, so took no action against him.

They spent some time discussing the haul of valuables. They formed a group which would make enquiries in the area to find the ownership of the jewellery. Any claim would have to be supported by witnesses, and the group would have the task of deciding whether the claimants were honest. If funds were left, they would be used for the whole community.

They spent a pleasant night under Rodor's roof, and late in the morning they assembled to break their fast. Rodor was a generous host.

The table groaned under pork, lamb and fish, with fresh bread, butter and honey.

'Up early you must have been preparing this!' said Deogol.

'We have already found some who are very grateful for your visit', replied Rodor, 'We have had townsfolk at our door since early this morning, with gifts of food to break your fast and for your travels.'

At Rodor's request, they fell to recounting how they had caught Brennos.

'It was really Claennis who accomplished it', said Ardith, 'with her tracking skills and her special weapon.'

Rodor's head turned. 'Special weapon?'

'It is a cross between a flail, such as farmers use for threshing, and a Roman mace', replied Claennis. 'It is simply two weighted handles with a rope between them. If you throw it properly, it spins in the air, then wraps itself around whatever it hits. I use it in Éire to bring down animals on our community farm.'

'No-one else like Claennis can so well throw it', added Deogol.

'Anyway it wasn't just me', said Claennis, 'Deogol distracted Brennos with his woman's voice... show them, Deogol!'

Deogol was embarrassed, but after some encouragement he demonstrated his high-pitched voice, which caused them all to fall about laughing.

When all had calmed, Rodor turned to Claennis and said, 'So, tell me, my lady, what is your mission in this land, and where is your destination?'

The three looked nervously at each other at first, then Ardith gave a nod of reassurance, 'I'm sure it's safe to say, and it might benefit us to ask for information about our journey.'

The story was told, each of the three taking turns to explain that they were headed for Lutetia to search for Claennis's cousin, Lufian.

'How long has he been gone?' said Rodor.

'Around seven months now', said Claennis, 'He was heading for Lutetia.'

'In that case', said Rodor, 'it is most likely that he has been taken by the Franks. They have recently moved south, and now control a large area between us and Lutetia. They do not take kindly to strangers wandering through their land.'

'Do you think likely it is that alive he still is?' said Deogol.

'The old king of the Franks is dead. He was a tyrant who would rather kill than make friends. His son, Clovis, is a very young king, and is rumoured to be more humane. He will kill if opposed, but it is said that his custom is to make servants of his enemies rather than kill them. That way, he gets some use out of them.'

'Does that mean we have to pass through Frankish lands to get to Lutetia, or is there a way past?' said Claennis.

'They say that Clovis has Lutetia nearly surrounded, at the north, east and west. There is a passage in from the southern road into the Burgundian lands, to Alsiodorum and Lugdunum. But you are not likely to be able to gain access that way.'

Claennis's face fell, and her brow furrowed. 'Then it is time we did some planning', she said.

Chapter Thirty-Eight
Ready for the Procession

Claennis disappeared into the town with Aia as her guide, giving no indication of what she was planning.

She was gone so long that Ardith and Deogol started to wonder whether they had got lost. Then, suddenly, she walked back in through the door, 'That's got everything. We need to ready our horses for the deliveries.'

Deogol looked at Ardith, then back at Claennis, 'Claennis, possible is it that we can know what you plan?'

'Rodor thinks we cannot sneak past the Franks to get into Lutetia. Fine. So we will not sneak, we will announce our presence as loudly as we can!'

Within two hours, large parcels were arriving at the door. Some contained colourful bunting and pennants, some contained bells and decorations for horses. Four long, slender spears came from one smithy, and leathers to mount them on the horses from the nearby tanners. Then came a huge bale of what looked like cloth.

With each delivery, Claennis became more and more excited; at this last bale she was squeaking with delight.

'What is it all?' breathed Ardith.

'You will soon see, and you will like what you see!' replied Claennis.

She beckoned them out to their horses, and started to unpack her purchases.

Deogol stared, 'Like a royal procession it is!'

With Rodor's help, they decorated the horses. Saddles were overlaid with gold cloth, bunting ran along the flanks, spears rose into the air with fluttering pennants, bells jingled.

'I have saved the best till last', said Claennis, as they finished.

She turned to the large bale of cloth and untied it. Everyone gasped when they saw rich garments tumble from it: decorated silken robes, shot through with gold, embossed leather belts, thick silken cloaks with gold fastenings.

Claennis turned to them. 'Now it is time for me to explain what we will do. We know we cannot easily bypass the Franks, so we will make a royal procession direct to the court of Clovis. I am Princess Claennis of Éire. Ardith, you are to be Queen Ardith, my aunt, and Deogol is one of our guards.'

'One of our guards?' said Ardith, 'then who is the other?'

'Ardith, have you not been watching?' laughed Claennis, 'How many horses have we made ready?'

'Four, because you have had Brennos's horse brought out. But who will ride it?'

Rodor stepped forward. 'I am the other guard. I am used to travelling these roads and know safe ways. I have encountered the Franks many times on my trading travels. Claennis asked my advice about her plan, and I asked, in return, if she would accept me as part of your escort. I also checked with Roveca, my beautiful wife', he looked sideways at her with a smile, 'whether she would allow me to go, and she gave her permission.'

They put on the clothes and stared at each other in amazement. 'Never have I seen you so much like a queen look!' said Deogol to Ardith.

'Well, my cousin was King of the Angles, and Claennis is descended from his family too, so you'd better get used to being with royalty!' giggled Ardith.

They were sad that they had to put all the finery back in the packs for the journey. The only parts which would be seen were the spears, one mounted vertically beside the saddle of each horse.

They set off the next morning. As they left, Claennis rode close to Rodor. She took something from her tunic to show him. From their gestures, she appeared to be consulting him about directions. After a brief stop for lunch, they diverted off the way, to the north. After an hour, they approached the bottom of a rocky escarpment. A deep valley was cut into the face of it like a scar. As they neared it they saw a wide river pouring down from the valley, falling the height of ten men and cascading into a rocky pool. The noise was deafening.

'Is this the place?' shouted Claennis to Rodor. He nodded.

They dismounted and Ardith and Deogol looked at one another, shrugged their shoulders, then looked at Claennis for an explanation.

'I wanted to keep quiet about this place, for I do not know whether we shall find anything here.'

The raised eyebrows of Deogol and Ardith did not lower, so Claennis continued. 'In the packs we took from Brennos's horse, there was a small piece of vellum, wrapped well in oiled paper.' She pulled the package from her tunic. 'The drawings on it seem like a map, and last night I showed it to Rodor. He said it resembled this place, with a waterfall from a high cliff.'

'But what here to find do you expect?' said Deogol.

'I honestly do not know, but it seems to me that such a man as Brennos would not have a carefully preserved map for no reason.'

She opened the map and spread it on a rock. 'Here is this cliff. Here is the pool at the foot of the fall, and... here is the mark I don't understand.'

'Seems it that under the waterfall it is', said Deogol.

They approached the foot of the fall from the right side. There was a pathway up a steep incline. Claennis confidently expected to find a pathway behind the fall, to where the mark indicated, but her hopes fell when, after climbing for some time, they found a solid rock wall blocking their way.

'We will try the other side!' she shouted over the roar of the water.

It took them some time to retrace their steps over the slippery rock, back to where their horses stood, then climb their way up the left side of the falls, but yet again they found a solid wall of rock. Claennis felt very downcast. She could have sworn that there was something important about this place, but there seemed no way forward.

'Down there!' Suddenly Ardith pointed downwards. They looked down onto what looked like a suicidal path, really no more than irregular narrow footholds, slippery with water. A hair-raising drop faced anyone so careless as to miss their footing.

All four of them looked at each other. Then, 'Well I'm going!' from the impetuous Claennis.

'Me too!' Rodor looked excited by the challenge.

Deogol looked down at his impressive girth. 'Sure I'm not that I could manage...'

'You stay here with Ardith', said Claennis, 'Ardith are you happy not to go down?'

Ardith laughed. 'I'm glad to say that my cliff-climbing days were over many years ago!'

Rodor went down first, facing the cliff, looking down for the next foothold. When he had gone down the height of two men, Claennis followed. Deogol marvelled, 'Ardith, see that, as nimble as a mountain goat is she!'

As Claennis looked down for a foothold, with a shock she realised that Rodor had disappeared from view. Alarmed, she looked through the spray to see if he had fallen, but could see no sign of him. Ten steps later her feet landed on a ledge. It was just less than an arm's length wide, but a welcome respite from the descent. She looked for further footholds below, but it seemed to be a sheer drop.

She turned towards the waterfall, fully expecting that there would be a pathway behind it, but yet again her hopes were dashed. The ledge ended some way before the rushing water. She stood, considering the situation and decided that if she tried to jump through, she would be swept away.

Suddenly she felt a touch on her shoulder. She jumped to the side so hard that she fell outwards from the ledge. An arm grabbed hers and pulled her back. It was Rodor!

'I am so sorry!' he shouted, 'But I had been shouting to you and the noise of the water is too loud!'

Claennis was still gasping from the near fall and could not reply.

'It's not through the waterfall, it's back here!'

Claennis followed Rodor towards the other end of the ledge. It seemed to peter out before a rocky outcrop, but as Rodor went near the rock face, he stepped round it and disappeared from view. Then a hand came out from behind the outcrop, beckoning.

Claennis stepped forward, took the hand and felt herself swung around the rock to land on a ledge the other side. She gasped, but Rodor was already pulling her into a crevice behind him.

'It's this way!'

Claennis followed into the crevice, which became a cave, which became a tunnel. There was easily enough space to walk, but she was surprised that the tunnel wasn't dark, and the waterfall seemed somehow louder inside than outside.

They had only gone a few paces when the roar got much louder still, and the tunnel widened to a large cave directly behind the falling water. Claennis was entranced by the downpour just in front of her face, but Rodor kept pulling her round and eventually she turned, There, high on the back wall of the shallow cave, was a narrow ledge. And on the ledge were six or seven large leather bags.

Rodor reached up and took one - and nearly stumbled under its weight. He undid the thong from its neck. Claennis knew what she would see. And she was pleased to find that she was right.

They packed the bags into their packs and unsteadily made their way around the ledge and back up. Oddly enough, Claennis found it easier than it had been on the way down.

Ardith and Deogol reached down and took their packs as they neared the top. Deogol gasped at the weight, 'I hope that heavy this is for a good reason!'

Claennis laughed, and she and Rodor explained what they had found.

As they returned to their horses, they discussed what they should do. Deogol was adamant, 'No matter it makes that this gold was Brennos's gold, before his it was, stole it he did from others. Our return to Sulis is required so that town elders decide what to do they can.'

Claennis looked at Deogol with raised eyebrows. This was the longest speech she had ever heard him make.

They all agreed, and made their way back to Sulis, arriving late at night. Roveca was delighted to see her husband again and bustled around getting a late meal and some drinks for them all.

Next morning, Rodor called the elders of the town together and told them what they had found. Their mouths dropped open as he undid the leather bags and poured out gold coins onto the table. 'Not even any silver!' breathed one of them.

'We think this was Brennos's main hoard, and he took out the silver from each haul to use as his ready spending money', said Rodor, 'But we would like you to decide what is to be done with this.'

The leader of the town elders spoke, 'Am I right in thinking that the capture of this thief was mainly due to this young lady?'

Nods of agreement from all who knew.

'And the discovery of this money...'

'Lady Claennis was responsible for that also', chimed in Ardith.

'And coming back here, to allow us the honour of deciding what should be done with it?'

'Thought we all that should so be', Deogol quickly answered.

The other three looked at him, but he shook his head. 'All of us it was', he insisted.

'Am I correct in thinking that you had already returned to us much gold and treasure from the thief?'

No response.

'And, I hear, you took no reward for your good work.'

Embarrassed faces.

'You recently bought a large amount of valuables from the town's merchants?'

Claennis nodded.

'And what funds did you use to buy those things, your own?'

Claennis nodded again.

'We will consult.'

The elders withdrew to a huddle at the far side of the room. There was a murmur of conversation, but the four could not hear what was being said. Then the elders broke and returned to the table.

'We well remember a holy man by the name of Patricius, who regularly passed through our town and sometimes stayed and taught here. He served the God who is alive. He taught that we should not be attached to great wealth, for God will provide what we need. So we have made a decision. We will take charge of the gold you have returned, and put it to good use for our community. But one tenth part of the gold will be given to Ro...'

Rodor burst out in objection.

'... -dor's wife. We know Rodor would never accept a reward, so we have decided to give it to Roveca. She will be more sensible.'

Roveca, across the room, looked as if she had just been made queen. 'Thank you, elders', she said.

The leading elder had not finished, 'And we have decided that one third part of the gold will be given to Claennis and her companions... NO, my lady, you may not object. We do not give you a reward because you need to receive it, we give it to you because we need to give it. Take it and use it for your quest.'

Chapter Thirty-Nine

Towards the Franks

As the morning had not passed too far, they left at once on the road towards Lutetia.

For a full fifteen days they journeyed. Each night they easily found inns, thanks to Rodor's local knowledge. He took care to interview carefully each of their hosts, often plying them with their own ale to ensure their tongues were loose enough. They were more than pleased to find guests for whom a ready supply of gold did not seem to be a problem.

At the breaking of their fast on the morning of the fifteenth day, Rodor addressed them all, 'According to all I hear, we will enter Frankish territory sometime today. They occasionally come to this place and trade. They have given assurances to the town elders that, while they intend to take this land soon, they will treat the townspeople kindly, provided they are not opposed.'

This was the moment they had all been waiting for. Excitedly they undid all their packs, decorating their horses with the bunting and bells, mounting pennants on their spears, and dressing themselves in the finery they had brought. They gathered a large crowd of onlookers, 'Never seen anybody done up like that!' shouted one from the crowd.

'I've never been done up like this!' replied Rodor, laughing, as he donned an expensive heavy yellow silk cloak, embroidered and embossed with pictures of exotic animals and dragons.

Eventually, the preparations were complete, and they all mounted, Rodor first, Claennis and Ardith riding abreast, and Deogol bringing up the rear. As they rode away the crowd broke into spontaneous applause. The four just could not help smiling and waving, as if their royal status had been known all along.

It all happened very suddenly. One moment they were riding along gently, bells tinkling, in warm afternoon sunlight. The next moment they were surrounded by warriors who had emerged from the trees, swords drawn, in front and to the sides.

It would be false to suggest that their hearts did not quail at that moment. But they gave very little sign of their apprehension. Deogol, who was lagging a little behind the rest, stopped his horse immediately. Ardith visibly shrank, her head a little lowered. Claennis, having anticipated this moment, straightened herself into a more regal pose, her head back and looking as haughty as she could manage.

But it was Rodor who surprised them all. He rode forwards with a wide smile on his face, and a booming voice, 'Good day! Good day! Good fellows all! We are well met at this hour! You are just the fellows to help us with our quest! We desire safe passage through your lands on our pilgrimage! And my friend at the back has the silver to recompense you for your trouble in conducting us!'

At the mention of silver, some of the sword points started to drop. There was quiet for twenty heartbeats. Then from the bushes to the left, a horseman rode out. He was young, possibly not many years older than his twentieth year, tall, with an aquiline nose and a stern face. He was dressed in what looked like old Roman armour.

'My men will have no need of silver.'

Faces fell around the circle of warriors.

'But I will need an explanation of who you are and why you wish to cross our land.'

Rodor's face was a picture. His beam grew greater still and he gently drew forward to meet the man, as if he were his best friend.

'Of course, my friend! My name is Rodor, from Sulis. I am a trader and Princess Claennis... ', he swept his hand around in an expansive manner, '...has engaged me to facilitate her travel, with her aunt and manservant, on her pilgrimage to Alsiodorum... you must have heard of the great holy man, Patricius of Alsiodorum?'

The Frankish horseman looked completely taken aback, his mouth opened slightly but no sound came out. The eyes of all the warriors were fixed on the drama being played out. Deogol's horse, very gently, moved back.

Rodor plunged on without stopping, 'Princess Claennis is from the royal family of a powerful Brittonic tribe. She has been sent by her tribe on a pilgrimage to Alsiodorum, and, as part of her pilgrimage duties has been required to distribute silver to those who aid her on her journey. All have heard of the great Frankish king, King Clovis, and it will be a delight for us to pass through his land and increase the wealth of those who live in his kingdom.'

It was all Claennis could do not to burst out laughing throughout Rodor's speech, despite the dangerous circumstances, but somehow she kept her face straight.

'And what', said the stern-faced man, 'would happen if I took you prisoner right now and had all your "silver" for myself?'

'Then kill you we would', said Deogol, quietly. His voice came from the bushes behind the horseman.

The stern-looking man whirled round, but Deogol had bow drawn and arrowhead pointing at the man's heart. To his credit, he did not so much as flinch, but appeared completely unruffled. Neither moved for several heartbeats, then, suddenly the man broke out into peals of laughter.

Now it was the turn of Claennis and her companions to sit, open-mouthed, wondering what was to happen.

'Let me introduce myself', said the man, wiping his eyes, 'I am the "great King Clovis". You have stumbled across one of my routine border patrols which I just happened to be inspecting. Now, you know that if you kill me, none of you will live; on the other hand I will not live either. So, for the sake of preserving the health of all of us, I would like to assure you that I have every intention of allowing you to pass unhindered through my lands.'

Deogol still did not move a finger's width.

Clovis continued, 'However, I do have one other proposition. I do not think my men have ever witnessed my "capture", as this excellent man has done', he nodded approvingly towards Deogol, 'so to smooth the way for them to tell this astonishing story to all the rest of my men, I wonder if you would accept my offer of hospitality? We are but an hour's ride from my headquarters. I have a pleasant Roman villa.'

Claennis looked at Rodor, then at Ardith. She decided to risk everything, and signalled to Deogol to lower his bow. She spoke as formally as she could, 'We will accept your gracious offer, in the hope that relations between our two peoples will be strengthened thereby.'

Chapter Forty

Rodor's Story

At Clovis's signal, they moved off to the east, the warriors walking behind them. Claennis rode next to Rodor. 'Rodor, your Frankish is very fluent!'

'It should be, I spent much of my early years as a Frankish slave. It is a long story.'

'It looks as if I may have sufficient time to listen to you. Please tell.'

My parents were British. They came over to avoid the waves of Picts who were raiding from the north. They crossed from Ceint to the north of Gaul.

At that time Gaul seemed very quiet, the Romans were still powerful and well in control. The Franks, Frisians and Belgae kept well to the north. The Juti, Ingwi and Seaxe were more interested in the east of Britain than moving south against the Romans.

It felt so safe under Roman rule that my parents decided to settle near the coast to the west of Lutetia. Nobody suspected the soldiers would suddenly be called home when the Visigoths attacked Rome.

You can guess what happened. As soon as the Roman presence lessened, the Franks took every opportunity to raid into western Gaul. Our little farm was hit almost immediately. My older brother and I were captured and taken north, deep into Frankish territory. He was about sixteen years old, I was ten. We were sold in a slave market, then held in a cell and beaten for several weeks. It was particularly difficult for him in the dim cell for he was only able to see in good light.

Eventually we were brought out in leg irons and made to work on the land of a Frankish lord. We worked there all summer, then I was separated from him and made to work in the Roman villa the Frankish lord had occupied. I heard later my brother had escaped, saying he was heading back to the west.

The odd thing was, what I learnt then has been the foundation of what I do now. My master's wife was very fond of pottery. She had a large collection. Whenever they travelled, she would bring more back. Some was beautifully moulded and kept for formal occasions or for decoration, some was plainer just for household use.

One of my jobs was to clean the villa and, in time, I was given responsibility for the pottery also. I found the variety of it very interesting. Much came from eastern Frankish lands, some came from Gaul, some from Rome, but there were pieces from Greece, and the eastern lands. I took pains to care for it well and my mistress rewarded me by explaining the origins of the pieces and their characteristics.

I was eventually trusted enough to accompany my mistress when she travelled to seek other pieces for her collection. Whenever I could, I took the opportunity to spend time with the merchants, and learn from them the nature of their wares. We travelled to far lands, even into Greece. My knowledge soon became so great that I was able to advise my mistress on her purchases.

Then I found that on the way back we would often meet merchants who wished to purchase what we had already bought elsewhere, so we used our journeys to trade.

After I had served her for nine years she became ill and unable to travel. So she started to send me in her place. As I was not Frankish, I was able to go more easily into Gaul and purchase from merchants far to the south, though I always made sure I took some choice pieces home to my mistress at the end, along with the full purses I had gained through trade.

You will say, 'And why did you not just run away?' and you would have a point. Yet by this time I was in my early twenties and had served the Franks since I was ten. I knew nothing else. I was so young when I was captured that I had no memory even of where I lived, so I would not have been able to just go home.

Then the day came when I decided to seek trade to the west. So, during my trip south, I loaded my cart high with both useful and unusual pieces, then headed there. As I arrived in that part of Gaul, I was surprised to find that people spoke the way I had done as a boy. I must have had a strange accent, to them, but I remembered my tongue tolerably well and found that I was able to talk and bargain with them. I found a ready market for my wares, and thought I was likely to sell everything I had.

Then I arrived in Sulis. I was invited to the house of an elder of the town, a rich man who owned much productive farmland. He asked me to show him what I had, and while I was bringing the pieces from my cart, in walked his beautiful daughter, Roveca!

The rich man was very pleased with what I wished to sell, and in turn, I was pleased with his daughter! I stayed three days. Roveca and I were able to spend some time together and we just talked. She is such an interesting lady, besides being so beautiful. She is clever and capable, and very brave.

I was very sad when the time came to leave, but I promised Roveca I would pass that way again when I could. With my nearly empty cart, and my bulging money purse, I made my way back east, into the Frankish lands. I came to the home town of my master and mistress, and paused in a mead hall for some refreshment before I went out to their estate. It was then I heard the news. My mistress was dead.

I do not know to this day whether what I did was right or wrong. I only know that it seemed the obvious course. I turned the cart right back round and headed to Sulis. I took the purse with me. Some would call it stealing, yet I had never had any pay for all my years of work, so others would call it my just reward.

I arrived back in Sulis, and before I even went to see Roveca, I bought a pleasant house near the river, adjoining her father's farmland. I spent two days furnishing and cleaning it, then sent an invitation to Roveca and her parents to dine with me.

It was only three months later that Roveca and I married. Her father graciously gave us more land near our house, and that is where we live now. In some ways I could not be happier. My only sadness is that I have lost my brother, my parents and my boyhood home.

Chapter Forty-One
Autricum

They rode in silence after Rodor had finished his story. Eventually, they arrived at a town, though by the size of it, Claennis would have called it a city. It had a huge wall around it formed by earth from a surrounding ditch being piled high and topped with stone.

'This used to carry the name of the local tribe, the Carnutes', said Clovis, 'then the Romans renamed it Autricum. It, ahem, "came into our possession" when the Romans left. The Carnutes were, by then, too weak to repossess the city and we were the only nearby people strong enough to hold it.'

They passed through huge wooden gates and entered a seething market. The crowd parted when they saw Clovis, pulling back and bowing low as they passed, but when they saw Claennis and her companions, royally dressed and riding beautifully bedecked horses, they fell silent and stared.

In the centre of the city they passed a beautiful grove of oak trees. Amongst the trees stood a large wooden building, and emerging was a giant of a man, dressed simply in rough brown cloth, with a round, florid face and thick, hairy arms.

Claennis was surprised when he did not bow low, as everyone else had done. Instead he held up his right hand in greeting and walked right up to the king. 'Clovis! It is good to see you back! Did you fare well on your round of inspection?' He turned and looked towards the royal party, 'And you have brought us some guests! Distinguished ones by their appearance!'

Claennis assumed Clovis would be embarrassed at being greeted so freely by such a roughly dressed person, but he seemed unmoved.

Then the man spoke directly to them, 'My ladies, my lords, I look forward to making your acquaintance over a meal in the King's house. Be assured you will enjoy your stay!'

Clovis at last found his tongue, 'This', he gestured towards the man, 'is Flavius, assigned here to be the bishop of Autricum.'

He stopped for only a short while, but it was enough of a gap for Flavius to re-enter the conversation, 'And will you introduce me to these grand personages, or must I do it myself?'

Clovis looked for a moment as if he would start speaking but Flavius just carried on. He walked up to the nose of Claennis's horse and looked up at her. 'Most distinguished lady, would you do me the honour of informing me who you are and where you are from?'

Rodor was riding by the side of Claennis, and at this point his impatience got the better of him. 'Allow me to introduce our party', he said, 'This is Princess Claennis of the Ingwi in Britain and Éire, her aunt, Queen Ardith, her chief steward, Deogol, and I am her official guide in Gaul, my name is Rodor.'

Deogol broke into a big smile at being called chief steward, but then realised that it may not be wise and suppressed it.

Rodor continued, 'We are on pilgrimage to Alsiodorum, where Patricius was taught.'

'Ah, the blessed Patricius, what a family! His uncle, Martinus of Turonensis, was great inspiration to all Gaul. Have you met Patricius?'

'We have come across him', said Claennis.

'What a man! What a ministry...!'

Clovis, at last, butted into the conversation, 'Yes, Flavius, might I suggest that we could discuss Patricius and his, er, kind, over a hearty meal which I will give tonight to honour our guests? You are, as always, welcome.'

Claennis later concluded that Clovis did not do well in conversation, being a man more of action than words.

They stopped before massive gates, which, at a shout from the lead horseman, swung open as if they were light as feathers. Claennis was open-mouthed. Rodor caught her expression, 'Roman engineering', he smiled.

The gates opened, and Claennis rode into a huge Roman villa, in its own grounds. She was surprised at the bustle of people walking back and forth. Some she could identify; that man entering a room to the right and covered in flour was obvious. The one racing away from her, dressed as a servant carrying jugs of liquid, he looked vaguely familiar, but then he was gone. There were two women carrying bedding towards a far room under a veranda, one man working in a huge herb garden off to the left, three warriors relaxing under the veranda with drinks, who stood to attention as soon as they saw Clovis.

Directly in front of her was a garden, rectangular, and about the same area as her whole house at home. It was planted with beautifully coloured flowers, but what stunned her was the sweetest smell which came from them. Even in her green Éire, she had not known such an intense fragrance.

'Corbus!' shouted Clovis. After a few seconds, a man emerged from a room to the right. He was not a young man, but he had a presence which held Claennis's attention. He was very tall, leaner than most of Clovis's men, with a short, greying beard. But it was his face which gripped her. Claennis had never been given to fancies, but she could swear his eyes looked - kind? She thought that in his younger days he must have had the women falling at his feet.

'I am here, my Lord.' Not a surprise this time, thought Claennis, his voice fitted his appearance perfectly. It was deep and sonorous and carried right across the courtyard, though he spoke only softly.

'Corbus, we have four guests. Please arrange rooms and tonight we will feast. Flavius also will be a guest for the meal.'

A look, semi-humorous, passed between Clovis and Corbus. 'His usual seat, my Lord?'

'Yes, Corbus, all as usual. Now, my new friends, my steward will take care of you. I will attend to my business.'

So, saying, Clovis dismounted and went into the main house ahead of them. Claennis got off her horse and stood staring at the house. She wondered at its colour and size. It was red, and made of rows of narrow oblong stones, with a white material between the stones. And it was so vast that she conjectured she could fit all of her Éire community in there.

'Have not you one of these seen before?' said Deogol.

'No, nothing like this, have you?'

Ardith smiled. 'We"ve seen plenty of them, though we don't get them in Éire, and there are not so many in Britain. But over here in Gaul, the Romans built many like this.'

A discreet cough sounded behind them. Corbus smiled benignly down from his great height (he seemed even taller close up, thought Claennis), 'My lords, my ladies, would you care to follow me to your quarters, a groom will take care of your steeds.'

They were shown to the most pleasant of rooms, not opulent, but clean and well presented, with better beds than they had had for some time.

'Allow me to show you the bath house, which you may use when you have settled into your rooms,' said Corbus. 'If the men would kindly wait, one of the servants will tell you when the ladies have finished.'

Deogol looked decidedly unimpressed by the thought of a bath, but Ardith seized Claennis's arm, 'Do come with me, you must not miss this, it will be an absolute treat!'

Some time later, Claennis's curiosity, which had grown since she had heard of it, was satisfied. Outside the main courtyard was a separate small house, with a beautiful pool, about four paces wide and six long, with steps down into the water at one end. It was completely covered in tiny tiles of many colours. Claennis looked at these for some time before she realised the tiles made pictures.

Ardith slipped off her tunic, 'Don't take all day, let's get in!'

Claennis stepped down into the water. Ardith laughed when she saw the look of surprise on Claennis's face, 'I've been waiting to see that! I knew you'd be surprised when you realised the water is warm!'

They assembled in the early evening for the feast. Deogol confessed to being surprised that the experience of being wet all over was pleasant. The four were seated on one side of the table, with Clovis at the head. Opposite were Flavius, Corbus and a tall young man with a likeable face.

The food was served one course at a time, rather than all being placed on the table at once, as Claennis was used to. The centre of the table was taken up with boards of bread and jugs of mead and ale. Servants approached from behind and placed a wooden board before each guest. Each board had a different type of food, fish, meat, sweet delicacies, the dishes seemed to go on and on.

Claennis thought she had never eaten so much. She was just resting after one course, when a servant leant around to refill the mead jug. She heard a whisper, 'In your room, ask for mead!'

Her head jerked round, but the servant had turned and walked away. She looked for him through the rest of the meal, but did not see anyone who she could identify.

The conversation flowed freely, mainly thanks to Flavius, who did not seem to stop talking, except to listen to the replies of others. He seems very good at learning the interests of others, she thought to herself. Even Clovis, possibly helped by the mead and ale, seemed to talk more freely. But the tall young man on the other side had not even been introduced. Claennis thought it a a little strange, so when there was a lull in the conversation, she took the opportunity to look at him and say, 'And what do you do here?'

The man, who had been silent while the conversation flowed around him, looked nervously at Clovis, but the king smiled at him, leaned back and said, 'Go on Elico, tell them the story of how you came to be one of my advisors!'

Chapter Forty-Two
Elico's Second Story

I was the advisor in Law to Chilperic, the King of Lugdunum. We were threatened with invasion by Gundric, Chilperic's brother. He ruled Vienne, to our south. Gundric had already swept around Lugdunum with his warriors and killed another brother who ruled Vesontio, to the north of Lugdunum.

Chilperic sent me to seek a treaty with Queen Denua, the Queen of the Parisii, to deal with the threat, but before I reached Lutetia, I was captured by the Franks.

I thought my life's work had ended, but for me it has turned out for the good. Good King Clovis is given to enquire who he has in his cells, and I soon found myself in his august presence giving an account of myself. He was so kind as to make some enquiries with his scouts and he recounted to me the news of what had happened to King Chilperic and my beloved home city.

After taking Vesontio, Gundric and his army, now swelled with those he could recruit from Vesontio itself, moved back south and laid siege to Lugdunum. The town had been well prepared by Chilperic and valiantly resisted Gundric, but eventually his troops invaded and captured Chilperic and his family.

They were brought to the river, where Gundric ordered that Chilperic be cut in two with the sword. Caratena, his wife, and Clotilde, his daughter, were forced to watch. Then Caratena was drowned in the river. Then the tyrant made Clotilde a prisoner in his stronghold in Vienne, where she remains.

Good King Clovis also informed me that Queen Denua had moved on from Lutetia to Alsiodorum, so the mission on which I had been sent would have been in vain.

Here Clovis interrupted, 'Now I wish to tell the next part!'
'Yes, my Lord, of course', said Elico.

This time Claennis was not surprised that the King was so ready to speak, as he had been emptying the jugs of ale throughout Elico's story.

'I like to have capable servants, and when I heard that this man knew the Law of the Burgundians, it struck me that perhaps we, the Franks, could do with some laws too! Isn't that so, Corbus?'

The imposing head of Corbus slowly nodded, 'Yes my Lord, I am sure it would be of great benefit to our people.'

'You see', continued Clovis, 'whenever there is a dispute, it is I who have to listen to all parties and settle it. It does not matter if the dispute is great or small, over land, marriage or animals, it all has to be attended to by me. I know that it is the duty of a king, yet I find it so tiresome. It takes so much of my life. Do you agree, Corbus?'

'I have often considered, sire', (Claennis found the sonorous voice of Corbus attractive to listen to, no matter what it was he was saying), 'that you would have accomplished even more in your already full life if only you had not had the constant call for your judgment on disputes and crimes.'

'So, if we became a proper nation, with proper laws', Clovis was almost giggling, 'tell our dear friends what difference it would make.'

'Well, my Lord, if there were a system of laws which you had approved...'

'Yes, go on...'

'...it would mean that every village elder could consult those laws to decide what had been done that was wrong, and what had been done that was right, and administer justice - on your behalf, of course - without having to consult you on each occasion.'

'Isn't that amazing?' Clovis looked at Claennis and her companions as if he expected applause. 'Laws mean other people can do my job, on my behalf! So, Elico, tell them what I proposed to you.'

'Very well, my Lord. As King Clovis was saying, he had reached the point of being ready to establish proper laws, and here was I, learned in the Law of Burgundia. My allegiance to my previous Lord has been removed by his regrettable death, so the good king proposed to me that I should serve him and produce a system of Law for the Franks.'

'Now tell them what was your reply to my kind offer!' Clovis spoke sternly, but with a hint of a smile.

'I have explained to my Lord that I would be glad to serve him in the capacity of Lawmaker, but before I commence that task, I would dearly like to travel to Vienne and rescue the beautiful princess Clotilde.'

'And I asked him exactly how he proposed to do that, all on his own! And what answer did he have?'

'None, my Lord.' Elico hung his head sadly.

There was silence for a while as this sunk in. Then Claennis looked pleadingly at Deogol, Ardith and Rodor. 'Can we defer our "previous mission" for a short time?'

To her delight, they returned nods of approval.

'My Lord, and my lord Elico, it may be that we can assist you. I am a trained warrior and tracker, my friend Deogol was once the captain of the Parisii guard, Ardith is a trained physician, Rodor is an experienced traveller throughout Gaul. We are travelling towards that area in any case. We will need to call in at Alsiodorum, but then we are free to help. If you, my lord Elico, would deign to be our guide, we would be glad to plan with you how we, together, might free this unfortunate woman from her imprisonment.'

'And this will need much planning.' To Clovis, ever the military expert, this was obvious. 'Tomorrow morning we will put some military options forward. - Corbus?'

'Yes my Lord?'

'At first light I want you to start examining how the kingdom can function without my presence for a few weeks. Put people in place who can handle responsibility, and you take overall charge. I have sat too long in a peaceful villa. This adventure whets my appetite. I will go myself!'

Chapter Forty-Three
Reunited

*T*hey talked late into the evening. They discussed laws which could be passed, what would be the advantages and disadvantages of each proposal. Flavius wanted the church to have a favoured position, but Clovis said, 'Look here, Flavius, you know I appreciate your company and wit, but just remember that I am not one of your flock, or even of your faith. You cannot have a special position. Your bishop of Rome may be powerful, but he does not rule in my lands.'

'Maybe not, but beware, my Lord, the One he serves rules in every part of the world.'

Clovis laughed, 'Oh my friend, we have been down this road many times and I still do not arrive at the same destination as you. My lady Claennis, what is your opinion of Flavius's God?'

Claennis swallowed hard, 'My Lord, I am privileged to possess a book which speaks about the God who is the creator of the world. The book teaches that we have all strayed from our creator, yet little more than four hundred years past, he sent his son to turn us back to him.'

'Is that the same "son" you talk about, Flavius?' enquired Clovis.

'Yes, my Lord', Flavius was smiling broadly. 'Please continue, my lady Claennis.'

'The son was executed by the Romans, but then witnessed to be alive days later. This is what Martinus of Turonensis and Patricius of Alsiodorum taught, because they also learned from this book. We are on pilgrimage to the place of learning of Patricius, in order to understand more about this man.'

Clovis looked puzzled. 'Here is what I can never understand. You talk about God, the creator, then suddenly change to talking about this man who died and was supposed to have lived again. Which one do you serve?'

'They are one and the same', said Claennis. 'The son shows us what his father, the creator, is like. When you serve the son, you serve his father. The son is also the creator along with his father and he is equal to his father.'

'Aha! Now, I have you there!' Clovis was so excited he was nearly shouting. 'I have heard that some followers of the son do not accept he is equal to his father. Is that not so Elico?'

'Yes, my Lord, for example the tyrant Gundric follows teachings of a man called Arius, who taught exactly as you say. But Gundric's evil actions are not a recommendation for that teaching. My previous master, King Chilperic, followed the understanding that my lady Claennis spoke of. He was a very different man.'

'What?' bellowed Clovis, 'Are you suggesting that whether you live a worthy or unworthy life turns upon the understanding you have of God?'

Flavius burst out laughing. 'My dear friend Clovis, of course we are suggesting that!'

Claennis interrupted, 'My Lord, fascinated as I am by our conversation, as we need to be planning early tomorrow, may I ask to be excused?'

She really wasn't that tired, but she had on her mind the strange message from earlier in the evening.

A servant was called to show her to her room. As she went in, she said to the servant, 'I am thirsty, please bring me some mead.'

'I will command the mead steward, my lady. He will be here shortly.'

Claennis took her pack and removed her dagger, placing it into its leather pocket inside her tunic. As she sat and waited, she marvelled at the simple comfort of her room.

A knock.

'Enter.'

Claennis gasped as the mead steward came in. 'Lufian!'

Lufian and Claennis embraced as if they had not seen each other for years.

Suddenly she pulled back and hit him with her fist on his shoulder. 'I have come all this way to rescue you and you are playing servant to Clovis? Don't you realise how worried we have all been about you? You don't have any idea what I have been through...'

Any further anger was silenced as Lufian kissed her, hard, on the lips.

He pulled back. 'Allow me to explain all that has happened, my sweet cousin, and you will understand.'

Claennis was shaken by the kiss. She had grown up with Lufian. Though he was her cousin, he had been more of a brother. They had played together, worked together, but she had never seen him as...

'You had better have a good story!' she said, through her teeth.

'But I also need to tell it to Ardith and Deogol - and who is the other man you have with you?'

'That's Rodor. He understands what we are doing and wishes to help. I will go now and call them here.'

Chapter Forty-Four

Lufian's First Story

J suppose it was really my fault. I was trying to warn my mother about the Franks and I got captured by them instead. I didn't know that they had made their way so far south. I even wondered about going south and heading north into Lutetia, but in the end, I decided just to head directly east.

One midday I nearly ran into a Frankish patrol. I was in the shade of trees, resting from my journey and eating. I heard the sound of voices and horses coming from the other side of the trees. I was so glad of all the work I put into my Frankish lessons as a child, or I might have been killed. I heard them say, 'Let us check around the other side of these trees.' I quickly picked up my pack, and as they came around one side of the trees, I led my horse around the other.

They must be useless trackers, Claennis, for I had left plenty of signs of my presence, but they came round the trees, then rode off in the direction I had come from.

I had been staying at inns on the way, but now I realised I was in Frankish territory, I decided to sleep in the cover of bushes and trees. My problem was food. I had enough for a day, but, because I had not expected to be in Frankish lands, I had stupidly made no provision for this situation.

I also didn't know how much land the Franks had taken. Had they taken Lutetia? For a moment I even considered going back, but then I realised that whatever had happened, my mother was still going to need my help.

It was then I made the worst decision. I rode near to a farm. It had a great barn full of hay. It looked so inviting, and I needed a good sleep. My firm intent to stay in the open at night evaporated and after dark I made my way in, snuggled into the hay and fell sound asleep.

I woke in bright daylight to a painful prodding in my leg. Standing over me were two huge men. One was sticking his pike into my thigh. I yelled and jumped up, swinging my fists at the man with the pike. I was too dull with sleep to notice the other man behind me. I can just remember a heavy blow on the back of my head. The next thing I remember was coming to my senses in Clovis's cells with a thumping head.

I was there for weeks! I despaired of ever returning to my earlier life. There were two other men in the same state as I. Disgusting food and stale water were shoved under our door each day.

One day, one of the men awoke, shouting. When he had fully awakened, he was relieved that it was only a dream. He desired to share with me what he had dreamt.

'I was in a huge eating-hall', he said, 'at table with Elico. We were both very hungry, and waiting for our meat. Then three servants came. They brought every kind of delicious food and drink but they placed it in front of Elico. I turned to see if food was being brought for me, but standing behind me were three soldiers. They grabbed me and lifted me from my seat, then dragged me outside. One of them took a huge sword and stood in front of me, preparing to swing. I tried to turn and run but my body would not move. He started to swing - and that was when I awoke. Was I shouting?'

'You were shouting very loudly!' I said. It was then that it struck me like a thunderbolt - you know what I'm going to say, don't you, Claennis?

Yes, you know. Understanding. Understanding struck me as if it were a blow from a fist.

Let me tell the others that, unlike Claennis, I had times when I did not wish El Elyon to rule my life. Since childhood I had found myself possessed of a strange understanding which would come over me, unbidden, a gift from El Elyon. I would be trying to lead my everyday life, when out of nowhere I would be struck by an understanding of events which had overtaken the lives of people around me.

Sometimes what was needed was to speak to those people, to warn them of what was to happen. Sometimes I had to make arrangements to deal with the consequences of the events which would overtake them. But all the time, when understanding struck me, I had to take the responsibility for doing something. As manhood came upon me, I began to resent this responsibility, and I am ashamed to say I sought to escape the burden that El Elyon had placed upon me. I decided I would live as I wished, and turned my back on him.

Yet though I turned my back on him, he never turned his back on me. And the gift never left me. It was declared over me by Patricius when I was a small child. Patricius was not its origin, he only saw that El Elyon had given it.

So whether I followed El Elyon or not, I was occasionally struck by deep understanding of what was to be. And so it was when Galba's dream...

'Galba?' shouted Rodor. 'Galba? The person who dreamed, his name was Galba?'

'Yes, that was his name. Do you know him?'

'Tell me. Did he have poor vision in the darkness?'

'Yes. How did you know?'

'Galba!' Rodor was still shouting. 'Galba is my brother!'

Lufian looked nonplussed, and Claennis helped him, 'Galba and Rodor were separated as children.' Then, seeing Lufian's face, 'It's a long story. We'll tell you later.'

'So, where is he?'

Lufian looked downcast. 'That is all bound up with the understanding.'

'But I do not have the understanding and I want to know where my brother is!'

Lufian's face fell further. He looked so sad that Claennis felt her heart wrench for him. 'Ah, my new friend', he said, 'I am sorry to say I have no good news for you.'

Rodor was silent.

Lufian continued, 'The understanding which fell upon me at that moment was the knowledge of the meaning of Galba's dream. I know it is a mistake to think that every dream carries a meaning; some are simply the mind wondering on the events of the past and worries for the future. But sometimes El Elyon himself, to accomplish his own purposes, gives a dream. And when he does, he can always be relied upon to give the understanding, sometimes to the dreamer, sometimes to another - or else what would be the purpose of giving the dream?'

'So are you going to tell us what Galba dreamed?' said Rodor, clearly impatient.

'Oh yes, Rodor, I'm sorry, this is what I understood. The three servants and three soldiers represented three days from the dream to the events which were in the dream. The sumptuous meal which was placed before Elico showed that he would be elevated to a place of high honour. But the explanation for poor Galba was that in three days he would be taken away to be put to the sword.'

'Oh no!' Rodor was overcome. 'And what happened?'

'Three days later we all were seized by soldiers and taken from the cell. I was given the duty of serving mead in the household. As you know, Elico has become one of the advisors to King Clovis. But Rodor,

I am sorry, as far as I know, the sentence on Galba was carried out. The Franks have no use for a blind man.'

Rodor's face creased, and tears fell freely from his eyes. 'I loved my brother! I lost him once. Now I have had him returned to me and then snatched away again, all in moments!'

Deogol, always a surprise, slid along the bench and put his arm around Rodor, who collapsed, sobbing, on Deogol's huge shoulder.

Chapter Forty-Five
Planning

They assembled the next morning to break fast. Clovis was at the head of the table. Claennis thought he looked as if life had become more exciting. By contrast, Rodor looked quite dejected.

'Right! Are we ready to plan?'

There were mumblings of assent from mouths full of delicious food. Meats, honey, bread, even some fish littered the table.

'My Lord Clovis', Claennis started, then hesitated, 'before we start to plan, I have a delicate request.'

'If it is in my power to grant it, my Lady Claennis, I will be pleased to do so.'

Claennis hesitated and gulped, 'If I may, my Lord, I would like... to... buy your servant, the one who serves mead.' The last few words came out all in a rush.

Clovis looked surprised, rather than angry. 'Buy my mead server? He has only been here a few weeks, I cannot recall even speaking to him. What is he to you, surely you do not need a mead server?'

'Good King Clovis, your mead server is my cousin.'

Clovis looked even more surprised. 'Your cousin! Then how did he come to be in my cells?'

'He was crossing Gaul, seeking his mother. He thought she would be in Lutetia, but we happened to know that she had moved on to

Alsiodorum to visit her children, who are studying at the place where Patricius studied.'

Clovis narrowed his eyes. 'Is there more to your journey than meets the eye, my lady Claennis? I had thought you were simply on a pilgrimage. This sounds more like a rescue mission.'

'You are very perceptive, my Lord. It has been difficult to describe the nature of our mission, so we have kept the explanation - how shall I put it? - rather simple.'

'Well, my lady, I think it is time for the complete explanation, don't you?' Clovis clicked his fingers to a nearby servant. 'Fetch the mead-server. Here! Now!'

Lufian came in hurriedly, but stopped short when he saw the whole group looking at him. 'Yes... Sire?' he said hesitantly.

'I think there is something that I have not known about you, mead server. Perhaps you would come and sit at table with us and tell us who you really are.'

'Yes, sire.' Lufian hesitantly sat at the table and gave a questioning look at Claennis.

'Go on', she said, 'we must now trust King Clovis.'

'My name, Sire, is Lufian. I am the only son of Kursa, who was, till his death, Joint Lord of the Ingwi-Seaxe. My mother is Denua, Princess of the Rhegninses in Britain, sister to their previous king, Wyrtgeorn, and one-time Queen of the Parisii. My cousin here, is Princess Claennis, she is the eldest daughter of Beorn, now Joint Lord of the Ingwi-Seaxe. Her mother is Princess Cwen, sister of Kursa and his brother, Hengest.'

Clovis rolled his eyes and leant back in his seat. 'So what you are telling me is that sitting here we have the royal families of half of northern Europa!'

'Yes, Sire. My mother, Denua, was invited by the Parisii to be an interim ruler following the death of Licnos.'

'I've heard of him!" said Clovis, 'Dreadful man, by all accounts!'

'Yes, my Lord, he was. The Parisii are well rid of him. He died in some sort of drunken stupor, from what I heard. The Parisii thought that having Denua as a temporary queen would give them time to decide on a replacement ruler.'

After she left to travel to Lutetia, we heard that the Franks - I apologise - you, my Lord, had moved south very fast. We were worried that Lutetia might fall to you, so I came over to be of help to her, should she need it. But I became your captive instead, my Lord.'

'So you are here to protect your mother from me!' Clovis was obviously very amused by this thought.

'Sire...' Lufian was now embarrassed, but Clovis laughed again.

'No matter, I would probably have done the same for my mother. But now, my lady Claennis, this begs an explanation of the real reason why you are here?'

'My Lord, my younger sister returned from her studies in Alsiodorum with the news that Denua had arrived, but Lufian had not. We thought that he might have had some difficulty and decided to set out to look for him. As it has turned out, we seem to have succeeded.'

Clovis pursed his lips and nodded his head. 'If I am to go on an expedition with allies, it is best if our alliance is based on telling the truth to each other. So I am glad that you have been honest with me. But now we must plan.'

'It strikes me that we should start by announcing what strengths each of us will bring to our expedition. I will start. My talent is the detailed planning of strategy and tactics, and overseeing their implementation. But I cannot travel as Clovis the king of the Franks for that will draw unwanted attention. I think I will travel in the guise of a Roman. Has anyone any suggestions for a suitable name?'

There was silence, and brows were furrowed. Then Elico spoke. 'My Lord, I think you need a noble-sounding name, for you are not travelling as a poor man. What about "Aurelian"?'

'That sounds excellent, Elico! I will travel as Aurelian the Roman nobleman, fallen slightly on hard times!' Clovis smiled. 'Now, who is next? My lady Claennis?'

'I am a tracker. I also have skill with the flail.'

Clovis nodded approval, 'Let us keep going round the table. Deogol?'

'Commanding of warriors. And I am in tests of strength so far unbeaten.'

'My lady Ardith?'

'Physician. I have some skills in ropework.'

'Elico?'

'I know the land and the city well and can act as guide. I am familiar with the building where Clotilde is said to be held.'

'Lufian. Apart from mead-serving, what is your strength?'

Lufian looked at Clovis, but the king was smiling. 'I am good with the sword, sire, though Claennis is often quicker. I have inherited some of my mother's skill with the bow. But the greatest skill I have is climbing.'

'Oh yes!' the words escaped Claennis's lips involuntarily.

'Save your cousin embarrassment and tell us, lady Claennis, just how good at climbing he is.'

'Yes, my Lord, he has been a powerful climber since he was a child. He is known for it throughout our community. There are sheer walls of rock near our home, with no obvious foothold. Lufian swarms up them as if he is walking on flat ground.'

'A talent that may well prove very useful' said Clovis. 'And Rodor. What talent do you bring?'

Rodor had recovered his composure from the previous night. 'I know pottery, my Lord, but that is not likely to be of assistance. I am well-travelled, but we have Elico as a guide. I think the only ability I can bring is a knowledge of Greek fire.'

There was a mixed reaction to this news. Claennis, Lufian and Ardith looked blank. Elico raised his eyebrows, but the rest of his face didn't move. By contrast, Clovis spattered the table with food as he suddenly bent at the belly and shouted 'What! You know Greek fire?'

'Yes my Lord. And in anticipation of a possible need, I have taken the liberty of bringing the ingredients with me.'

Clovis was so overcome that he stammered, 'B-bbut how do you know? I thought Greek fire was only a legend!'

'I am delighted to recount the events, but it is quite a long story, my Lord.'

'I cannot leave this table without knowing. You had better tell the whole.'

So Rodor began.

Chapter Forty-Six
Rodor's Second Story

*I*t was my fourth trip as a slave with my master's wife. Under my influence, she had changed from just collecting pieces to trading. With our combined knowledge, we ran a very lucrative business. We travelled far to the east in Frankish lands, then we went south across the river Danuvius into Roman Dalmatia, but we found that all the Roman soldiers had left, having been taken south to reinforce Rome against the East Goths.

We travelled south into Dalmatia for some weeks. We were buying as usual, and with the absence of the Roman armies, the local trade was very poor, so we were able to negotiate very good prices. We soon had a cart full of good stock, some of which my mistress marked down for her own use, the rest we should be able to sell at a good profit as we returned.

We came across a pottery trader. He mentioned that we should visit a town on the coast of the Ionian sea called Dyrrachium. He was one of those people who say things, then look at you to see if you are suitably impressed.

'Dyrrachium was the headquarters of Pompey's army when he fought Julius Caesar!' he said. 'It is noted for its pottery! It has large clay deposits which are just right for fine pottery making! You ought to see the Roman amphitheatre!'

We made suitable noises and faces, to show that we were, really, impressed. But as soon as we heard his words, my mistress would not rest until we had visited it.

It was in the afternoon, three days later, when we approached Dyrrachium along a ridge of land. The town was set on a promontory. True to what the trader had said, it had been a Roman fortress and, though it had fallen into disrepair, it still had thick stone fortified walls. To the west there was a steep drop to the beautiful blue of the Ionian sea.

We passed a large Roman amphitheatre. I recognised what it was, of course, as I had come across many of them, but I had never seen one of this size. The vast walls consisted of alternating brick and stone layers; we found out later that this was to better resist the earthquakes which are frequent in this area. Gladiatorial contests had ended only about eighty years before and two of the galleries were now used by Christians as their meeting places.

As usual we asked directions for a good inn. It is my experience that an innkeeper, suitably rewarded, is the best source for information about any aspect of the area. We were recommended to an inn near the centre of the town, and found ourselves in a pleasant hostelry with the irresistible aroma of cooking meat. We left our horses in the care of the stable lad, and enjoyed a tasty meal of lamb and local vegetables washed down with good ale. You can tell how good it was, I still remember it!

Despite the good food, I noticed that there were few customers. I paid the innkeeper for a drink for himself and asked whether trade was usually better than this.

'Normally we are full at this time', he said - rather sadly, I thought - 'but since the raids, many have left their homes, or at least do not venture out towards evening.'

'Raids?' said my mistress. I could tell by the sound of her voice that she was nervous. In some ways she was adventurous, yet she would travel far out of her way to avoid trouble.

'Have you not heard?' He pulled at his ale. 'Just to the north of us is a hotbed of Illyrian tribes who care for nothing but their own wealth. They have been pirates between here and Italia for centuries, but the Romans suppressed them. For some time they turned to using their ships for honest trading, but since the Romans left, they have gone back to piracy.'

'Are they likely to come here?' My mistress's voice had gone a shade higher.

'Oh, I see.' The innkeeper had only just noticed her unease. 'Do not worry, my lady, up here we are quite safe. This used to be a Roman fortress and it is still a good stronghold. It takes some climbing of the hillside to reach us, and we have lookouts posted.' He paused for a moment, and took another long pull at his ale. 'Only last week we repelled two ships with Greek fire.'

Now my attention was caught. 'Greek fire? I have not heard of that before, what is it?'

'Ah, that is our secret.' He put his finger to the side of his nose. 'We do not tell how it is made.' He drank the rest of his flagon of ale and I put the price of his next on the table.

He bumbled around the ale casks for a while, but eventually returned with his refill. 'Mind you, I can tell you that around here I am the only one who knows all the secrets of its manufacture.' He smiled and seemed to swell with pride at his knowledge.

'I hope it is effective', said my mistress, 'What if it fails?'

'Fails? Greek fire? You evidently know nothing of it! Greek fire cannot fail.'

'How can you be sure of that?' I saw that my mistress had detected my interest and was assisting me in turning the conversation.

'I suppose, once we are finished here, I could show you the vessels and nozzles.'

'I would like that very much', I said. 'Have another drink on me.'

An hour later, we stood on fortified ramparts at the top of a steep slope dropping down into the Ionian sea.

The innkeeper - we now knew him as Demetrius - waved to a lookout and we walked over towards him. The lookout was standing next to an odd-looking machine. There were several of them dotted about on the edge of the ramparts. As we reached him, the odd thing was that he ignored us and peered out to sea.

Suddenly he leant and picked up a large ram's horn, blowing a series of blasts.

'Now you will get some answers to your questions!' shouted Demetrius, running to one of the machines, 'We are under attack!'

I looked out to sea. There were five small ships, sailing very fast into shore. Despite its speed, each one was loaded with men, bristling with spears.

Men from Dyrrachium came rushing onto the ramparts, manning all of the machines. Fires were lit under large metal barrels, each about the same size as a wooden ale barrel. Projecting from the bottom of the barrels, out from the ramparts, was a long metal tube with a narrow nozzle pointing out to sea. A man sat in front of each barrel, holding the tube with thick leather gauntlets. Another man sat near the end of the nozzle, with a flaming torch. Two more men went to the back of each machine, and seemed to operate huge wood and leather bellows with pipes to the top of the barrels, forcing air in.

The two lead ships had nearly reached the shore below when I heard Demetrius shout an order. Each man with leather gauntlets turned a tap. The pressurised liquid jetted from the nozzle and immediately caught the fire of the torch. The men turned the nozzles and the jets of burning liquid squirted forwards, then fell, seemingly slowly, like water from a waterfall, right onto the two ships below.

There was pandemonium on the ships. At our distance above them, I could hear the screams of men burning. The ships flamed immediately, as if they were dry tinder. I could see men rushing to throw water onto the fires, but it made no difference. The fire was unstoppable.

Although these men had come to attack us, I felt pity for them. They did not have any chance against the Greek fire from the defenders. Within a short time, the remains of the two ships were sinking and the other three ships were running back out to sea.

It was some hours later when we reassembled at the inn. This time, Demetrius was plying us with drink, in celebration of the rout of their invaders.

I took the opportunity, given his elated state of mind, to press home my enquiry about the constituents of his fiery liquid. And eventually, I elicited from him a description of the recipe. So I have brought the ingredients with me, in case they are needed. You do not have to use an engine to squirt the fluid, and my hope is that at some point my knowledge might be useful.

There was silence for quite some time when Rodor finished his story. Then Clovis said, 'So, tell us, what is your fiery fluid made from?'

Rodor hesitated for a moment, 'My Lord, you do realise that the users of this liquid consider the recipe to be a highly guarded secret, known to only a few, because of its great power?'

'Yes, of course I realise that! And I demand, as King of the Franks, that I also be admitted to the ranks of the few who know. Now, tell me!'

Rodor said, 'Indeed my Lord. But in order to obey your instruction, it will be easier if I show you what I have brought with me.'

He went out, and returned with a leather bag and two large, flat clay pots from his packs. 'In this, my Lord, is powdered brimstone.' He opened the leather bag and showed some yellow powder, which smelt foul. 'In this pot is resin from pine trees.' He took an oiled cloth from the top of the pot and tilted it to show a viscous liquid which smelt fresh and heady. 'And in this one', he picked up the third pot, 'is a powerful liquid called naphtha.' The cork seemed to be sealed onto the pot. He broke the seal and poured out a tiny amount of the liquid. It was pale in colour, with a very strong, unbreathable smell, and within a few moments it had disappeared into the air.

'That is good, but not good enough!' said Clovis. 'I need to know where to get these from. And I don't have any difficulty with the pine resin. I know how to get that.'

'The brimstone is easily available, my Lord, being mined in several places, and sold to anyone who can afford it. It is the naphtha which is the secret ingredient, although it is easy to obtain if you have the knowledge. In Augustonemetum to our south are pits which bubble up tar. You need a special pair of flasks and an unusual connecting piece. You fill one flask with tar, and heat it very gently, the first liquid which runs into the second flask is naphtha. Mix this with the brimstone and resin, and you have Greek fire.'

'And, if I understand correctly from your story, the main problem for the enemy is that it is very difficult to extinguish.'

'No, my Lord, not "very difficult". Impossible.'

'I think that will suit our purposes admirably, Rodor', said Clovis, visibly brightening.

Chapter Forty-Seven

The Journey Starts

They took the rest of the day to prepare, at Clovis's instruction, for the journey. Horses were made ready. The servants brought a good cart and Clovis selected two horses to pull it, and one to follow, which gave an opportunity to rotate with those being ridden. Servants brought provisions; seemingly an endless supply went into the packs. Clothing was selected, such as traders wore.

Claennis was still perplexed, if she allowed herself to think of it, by Lufian's kiss. Yet she had not a moment to question him about it. His duties seemed to keep him running to and fro; whenever she saw him, she had the impression that he was too busy to talk - or maybe avoiding her?

Early the following morning they set off, Clovis and Elico at the head of the group. Claennis and Ardith followed. The cart was next, with Rodor driving. Deogol and Lufian rode at the rear with the spare horse.

They headed southeast on a totally straight road. As they left the town, Clovis looked round at Claennis. 'Here's one thing we have to thank the Romans for!', he said, 'They made the best roads in Europa! Elico says this road will take us one fifth of the way.'

Elico had allowed for four hours travelling each day. He reckoned they would arrive in Alsiodorum on the fifth day. At the end of the first day they reached a village where the Roman road turned south.

'This is where we turn off this road', said Elico, 'so we stop here for the night.'

They pulled into the yard of a large inn which sat on the crossroads in the village centre. The innkeeper and his wife were surprised to see such a large group, but rooms suddenly became available once they saw Clovis's gold. The stable lad took the horses and the cart to the rear of the inn. Rodor volunteered to sleep with the cart, for security. They ate well, and slept well, and were ready to go early the next morning.

Next day they found a misty morning, the sun valiantly trying to break through. Elico set a constant pace, but not a fast one.

Claennis took in the moist beauty of the trees lining the road. Her thoughts turned to Lufian. Since she had not returned his sudden kiss, he had retreated slightly. He had always been her best friend, but now he seemed careful not to come too close.

As she thought back on - the kiss - her mind constantly switched emotions. She was angry with him that he had disturbed their relationship. And she was confused. Had he kissed her on a whim of delight at finding her? Or were there - other feelings - behind it?

And there was something else inside her. Yet another feeling. When she pictured Lufian kissing her, it warmed the base of her belly.

The morning was getting warm. They rode gently through an avenue of trees. The movement of her horse was soporific. Her thoughts drifted to her childhood...

Padraig, for that was what they called Patricius back in Éire, looked down at Claennis and Lufian. With his white beard and wild hair he looked quite frightening, thought Claennis. But then she thought something else. She remembered that she had been brought up not to be frightened of people. And though she was only six, and in a strange land, with a strange language, she was standing next to her friend Lufian, so she felt quite brave, today.

Padraig started to talk. Claennis almost jumped. He had such a beautiful voice! It was like - like - what was that she sometimes ate? Honey! That was what his voice was like.

What was he saying? 'You are destined to be Royal servants of the Most High God. From you will come two Royal Houses. But you must remember this. Be you ever so high, higher than all you rule, yet you are still only a servant to Him. So you must keep your hearts humble, as a servant is humble. Keep this in mind when you administer justice.'

What? What did he say? Remember? I'll never remember all that. Something like 'humble.' I'll ask my mother afterwards.

Lufian was her best friend. Well, actually he was her only friend. There was no-one else. She enjoyed playing with him. She enjoyed fighting with him, too. Her sword, it was only a wooden one, usually hit him before his hit her. She was very proud of that. But he was very good at Latin; his mother and father sometimes spoke it around the house, whereas her father was still struggling with Éireann. She would have to try harder at their community school.

A sudden shout broke her reverie. Armed men were streaming out of the trees on their left, surrounding them. Not again, thought Claennis, then she realised these could not be Franks, Clovis was here!

'Halt! And state who you are and your business travelling through our land!' The man who drew forward out of the group had a stentorian voice.

'We are but traders in cloth, with our wives and servants' said Elico. He spoke in an oddly humble tone of voice. 'We travel to Alsiodorum' he continued, truthfully.

'You travel nowhere without our permission! We will search your packs and your cart. If we find you are lying, you will all die.'

What happened next happened all at once.

A huge man swung down from a tree on the right side of the road, and landed directly on the one who had spoken. They both fell heavily to the ground. 'Elico! Go! Now!' he shouted.

Simultaneously, a shout of 'Trymian!' came from several of their attackers.

Clovis shot forward like an arrow from a bow, a sword appearing in his hand as if by a miracle. He dropped from his horse and held his sword at the throat of the leader. 'All of you! Stop where you are! If anyone moves, he dies!'

Lufian and Deogol appeared with swords.

Elico shouted 'Galba!'

Deogol shouted again, 'Trymian? Is it you?'

Rodor, did not move from the cart, his eyes widened 'Galba?' he said, weakly.

'What is going on here?' demanded Clovis angrily. 'Does everybody know everybody? Somebody explain. Now!'

'My Lord, the name of the man from the tree is Galba. He was in your cells with Lufian and me' said Elico. 'We thought he had been executed. He must have escaped.'

'There was a blind man who escaped, wounding one of my guards; but this can't be him, this man can see!' Clovis turned to the man on the floor, 'What is your name, man, and how do you come to be here?'

'My name, as Elico has said, is Galba, my Lord. I am blind only when I am in dim light. In daylight, I can see. I was led out for execution, but because they thought I was blind, your men did not watch me carefully enough. So I snatched a sword, struck a guard and escaped. I was hiding in the trees when I saw your party being stopped by these men, and because I recognised the voice of Elico, I knew he must be in danger.'

There was silence for a moment while Clovis absorbed this.

Then a weak voice came from the back, 'Galba is that really you?'

'Yes, I am Galba. And you speak with a Brittonic accent. Do I know you?'

'I am Rodor.'

'Rodor!' Galba sprang up, raced to the cart and fell upon his brother, weeping.

Clovis turned from that scene to find Deogol jumping round hugging the leader of their attackers. 'Deogol!' he said, testily, 'So what in the name of the gods is going on here?'

'When I was a young man, my Lord, and Trymian was a small boy, into slavery we were taken by... I am sorry my Lord, by some Franks...'

'We are again the wrongdoers, it seems' said Clovis in a resigned voice. 'Go on.'

Trymian's deep voice interrupted Deogol. 'This man became a father to me when we were slaves. Then King Bricius of the Parisii bought us and freed us. When he died, and the evil Licnos became king, Deogol helped Queen Denua to escape. I have not set eyes upon him until now.'

Now Deogol interrupted. 'Trymian still only a boy was and remained in Lutetia. I would not his face have recognised, but I hear a faint Ingwi accent, and when I hear his name shouted, him it had to be.'

Clovis looked at Trymian's men who still surrounded them. 'Well, Trymian, as we seem to have, how shall I put it, connections, will you now allow us to go on our way to Alsiodorum?'

Chapter Forty-Eight

Lufian's Second Story

Trymian proved more helpful than Clovis had expected, for he and his men escorted the group, which now included Galba, for several hours. Eventually they arrived in a village. Trymian halted the group by the gates of a large house. 'This is the edge of Parisii lands', he said, 'and this is the house of Vortrix. He was a Parisii warrior. He served for years as captain under the rule of King Bricius, but when Licnos took over he retired here with some of his men. They guard our southeastern flank against Gaulish raids. His house functions as an inn, though he welcomes only those whom we vouch for. I will go in and speak to him about your party.'

That night, by courtesy of a very hospitable Vortrix, they feasted again. Claennis remembered her last mouthful of bread at her breakfast in Éire, when she wondered if she would be eating at all on her journey. Now, on the contrary, it seemed as if they were feasting every night! She had a fleeting hilarious picture of her horse, with a hollowed back from her weight!

That night, she and Ardith were to share a room. She generally had no secrets from Ardith, and wondered whether to tell her about the kiss.

'Ardith... I was just wondering whether... you might give me some advice.'

'Of course, Claennis. You look so worried. Whatever is the matter?'

Claennis poured out the story of the kiss, and the way that Lufian seemed to be avoiding her since.

Ardith's eyebrows rose. 'Lufian, eh? Well...'

'What do you mean, "Lufian, eh"? Have you been expecting something?'

'No, no, my dear, nothing like that.'

Claennis felt herself get more agitated, 'Well? What should I do about it?'

'There is only one thing to be done in these circumstances', soothed Ardith, 'You will have to ask Lufian. And don't pull that face at me. Find a time when you have a quiet few moments. Tell him how you feel and ask him what is going on.'

Next morning, they met with Trymian at breakfast. He wished them God's blessing on their travels, and bade them take care for they were soon to pass into Burgundian lands. 'Elico', he said, 'As you seem to be the guide, can we have a few moments together to check through your planned route to Alsiodorum?'

The breakfast broke up gradually. Clovis excused himself and left to 'make arrangements'. The others drifted away to prepare for the journey.

Quietly Claennis said to Lufian, 'Cousin, would you walk with me?'

They went outside into a large grove of fruit trees, 'It's about the kiss, isn't it?' said Lufian.

'Of course. What... why... I don't know how to even ask.'

'And I don't really know how to tell.' Lufian tailed off, looking more dejected than she had ever seen him.

Claennis gave him a playful punch on the shoulder, just as she had always done when she had got frustrated with him. 'Well, you can't leave me like this! Tell me what has happened to you. You''ve kissed me lots of times - but never - like that. Did you mean to kiss me that way? And why have you been avoiding me? And tell me why you are looking so sad!'

Lufian laughed loudly, 'Same old Claennis! Always asks the next question before you"ve had a chance to answer the last one!'

Claennis was so glad to see him laugh, in his old way, that she could almost have forgiven him for putting her through her mental torture. But she had started, and she had to see it through. 'So, are you going to make a start on my questions?'

'Yes, you"re right that something has happened to me. While I was in Clovis's cell, not knowing whether I was going to die, or live out the rest of my days in that dismal place, my mind returned to the happy times of my life.

I was taken back to our life in the green beauty of Éire, our schooldays, learning to teach others what I knew, working on the land, being with our families, our community, and...'

He quietened. His eyes were downcast, his face looked so sad that Claennis didn't know whether to hug him or hit him. 'Yes? And?'

'And you.'

'Me?'

'Yes, you. It seemed impossible that I would ever see you again. And... ', Lufian took a deep breath, 'that made me very sad.'

'I see.'

'No you don't. That's the problem. You don't see.'

Claennis could no longer hold in her irritation. 'Lufian, will you please tell me in plain simple words what is going on or do I have to hit you again?'

'Alright. Do you remember the day, we were fifteen, when our families had the archery contest?'

'Vaguely. We were one team, my mother and father were another, and Denua and Kursa were the third. What of it?'

'You know I am in awe of my mother's ability with the bow, and have always felt I can't quite live up to it? Well. Remember how it all came down to that last shot? Cwen and Beorn were well behind and my parents were one point ahead of us, mainly due to my mother's amazing shooting, and I had to shoot the last arrow.'

'And you were shaking, and then you got control of yourself, and then you fired the last shot and we won. I saw it all.'

'And then?'

'Then? What?'

'What happened next?'

'I don't know - we celebrated, didn't we?'

'What happened next, my sweet cousin, is that you threw your arms around me and hugged me. And then you kissed me.'

'Only on the cheek!'

'Yes, only on the cheek. But from that kiss, I started to feel - differently about you.'

Slowly, the light dawned. 'You mean - not like I was a sister.'

'No.' All of a sudden words poured out. 'Not like a sister, more than that, like you were my... my...'

'Lover.'

'Yes, lover. That day, I suddenly realised you were - you are - beautiful.'

'Hah!'

'So even though outwardly I treated you as if you were my sister, I just wanted to keep looking at you. And when we were together, I felt as if I wanted to be with you forever.'

Claennis stood, stunned.

'But even though you have found me and rescued me', Lufian continued, 'I still know it can never be, and that is what makes me feel so low.'

Hesitantly, knowing she was in a delicate position, Claennis said, 'It can never be?'

'Because I know well that you don't think of me like that. I am your cousin. We grew up together. I'm like a brother to you.'

'So why did you kiss me?'

'A moment of madness. I was so glad to see you, my whole world had just turned the right way up again. Your beautiful face was mine to gaze on again, when I thought I never would, I just suddenly acted the way I felt. I realised I shouldn't have, but then it was done. I thought I had better keep my distance from you after that, so as not to put pressure on you.'

They walked on in silence to the end of the grove of trees, and turned back.

'Lufian.'

'Yes?'

'You obviously realise that all this is a bit new to me.'

'Yes.'

Claennis spoke slowly. 'But I need to tell you that, as we have been on the road, I have thought about what you did.'

Lufian slowed and looked at her.

'And when I think about that kiss, I get a strange feeling in my stomach.'

'I'm so sorry, Claennis, I never meant you to feel bad.'

'It doesn't feel bad. It feels good.'

Lufian stared.

'So first I need to ask you not to feel downcast, then give me opportunity to consider all this. It may take me some time, but while I'm thinking, please', Claennis smiled and gave him another punch on the shoulder, 'I'd like you to treat me as your sister again for now. I want the old Lufian back!'

Chapter Forty-Nine

Alsiodorum

The group left the house of Vortrix, grateful for his care. Clovis paid him with more gold than was owed, which caused his eyebrows to rise. 'Really? You are very generous!'

'I have a clandestine reason', said Clovis, archly.

'Oh yes?'

'There is a distinct possibility that in not too long a time, we may be heading back this way in some haste. We may need to call upon your hospitality again.'

'You are friends of Trymian. You are welcome here at any time. We are glad to render any service we can.'

'Perhaps we can talk for a moment about what help you may give?'

'Certainly.'

Clovis and Vortrix moved away and talked together for some time. Then the whole group bade their farewells and set off.

Elico's directions seemed to become more confident as they journeyed east. He kept shouting triumphantly to Rodor when he recognised landmarks. For the next three nights, they managed to find a suitable hostelry and on the sixth day they found themselves entering hilly country, with thick forests dotted along the way. Occasionally bare rock broke the surface. They passed through a scatter of small villages. 'We are approaching Alsiodorum', intoned Elico.

They rose higher, with glimpses of mountain blue far in front of them. The road wound upwards to large studded gates in a thick wooden palisade. 'We are here', said Elico, unnecessarily.

'What is your business?'

Elico shouted up to the gateman, 'We visit the abbey of St Germanus. We have business with Queen Denua of the Parisii. Give the names Lufian and Claennis.'

'You will wait.'

Less than a hundred breaths later, the gates swung open and there stood Denua, looking resplendent in gold and green - her favourite colours.

Lufian and Claennis rushed at her, Deogol and Ardith were close behind. Clovis, Elico, Rodor and Galba hung back. This was a legendary Queen. They would wait to be invited into her presence.

Once the hugging had subsided, Lufian took his mother's arm. 'Queen Denua', he announced, 'I would like you to meet one of our party, travelling as Aurelian, a Roman. However, his true identity may be known to you. Allow me to present to you Clovis, King of the Franks.'

Just then, Lufian distinctly felt Denua's weight suddenly pull on him, as if her knees had buckled slightly, but she recovered within a few heartbeats. 'King Clovis, it is a great honour to make your acquaintance.' Her deep tones were soft but firm.

'I have heard much of you, my lady, and also the fine men, Bricius and Kursa, who were privileged to call you wife.'

Lufian continued his introductions. 'And this is Elico, one time legal advisor to Chilperic of Lugdunum, now legal advisor to King Clovis.'

'Elico, I know of your previous lord. I am sorry to hear of the dark times which have overcome his family.'

'Thank, you my lady', said Elico. 'We travel with the aim of alleviating some of their suffering.'

'Rodor, trader in fine pottery, and his brother Galba.'

'I am pleased to meet you, Rodor and Galba. Now perhaps you would all like to be my guests at St Germanus's abbey. My friend Patricius studied here, as do many of my family.'

They walked their mounts through narrow streets. The people obviously knew Queen Denua, and drew back respectfully as she went past. A large stone-built abbey came into view, with beautiful gardens and a river visible just to the side. Denua led the way to a large villa by the side of the abbey. 'This is where you will stay; please rest and refresh yourselves. We will eat later, and you will tell me of your mission.'

They entered, but within a few moments, the door burst open and five young people ran in and threw their arms around Claennis, Lufian, Deogol and Ardith.

'These are our family, our brothers and sisters', explained Lufian to the others.

They sat with Denua for most of the evening. Lufian and Claennis explained the journey they were on, and their aim to rescue the princess Clotilde.

'If that is the case', Denua was speaking very loudly, 'I wish to be part of the rescue myself! It has been a long time since my bow has seen action!'

The next morning, Claennis noticed Clovis, Denua, Rodor and Galba in deep conversation. A short time afterwards, Rodor's cart was being driven out of the yard. Half a morning later he returned with several large objects on the cart. Everyone went out to see what he had bought. Claennis was disappointed to find that she did not recognise a single thing.

She went out to help to carry, and in response to her raised eyebrows Rodor said, 'As I have found my brother again, we have decided to prepare two lots of Greek fire. I am going to teach him how to make it.'

In the main hall, Rodor and Galba poured a prodigious quantity of black sticky liquid into a big metal pot. It had a neck set over to one side. They lifted it and set it over the fire, which was only smouldering, with its neck pointing out of the flames. A large glass flask was placed to one side on the floor.

Then Rodor, with an air of triumph, pulled from a sack a metal object, nearly half his size, looking like a helmet with a long tube sloping out from one side. 'At last I have managed to obtain one!'

'What on earth is it?' wondered Claennis, out loud.

'It is a fine quality alembic!'

'But that leaves me none the wiser!'

'Watch!' Rodor inserted the opening of the big metal pot into the bottom of the alembic, then dropped the sloping tube into the top of the glass vessel on the floor.

'Now get the embers going!' he instructed. 'Not too much, or you'll have the whole place on fire!'

Bellows lit up the embers. For a long time nothing happened. Then Claennis noticed that a light brown liquid was dripping into the glass flask.

'Naphtha! We have naphtha!' Rodor was nearly dancing with delight at his success.

They boiled the pot for most of the afternoon, nearly filling the flask.

'I have brimstone in that jar, and pine resin in that!' Rodor was so excited. 'Now I have naphtha, I can make Greek fire!'

Clovis came into the hall just at that time. He bent over the flasks and the alembic to examine what they had made. 'How does it do that?'

'I have not the first idea', said Rodor with a wide smile.

Chapter Fifty
Approach to Vienne

The whole group set off early the next day. Elico and Clovis rode at the front, then Lufian and Claennis, who had decided to ride together, then the cart with Rodor and Galba. Denua and Ardith followed, and Deogol was the rearguard.

They rode on, day after day, camping in woods and thickets for safety at night. Lufian surprised them all by producing the most delicious repasts each evening from the food they had packed in Alsiodorum. At one meal, Clovis put down a bone he had been gnawing and said 'If I had known what you could do with food, you would not have been only a mead-server!'

Their journey passed quietly, apart from one incident when they were attacked by a small group of men who ran at Clovis and Elico brandishing swords and spears. Denua was their salvation. She spotted the approaching band and let fly such a thick volley of her short arrows that they turned and ran.

Elico led the company on a curved path which skirted far to the east of Lugdunum. They passed through wild country of forests and lakes. The roads were often steep and treacherous, overgrown with foliage.

'Are there not easier ways?' a grumpy Clovis was heard to demand of Elico, at one point where the road was nearly impassable.

'Yes, my Lord, but all the easier ways will be frequented by Gundric's warriors. We must also keep east of the river Rhodanus. Vienne lies on its east bank, and we will not be able to cross from the west without attracting attention. If we approach from the east, we will be able to arrive at the city more easily, but that route takes us on these paths.'

'But how do you know we are even going in the right direction?'

'My Lord, I, like all the children of Lugdunum, used these hills as my playground. I know these roads as I know my own home.'

The day arrived, when, in the early afternoon, they crested a range of hills, and stared down into a small depression. There, next to a curve in the Rhodanus river, lay Vienne. From the hill, they could just make out Roman features. Heavy stone ramparts were now broken down in several places and replaced by a wooden palisade. In the centre of the haphazardly laid out town was a huge romanesque building, with some kind of pointed monument by its side. Slightly nearer them was the semicircular shape of a Roman theatre, its walls half demolished.

Despite the distance and the worn-out appearance of the town, it was easily possible to imagine the grandeur of its Roman days. They all were silent, hardly breathing as they took in the sight.

'The building in the centre is the old Roman temple', said Elico, his voice little more than a whisper. 'It is now being used by a follower of Arius as his church.'

Claennis spoke quietly. 'Is that why Gundric was given this town when his father died, because he was also an Arian?'

'Nobody really knows', said Denua. 'Is that right, Elico?'

Elico nodded. 'But did you also know that this is where they sent the Roman Prefect of Judea? That pointed monument is reputed to be his memorial.'

'Oh', sounded from several mouths.

'Really?' Denua hardly breathed the word.

'So, help me out', growled Clovis. 'You all obviously know what Elico is rambling about, will anyone explain it to me?'

'My Lord', said Denua, 'I think it would be good to discuss that at leisure over one of Lufian's meals.'

This met with general approval. They retraced their steps away from the town into the forest by a good mile, finding a small clearing where they built a fire for the meal.

They sat, satisfied, around the fire. Denua looked at Clovis. In his voice and demeanour, he gave the impression of being an older man, but she judged that he could not be much older than twenty-five years. She looked around the group, and realised they were all looking at her. Indeed. This was to be her task. Once more she would need to rely on El Elyon. She spoke to Him in her mind, and simultaneously took a deep breath to speak to Clovis.

'My Lord, may I speak about our earlier subject?'

'Of course. It is a pleasure to hear your voice. But, I appeal to you, do not expect me to suddenly change my views and think otherwise than my upbringing has taught me.'

'And one day, my Lord Clovis, perhaps you will tell us of your youth?' - through Denua's mind flashed pictures of her own youth, how at a very similar age she had been a Princess of Rhegin, then Queen of the Parisii - 'and how you came by your views?'

She commenced her story:

'There was once a Roman Prefect of a distant land, at the eastern end of the southern sea. He came from a rich and well known family, the Pontii, named from an eastern region called Pontus. His own name was Pilatus, which means "armed with a pilum". You know this Roman weapon, my Lord?'

'Who doesn't? A vicious thin bladed throwing spear! I have had to evade more than one of those in the wilder times of my youth, though thankfully only thrown by locals who had found some old Roman weapons and didn't know how to use them properly.'

'The wilder times of my youth', thought Denua, and here he was, still only in his twenties!

'As a young adult, Pilatus of the Pontii rose to become a Roman official. He was sent to administer the land of Judea, which had been the home of the Hebrew people since the early days of the world. At the time there was a young teacher who was being followed by thousands of the Hebrew people.'

'Is this the god-man you all talk about, who died and came to life again?' interrupted Clovis.

'Yes. He was known, not just for his teachings, but for miraculous events, generally well attested by many witnesses. He was also famous for his surprising way of life. In some ways he broke with the laws of his people. For example, although he observed a day of rest, he enraged his enemies by healing on that day. Yet at the same time, all except his enemies agreed that his general conduct was above reproach.'

'But he did accumulate enemies. His great following caused those who held the reins of power in that land to fear for their position, and they plotted against him. You already know that they had him killed, but they had to ask permission of Pilatus. He examined the man, and could find no cause for execution. Nevertheless, the pressure from the man's enemies was so great that eventually Pilatus washed his hands of the whole matter and handed the man over to be crucified.'

'Crucifixion, eh? The Romans were well known for it. Particularly cruel. I never could abide it myself. I have no reluctance to dispatch a man if it is needed, but I prefer it to be quick. That is certainly what I would want when my time comes. But then, the Romans crucified many people. Why do you pick out this one?'

'Because a few days after his crucifixion, he was seen alive again. And not just by his followers. On one occasion over five hundred people saw him alive.'

'And you don't think the Romans could have made a mistake?'

Denua spoke quietly and slowly. 'Are you aware, great King Clovis, of the Romans making "mistakes" when they kill a man?'

Clovis tilted his head, pursed his lips and raised his brows. 'I suppose I must agree with you there. It is hard enough to imagine Romans making an error with any slaying, but nobody wakes from crucifixion.'

Denua was silent, not wanting to say more than Clovis could accept. But then Clovis leant forward. 'So, what happened to these two men? I presume Pilatus ended up here, from Elico's words.'

Denua looked over at Elico and raised her brows. 'Elico?'

'Yes, my Lord, the understanding which has come down to us is that after the events my lady Denua described, Pilatus was moved here by his Roman masters. The monument by the large church is called "The Tomb of Pilatus" to this day.'

'And what happened to the other one? The god-man?'

Denua took over again. 'He was seen for forty days upon the earth. He spent time with his followers, as he had before, and explained many things to them, much of which they wrote down. There were more miraculous events, seen by many. On the fortieth day, he took his closest band of followers to the top of a hill, and they saw him being taken up into the clouds. Suddenly two men appeared by them, who told them that one day he would come back to earth again, in like manner.'

'And has he come?'

'Not yet my Lord, but all his true followers look for that appearing.'

'That is the most ridiculous story I have ever heard!' exclaimed Clovis.

'I have to admit, my Lord, there are many who share your view.'

'And why do you not share my view, good Queen Denua?'

'Because I have met him, my Lord.'

Clovis looked startled. 'Met him? But you have just said he has gone!'

'His body has gone into the Heavenly World, but he is God. His Spirit can come and live within us. He transforms us to be more like him.'

'I thought your previous story was preposterous, but this is now even more so!' Clovis looked around at the rest of the group, warming by the fire. 'Surely the rest of you don't believe all this?'

Lufian spoke gently, 'I have had the same meeting with this man as Queen Denua, my Lord.'

Clovis visibly started, then looked at Claennis with the obvious question on his face.

'And I my Lord.'

'Deogol, Ardith?'

'The same, my Lord', they spoke simultaneously, then looked at each other and laughed.

'But what about the Gauls? Rodor, Galba?'

Galba replied first. 'When I was a little boy, my Lord, a man called Patricius passed through our village and taught us just as you have heard Queen Denua speak tonight. I found my little childish heart was transfixed by the man he spoke of, and I set my mind to follow him. I have not always been as true to that as I should, but the older I get, the more that is my desire.'

Rodor spoke as Galba finished. 'I experienced a touch of this man's hand upon my life as a child. He saved me from an unpleasant fate. I have followed him since.'

Clovis's brow was becoming more furrowed with each account, though he still had a half-smile, and spoke lightly, 'Elico! Come to my rescue! You are my last hope! I am surrounded by believers!'

'And I am very sorry to tell you, my King, that I am another one. From my youth in the court of King Chilperic of Lugdunum, my master, Senaculos, taught me of this man. He said it was because of him that he had no fear of his own death, for it was but passing through a door to meet with his Lord. I also came to know him, as I surrendered my life to him, to work for him. And I have come, not just to know him, but to love him.'

Claennis could have sworn that she saw a glisten in Clovis's eye in the firelight, but he gruffly shook his head. 'So I am alone! No matter, you have all been good friends also, and with your help, we shall complete our mission tomorrow. I will think on what you have said some other time.'

'And your story, my Lord?' Denua spoke with a smile. 'We would like to hear it, though perhaps it is a little late tonight.'

'Yes, I'll tell you when we have more time.'

Elico suddenly spoke from the darkness, 'We will look forward to it, my Lord.'

Chapter Fifty-One

Rescue!

*T*hey woke on a bright autumn day to find Clovis already risen and constructing some sort of display with stones and pieces of wood.

'Break your fast, everyone, then come and join me. I will be ready by the time you have eaten.'

Lufian and Deogol broke a cold but tasty repast from their packs on the cart, and soon they were making their way over to Clovis.

'It is a model of Vienne!' exclaimed Claennis.

'Precisely. Today we will rehearse my plan.'

They spent the whole of the morning working through Clovis's plan. Every now and then, some detail proved to be difficult, and Clovis made a small adjustment. They had a break for a midday meal, then came together again.

'We will run through this twice more', announced Clovis. 'I want to make sure you can do it both times, exactly the same, without me prompting you.'

An hour later, and Clovis was satisfied that everyone knew what was required of them. 'Now you must rest. Try to sleep if you can. We move down to the town just before dusk.'

By late afternoon, they all stood on the hill overlooking Vienne. Fires were glowing within the walls and the roads outside were largely empty.

'Everybody ready?' said Clovis, unnecessarily, 'Rodor's team, move!'

Rodor's cart left, with Rodor driving, and Galba by his side.

'Count!' instructed Clovis. All those left behind placed one finger against their temple and started to count the pulse they felt. Some started to count slightly faster than others, but gradually they came to a consensus on the speed.

'Two hundred and ninety eight, two hundred and ninety nine, three hundred.'

'Now! Elico's team! Go!' instructed Clovis.

Elico led the way, with Lufian and Claennis behind and Denua at the rear, bow at the ready.

'Count again!'

Ardith and Deogol repeated the counting, but this time to only two hundred, before Clovis again said, 'Go!' All three left along the same route the others had used.

As dusk fell, Elico led his team down a track off the main road to the town, travelling down a path to the left. They approached one of the areas of broken down Roman wall, which had been replaced by a wooden palisade, about the height of two men.

'There is the tower', whispered Elico, pointing at the top of a building, visible over the palisade. It looked like the top of an old disused flour mill. There was a tall, narrow gate in the palisade just in front of the building, but it was closed.

They stopped in the gloom, just by the side of the gate.

'Count!' said Elico, and again they started their count.

They reached around two hundred. Elico broke off and said, 'Well it should be around n...'

Suddenly shouting was heard from the direction of the main gate, some way to their north. A bright glow sprang into the sky, accompanied by uproar and shouts of 'Fire!' from within the walls.

'Lufian.'

Lufian stepped back three paces, then ran at the palisade. His arms and legs spreadeagled like a spider, he seemed to float upwards. Then one hand found the top and his whole body swung upwards and sideways. For just a moment he was poised on the top, his eyes darting around the scene on the other side. Then he was gone.

'Gate.'

Elico, Claennis and Denua grouped around the gate, Denua near the hinge, her arrow pointing towards the side due to open, Claennis was in the middle, slightly further back, her flail at the ready, and Elico stood right by the opening.

Clovis, Ardith and Deogol appeared out of the darkness behind them, and at the same moment, the gate swung open. Denua's arrow point swept round as the gate opened, but, as they all had hoped, there stood Lufian, smirking slightly.

He stood back with a bow and a smile. 'Welcome.'

His face changed to horror when he saw Denua point her arrow directly at him and release.

She missed!

Thoughts flew through his mind like birds racing through the sky.

But my mother never misses! There must be some other explanation. Where did the arrow go? Behind me.

Need to turn and drop low. Why is my body moving so slowly?

Another arrow, I heard the sound as it flew past my ear.

There, two mounds on the floor.

Lufian felt strong hands under his arms, lifting him up and away.

'Don't worry, lad, got you we have.' Deogol's mangled grammar was a great relief to Lufian's ears.

'All under control now?' whispered Clovis.

'It seems so, my Lord.' Elico's measured tones brought back calmness to the group.

Lufian looked back at the lumps on the ground. Two men lay there, swords unsheathed.

'I didn't see them when I went over the palisade.'

Clovis grimaced, 'But they saw you. Be thankful for your mother's speed and accuracy. I have rarely seen the like. Now let us carry on. Elico, is that the old mill tower?'

'Yes, my Lord. Just around the tower to our left is where the watchman usually sits. But he will be on his guard because of the fire.'

'Thank you, Elico. Now, Claennis, Ardith, Deogol.'

The three ran silently to the side of the huge stone mill tower, then edged slowly around, Claennis leading.

Clovis allowed himself the luxury of moving to his left, taking cover behind the corner of a house, from which he had a view of the open ground in front of the main door of the tower. There stood the watchman, holding his position, but staring off to the flames rising from the far side of the town.

Clovis watched as something like a large piece of cloth sailed from behind the watchman and wrapped itself around his head. He never failed to be impressed with the fighting skills of this family. Who would have imagined this use for a flail?

The watchman fell, struggling to free himself, making muffled noises. Then Deogol held him down while Ardith pulled back the cloth and held something against his face. He went limp.

Clovis looked behind him. 'Go!'

Denua, Lufian and Elico raced to the front of the tower.

'There!' whispered Elico. 'High on the tower. There's the ring. Can you get through it?'

Right at the top of the tower a metal ring hung from a peg set into the stone. It had been meant for lifting sacks of grain to an opening near the top.

Denua had already set her arrow on her bow. She looked sideways at Lufian, who held a coil of twine loosely over one hand. He nodded at her. She lifted her bow, seemed to aim for only a single heartbeat then let fly her arrow at the ring.

'Clean through! That is amazing!' Clovis could not help muttering aloud as he saw the feat.

The twine had been pulled through the ring by the weighted arrow, which now dropped to the floor.

'Deogol.'

Deogol leapt forward, grabbed the twine and hauled it through, pulling a length of heavier rope tied to the end of the twine. He wrapped the end of the rope around his right arm and nodded to Lufian.

'Lufian.'

Lufian swarmed up the rope until he was level with the opening in the wall, the height of six men. He glanced down at Deogol, who nodded back, then he began to swing. After only three swings he came near the opening and leapt inside.

Only moments later they heard a grating sound from the huge door at the bottom of the tower.

'Inside.'

They all ran through the open door, which swung to behind them. Elico, Claennis and Clovis raced up the uneven wooden tower stairs, passing through a trapdoor in an upper floor. In the light from the opening that Lufian had used they could just make out more stairs leading to another trapdoor above them. Heavy bolts held it shut.

'You first, Elico.'

Elico went up the stairs and spoke as loudly as he dared through the trapdoor, 'Clotilde! My lady Clotilde! Are you there? It is Elico!'

There were sounds on the floor above, 'Who is that?'

'My Lady, it is Elico! We have come to get you out of here! Please move away from the trapdoor!'

The huge bolts slid surprisingly easily and the trapdoor opened. Elico went in first. 'My Lady, these are friends to help me. Are you ready to come?'

Clotilde looked at the three. Elico looked older and greyer, but unmistakably it was him. Beside him stood a young woman who might be called beautiful, but she had a face like a warrior. The third, a tall man, wore drab clothing but radiated an air of authority.

Claennis looked at her. She was thin and filthy, her dark hair matted and she smelt dreadful.

Clovis spoke. His voice was deep and quiet. 'My Lady, we are here to rescue you from this prison. Would you please come with us.'

They half carried her down the steps, Claennis one side, Elico the other. Lufian gasped when he saw them arrive at the door. The woman they had brought down looked more like a tramp than a princess.

'Deogol, Ardith, Lufian.'

Deogol and Ardith went around the tower away from the side-gate. Lufian headed around the tower the opposite direction. All the rest headed towards the side-gate. Elico and Clovis almost carried Clotilde, who was much too weak to run.

'Who's that?' A voice came from a side passage as the group passed.

'Boys! Over here! Want some fun?' A woman's voice came from the shadows. Two men had come from the passage. They hesitated and turned to the sound of the voice.

Lufian leapt from the side and pushed them to the ground. Deogol appeared from the direction of the 'woman's voice' and clamped his hand over the mouth of one of the men. Ardith leant forward and held a pad of cloth over the mouth of the other, then the first. Both lapsed into unconsciousness.

They all emerged from the side-gate to find a chortling Rodor and Galba on the cart outside.

'Gate', ordered Clovis. Deogol and Ardith closed the gate.

'Cart.'

Claennis climbed onto the cart. Elico and Clovis lifted Clotilde on then jumped up themselves. The cart rattled off into the night.

Denua, Lufian, Deogol and Ardith set off to walk back up the hill.

Suddenly, Lufian elbowed Denua. 'Look!' Denua turned her head to see a man looking at them over the palisade. He lifted a trumpet to his mouth, then fell backwards.

Lufian looked sharply at Denua. She lowered her bow. 'Let us get out of here quickly.'

Chapter Fifty-Two
Aurelian's Entertainers

*L*ate that night, they all met in the forest clearing. Clovis addressed the group. 'All assembled? All safe? Rodor and Galba, did you enjoy that?'

There were nods from everyone, and big smiles from Rodor and Galba.

'My Lady Clotilde, I realise that you do not know what is happening, or who we are, apart from Elico.'

Clovis was speaking in an unusually gentle tone, thought Claennis. She watched his face as he continued. He seemed quite fixed upon the dirty face of Clotilde, almost as if he cared for her.

'Rest assured that we are your friends, and we have travelled here to liberate you from the clutches of Gundric. You will get to know all of us as we travel. You will wish to, er, restore yourself, but it is better to stay as you are until we are well away from the area.'

Clovis looked around the group, 'We need to work on the assumption that, just at this moment, we are being pursued. They won't be able to track us properly till daylight, but they will be able to send out search parties with some idea of the routes we may have chosen. One of those parties could easily come upon us. Therefore we must move out of here immediately. We will travel tonight while we have the moon, then rest in the day. Please make your mounts ready. Princess Clotilde, you will travel in the cart. We will attempt to make you comfortable, but we must also be able to make you invisible.'

The group broke up to ready their horses. When they reassembled, Clovis continued. 'Elico and I have devised a route which will give a false impression of our direction. We will stay together. We will head southwest, then double back. We must not stop until we leave Gundric's lands. If we get separated, we meet at Geneva in East Burgundy. It is about five days' journey. Before we left Autricum, I sent messengers to Princess Clotilde's uncle, Gisel, who rules Geneva, and received assurances that he would support our mission and give us hospitality. Does anyone have questions? Then let us move out.'

They travelled slowly, at the pace of the cart. At first Claennis worried that they seemed to be getting nearer to Vienne, but then, after a patch of stony road, they turned eastwards, away from the town.

They travelled through the night, on mountainous tracks, stopping in a copse of trees at dawn and sleeping well thanks to exhaustion. They set off again at dusk. Next afternoon, as they were dozing, they were jerked awake by shouts, and then found themselves surrounded by about thirty poorly dressed men and women, armed with sticks and hoes. More people were arriving behind them, from the direction of a nearby hamlet.

'Who are you and what are you doing here?' shouted a man.

Clovis was on his feet in a flash. 'Welcome all, welcome to "Aurelian's Travelling Entertainers"!'

He took three apples from his pack on the floor and threw them in the air, catching each one in turn before throwing it up again. The villager's eyes popped.

'My name is Aurelian, and we are entertainers, roaming these lands trying to find people of discernment - like yourselves - who seek only the best entertainment. We have acts which will astonish you!'

I am already astonished - but maybe not all that surprised, thought Claennis to herself.

Clovis, still juggling the apples, walked around the crowd and continued. 'We have the Great Fire Thrower - Rodor and his able assistant Galba. Please be ready, Rodor! Empty the cart!' Rodor and Galba scuttled away to the cart, realising what was going on.

Clovis didn't stop, 'But first we have a demonstration by Lufian the Human Spider, and Denua the Accurate Archer. Lufian will climb this tree, with...' Clovis reached into the crowd and pulled a cap off a young boy's head, 'this cap. Don't worry sir, we will see that your son gets his cap back, and he will tell his grandchildren of the great feat he took part in today.'

Lufian looked at the tree Clovis had pointed to. Was the man mad? The thin trunk was dead straight with no handholds, and the crown was the height of five men.

'Here is the cap Lufian', said Clovis, then under his breath, 'and you might want this belt.' Clovis handed the cap and a huge belt which Lufian realised was Deogol's. How had Clovis...?

Lufian gave up wondering and paid attention to his task. He put the belt round the tree, tucked the ends through his own belt and tied them.

The crowd gasped as he threw the belt up the tree, then pulled himself up, gripped with his feet on the trunk and threw the belt higher again. He was in the crown in a few heartbeats, waving down with the boy's cap.

'Keep waving the cap!' shouted Clovis. 'Now, ladies and gentlemen, Denua will perform a feat you have never seen before and may never see again!'

Denua hardly looked up at the waving cap. Suddenly her bow had lifted and the cap was flying through the air. Clovis dropped his apples, ran below and caught it as it fluttered down, the arrow still embedded in its padding.

Denua 🜲 *Warrior Queen*

'What have we here?' called Clovis, in a voice which, Claennis thought, was becoming even more like an actor than at the start. 'It is the cap! But look! Oh dear! There is a hole in it! Well sir, your son will need recompense for that! Let me see...' He reached behind the young boy's ear and drew out a small silver coin. 'Will this cover the damage, sir?'

That will feed the family for a week and buy a new cap as well, thought Claennis, who was beginning to enjoy the event more than anything she could remember. Her smile faded when she heard the next announcement.

'And now we have a fight! It will be between Deogol, the Strongest Man on Earth, and Princess Claennis - the master of the flail! Deogol! Show these good people your strength! Pick up this cart!'

Deogol gave secret thanks that Rodor and Galba had unloaded the cart. He approached the cart from the front, raised the shaft into the air, and worked his way underneath. He grunted as he found the centre and started to lift, but the whole cart came off the ground. The crowd roared.

'And now the match you have been waiting for!' Clovis was almost dancing in front of the villagers. 'Are you ready? Fight!'

Clovis darted away towards where Clotilde was hidden.

Deogol approached Claennis menacingly. She danced away, and took an object from beneath her tunic. She twirled it in the air, faster and faster, then, leaping high in the air (just for effect, she thought), she launched it at Deogol's legs. It hit, wrapped itself around, and brought him crashing to the ground. In a flash, Claennis was sitting on his chest, her small dagger at his throat. Applause erupted from the crowd.

'And now! Magic fire puts an end to... the Swamp Woman!'

An eerie scream rose from behind a nearby bush. Rising into the air above the bush was a hideous apparition, with the form of a woman, but covered with moss and foliage. Rodor and Ardith walked, unafraid, towards the bush, then suddenly bent and seemed to touch the ground.

Fire sprang up before them and flashed into the bush, which exploded in flames. When the flames died away, the Swamp Woman had gone!

The crowd stood, open-mouthed.

'And now that is the end of our events for this afternoon. But there is one more thing. We would like you to tell your friends about our excellent entertainment! And to reward each of you for spreading the news about us, not only is there no charge for what you have witnessed, but we will give each family a small reward as you leave!'

I wondered how he was going to make them go, thought Claennis.

'I would like each family to pass my good friend Elico, who will give the rewards.'

Elico had made his way back from hoisting Clotilde above the bush with Galba, then hiding her behind the group. He stood between the group and the village, handing out tiny silver coins to the delighted villagers.

Chapter Fifty-Three

Gisel

*I*t took another night's travel before a local farmer confirmed that they had left the lands ruled by Gundric and were in the kingdom of Geneva.

They looked back from the hill they had wound their way up.

In the distance they saw a large band of men on horseback. Suddenly another group of men rode out from the cover of trees nearer to them and encountered the first group, who turned away and fled back the way they had come.

'I am not sure whether this is good news or bad news', said Clovis, 'But my calculation is that the first band we saw came from Vienne and were tracking us. The question is who are the second band? Friend or foe? We must be very careful, but if I am right, the second band may not be too ill disposed towards us. I think we can relax far enough to stay in an inn tonight.'

That night they stayed in a local inn which the farmer had recommended. It was in the centre of a large village. The farmer said that the inn was regularly used by travellers over the hills, and even had its own bath house. He gave this last information very proudly, as if assuming that none of the company would ever have so much as seen one.

'At last, my pretty one', said Clovis to Clotilde, 'You will be able to get rid of your rags and resume being a princess.'

'My pretty one?' the words went through everyone's minds.

Clotilde had said almost nothing on the whole journey. She had got to know their names and where they were from, but had remained silent about herself. She had obviously been seriously maltreated by her captors, her uncle Gundric and her guards.

Suitable clothes for her were found in Claennis's pack, slightly more generous in size, but with a belt which would serve to fit. Claennis and Ardith went with her to the bath house. It was two hours before they emerged. The rest of the group were sat at the table, starting on a hearty meal which the innkeeper had arranged as soon as he saw the colour of Clovis's gold.

Claennis had guessed the effect their entrance would have. She was right. Eating stopped and jaws dropped all around the table. There was indrawn breath. 'Ohhhh' escaped the mouth of Clovis.

Into the room had walked the most beautiful woman he had seen. He had felt warm towards her on the journey but he had assumed that was just compassion for her plight. Now he was overtaken by another feeling. He was used to the presence of women, they came and went in his court at Autricum - but none had ever taken away his breath.

Clotilde's jet black hair was topped by a small green and gold bejewelled clasp. She wore a simple yellow dress with full sleeves, a fine gold necklace and long gold earrings. Her face was thin from her deprivations, but she stood, tall and slim, with a degree of regal composure that he had not noticed before.

'Ahem.'

Clovis was jerked back to reality by Ardith's implied rebuke. He realised that he had been staring at Clotilde for quite some time, and she still stood in the doorway. 'Come in! Come in! Please sit and eat with us! What -' Clovis hesitated a little too long, '- a transformation!'

Clotilde, followed by Claennis and Ardith, joined the others at their meal.

They ate heartily of the good meat the innkeeper had provided. Claennis sat opposite Clovis, with Clotilde to one side. It was obvious, now, what they had suspected before: Clovis was transfixed by Clotilde.

The food dwindled. As they rested, Clotilde looked at Clovis and said, 'My Lord, may I speak?' Her voice was stronger and more confident than anyone had expected.

Clovis extended his hands in a welcoming gesture.

'You all know that my poor parents were killed by that evil man, Gundric, in front of my eyes. He then held me a prisoner, though my family and I had done nothing against him. Elico and I have lost everything we had. For eight of you, Queen Denua, Claennis, Ardith, Lufian, Rodor, Galba, Deogol and' - here everyone noticed a sideways glance at Clovis - 'King Clovis, my plight must have meant nothing. You did not even know me or my family. Yet you all have travelled for weeks and risked your lives to rescue me. To say I am astonished would be far too little. You may know that I am a follower of the living God, and his son, who died and lived.'

Claennis caught Denua's eye and both smiled.

'I first thought that you were his angels, come to take me to him, but now I know that you are of human stock, I can only imagine that the Creator himself sent you in answer to my many prayers. I praise him that he is so faithful, and I pray that he will pour out his own Spirit upon you all', Clotilde looked at each one seated around the table, with her eyes alighting last on Clovis, 'and fill you with his Presence, and bless your lives for the good you have done for me, his servant.'

There was silence around the table for some time, then Denua said, gently, 'And we also follow the same Lord'. A loud 'Ahem' from Clovis interrupted her, and she restarted, ' "Most of us" follow the same Lord, and we rejoice that he has used us to answer your prayers.'

Silence reigned again.

After some time, Rodor spoke, 'I am warm and well fed; one thing will complete my comfort and that is my bed, may I bid you all a very good night.' So saying he rose and left the table.

Slowly the rest departed, one by one, leaving Clotilde and Clovis talking in front of the great fire.

The next day they stood on a high hillside looking down into a beautiful valley. Far away in the valley they could dimly see a great city. Beyond it was the glint of water. A river flowed from the lake, to the left of the city, and past them.

'That is the great lake of Geneva', said Elico. 'That city was built by the Romans to land goods from boats crossing the lake. You will appreciate that is a lot faster than using these mountainous pathways. The river leaving the lake is the Rodanus, which we saw near Lugdunum and Vienne.'

They set off down the track, which gradually dropped and wound its way from the hilltop, then the land opened out into wide lowland fields. Cattle were grazing, and here and there crops were growing.

Suddenly Clovis hissed, 'Everyone! Right and left! To arms!'

They had learnt to trust Clovis. Their weapons were raised before they even turned their heads to look. Each side, just beyond bowshot, was a line of warriors, maybe forty in all, riding parallel to their track.

The leader of the left side line turned his mount towards them and raised his right hand. 'Ho! Aurelian! We are sent by King Gisel of Geneva to escort you in safety! For your own reassurance you may keep your weapons raised as we approach.'

The second in the line shouted something to the man who had first spoken and he spoke again. 'We only ask that the lady in the centre of your group lowers her bow. It is making my men nervous.'

The two rows of warriors converged on the group. When they got to speaking distance, the leader introduced himself. 'My name is Catuvalos, I am the captain of Gisel's men. We have been watching you for two days, since you entered our lands. Would you confirm that you are, indeed, Aurelian's party, and give me the agreed passwords?'

'I am Aurelian', Clovis spoke up, 'And the words you seek are "Greek Fire". '

'My Lord Aurelian, here is the proof of our authenticity as servants of King Gisel.' Catuvalos handed Clovis a scroll. 'You will recognise the King's seal, which matches the one you were sent some weeks ago.'

Clovis took the scroll, broke the seal and spent a few moments reading. Then he looked up with a smile at Catuvalos, 'All seems in order, we will follow your lead.'

The warriors from the left now drew in front, the rest fell behind Clovis's group. The track they had been following became a good, paved Roman road. They crossed a tributary of the Rodanus and entered the town. It was obviously wealthy, with large residences and wide streets. They turned this way and that, and eventually came down by the lake. They turned right along a quay with many boats tied up, men working on nets in some, and cargo being transferred in others.

They slowed as they picked their way past, and Claennis got her first view across the lake, the water sparkling blue-green in the sunlight. On the far bank was a low green forest, with blue hills rising high behind. 'Oh it's so beautiful!' she exclaimed to Lufian, who was riding next to her.

'It makes me homesick for Éire', he replied.

Halfway along the quay they turned away from the lake into a large garden with a palatial Roman building at the far side, looking back over the lake. Built into its front were two massive pillars of rock. In between the pillars were thick double doors, heavily decorated and studded with iron. Wide steps led down from the doorway to the pathway they were on.

As they entered the garden, the warriors pulled back and Catuvalos indicated to Clovis that he should take the party on towards the door.

They got about halfway down the pathway when the doors were thrown open and a giant of a man dressed in purple and gold emerged and stood at the top of the steps. His height and girth dwarfed even Deogol.

And he was laughing! His head was thrown back and tears were running down his face.

As they neared, he was visibly making a supreme effort to control himself, but still lapsed into guffaws between words, 'My dear friends, welcome!'

Clotilde jumped from the cart and ran to him. He hugged her, then tucked her beneath his left arm and held out his right hand to Clovis, who was the next to approach. 'You must be "Aurelian"!' He made a great play of winking one eye, knowingly, at Clovis. 'You simply do not know what a great blessing you have been! You have rescued my niece, and you have rescued me and my men from undertaking a raid against my brother which we had no idea how to complete! Come in and take your rest, and you may relate the whole story to me over the best fare I can put on my table.'

Claennis looked at Lufian, who mimed his belly growing. Both laughed.

Gisel welcomed them into his palace, which, by its design, was obviously of Roman origin. That evening they were summoned to his table in a great hall. There sat Catuvalos, the captain of Gisel's guard, next to an older man, slim and tall, dressed plainly, but immaculately, with a shock of grey hair and a thick grey beard.

Clotilde spoke, 'My dear uncle, may I introduce my rescuers?' She introduced all of their party, beginning with Clovis and Denua.

'And allow me to introduce you to my friends', said Gisel. 'Bishop Dormian is in charge of the church in Geneva, and a good friend to our city. I advise you to listen carefully to all he says, as I have never found such a good teller of stories. Catuvalos you already know.'

Dormian smiled around at them all, 'Gisel is too kind, though I will admit I enjoy stories. I hope to hear some of yours...'

'There are some of us who owe stories', said Denua, looking at Clovis in mock disapproval. 'My Lord, who are you and where are you from?'

'Ah yes', said Clovis, 'I promise to put right my omission.'

'I would like to hear that', said Gisel, 'Your reputation goes before you, but it reveals little of the man who has helped to rescue my niece. We have a good meal, a good fire, and the whole evening.'

'Very well, can I warn you that we will need all evening? I must begin with my family...'

Chapter Fifty-Four

Clovis's Family

J am Clovis, son of Childric, son of Marvig. I never wanted to be a king, I much prefer to be a travelling warrior.

When I was very small, my father would tell me stories of two friends. Marvig, my grandfather, and Aegid. Aegid was born locally, but of Roman parents. Marvig and Aegid fought for the Romans since they were young, and both learnt well the Roman battle strategy.

When the Romans left our lands, Aegid decided to remain in his home town of Noviodunum where he became a local ruler. His lands bordered ours, and his friendship with my grandfather grew.

As the strength of the Roman rule lessened, the Franks were regularly raided by the Belgae from the south, and the Frisians from the north. The Franks needed to unite to fend them off, but they were split into separate clans, always fighting with each other, and so were too weak to resist. Eventually things got so serious that our clans gathered to choose a chieftain.

They chose my grandfather. Marvig asked his friend Aegid to be his advisor. Under their leadership, the clans easily fought off the raiders and brought peace for our people.

My grandfather died before I was born, when my father was only twenty-one years old. The old man's death threw our clans into confusion. They knew that when the Belgae and Frisians heard of it, they would raid again.

After much discussion, our people decided to replace Marvig as Chieftain so the surrounding tribes would assume that we were still strong. They chose my father Childric, despite his youth, but they insisted that Aegid stayed on as advisor. The strategy succeeded, the Belgae and the Frisians kept their distance.

But soon afterwards there were attacks from yet another tribe, the West Goths, who were gradually advancing towards our land from the east. They had already attacked our Frankish cousins on the east side of the River Rhenus. The Goths had been driven slightly south, but still poured towards us.

They would have overwhelmed us, I think, but Aegid called on all his old comrades who lived thereabouts, and joined them with the Frankish warriors. Together Chilperic and Aegid drove the Goths far to the south.

Peace returned to our people, but not for my father. He had always been - how shall I put this delicately? - one for the ladies. When he returned from his battles and was in residence at court, no man's wife was safe. If he had been a despotic ruler, he might have continued to have his way, but the clan chiefs had power. And they had an alternative candidate for ruler.

Aegid was that man. He had proved himself capable in battle. They had no hesitation in appointing Aegid and sending Childric into exile; his reign was now at an end. My father fled across the River Rhenus to his cousins in Thuringia.

Seven years passed. Slowly, our people realised their mistake. What Aegid really wanted was an Empire - like the Roman Empire had been - with himself as the Emperor. He merged his own lands around Noviodunum with all the Frankish lands and proclaimed himself the ruler of all. He might have got away with this, but he couldn't hold himself back from increasing taxes. He was draining Frankish coffers to fund his own ambition.

Then, the Franks heard that Childric had married Basina, the daughter of a Thuringian chief. They wondered whether Childric's waywardness might have been tamed by his wife. Many wanted to invite him back, so they sent a messenger to enquire of his intentions.

As luck would have it, the West Goths chose just that moment to attack Aegid. As he had taken their riches, the Franks had no desire to come to his aid.

Then Childric arrived with his new wife. He took command of the Franks, and persuaded them to help Aegid, as then they might regain their riches by plundering the Goths.

In return, my father made Aegid agree that he must surrender all plunder, and take none for himself. He also had to to give up all his influence over the Franks and return to his own lands after the battle.

Together, they fought the Goths in a huge battle at Aurelianum, south of Lutetia. As my father had hoped, the result was total defeat for the Goths and great plunder.

Of course, Aegid tried to renege on the agreement, but by now the Franks were fervent in support of their returned king.

Many Franks took home more riches than they had ever seen in their lives, and went back to a renewed peace and a new level of respect from the surrounding tribes. They publicly appointed my father as King of the Franks, rather than just the chieftain of the clans. They even made a golden signet ring for him. It had the face of a warrior in the centre, and the words 'Childric Regis' around the edge.

A year later, Aegid died, and the next year I was born.

So, how did I come by my own great ability in strategy and tactics, I hear you ask?

If you think that sounds immodest, it is only because I have much to be immodest about.

I owe it all to Aegid. The man who I never saw, who died the year before I was born, I owe him all my military success, and much of my ability to rule my people. I have also learnt from his mistakes. I do not tax my people beyond what they can bear; instead I share my plunder with those I rule. The people will always love a ruler who makes them rich.

Aegid trained my father from early childhood in the accomplishments of leadership of men. Though my father spent seven years in exile, he spent twenty-two years under the tutelage of Aegid before that.

When Aegid was gone, and I was born, my father determined to pour all he knew into my head. From the time I could walk, I was taught to command others, to direct and control, to achieve the desired goal.

Though I learnt languages with my tutor, my main learning was done in the fields, with groups of boys and men. I had to instruct them to perform a myriad of different tasks, cross a river, scale a wall, surround and capture another group, the list was different every day.

I was but nine years of age when my father took me to battle. I was kept far back, but I was given a duty to observe what took place, to deduce whether our actions were helpful, or could be improved.

After the battle, I reported my analysis to my father. He then made me report it all over again to the clan leaders. I am pleased to admit that I provoked some astonishment with my suggestions as to how we might have done better. I think they found my proposals daring and innovative.

So I was given command of warriors from a very early age. As you can see from my frame, I am not the strongest warrior, yet it seems that when I command warriors, we prevail.

When I was fifteen, only just out of boyhood, my father, Childric, grew suddenly weak and died. Despite my youth, the Franks took me immediately as their king. The clan leaders had been watching as I learnt my skills. They had seen my ability to command and to direct men effectively.

They took my father's signet ring from his hand and put it on mine as a sign of my new position. My mother wept when she saw it, so when my father was put into his tomb in Turnacum, I placed the ring by his hand. I decided then that my kingship is not to consist of outward symbols, but effective leadership for my people.

Chapter Fifty-Five

Replenishment

A mead server came in to replenish the cups.

Denua looked at Clovis. 'My Lord, may I say, your story so far has moved me. But you are still only fifteen years of age. Are there more adventures to come?'

Chapter Fifty-Six

Clovis's Battle

*M*y Lady, if it so be that you are able to hear more, I have more to say!

And so I came to my first and my greatest test. It was also my greatest success - so far! And in a strange way, I owe that to Aegid as well.

For he had a son. His name was Syagrius. Aegid had sown seeds of self-importance and the stories of the greatness of Rome into Syagrius's head. So after his father died, he wasted no time in consolidating all their lands and creating a new Roman Kingdom, which he called Suessionum. He appointed his home city of Noviodunum as its capital. He called himself the King of the Romans, and Duke of Suessionum.

As you can imagine, with titles like that, his ambition was great. He considered himself a god among men. In his own eyes, he was a Roman Emperor.

He immediately started lording it over all the surrounding peoples, not only those in his new kingdom, but those outside. He would threaten small tribes till they gave in, then take their lands for his kingdom.

Soon, I received appeals for my help. Envoys arrived with gifts to persuade me, but they also told distressing tales of the unnecessary violence which Syagrius seemed to enjoy.

I called together my clan chiefs, but I already had done my research, and I knew full well that we had not enough forces to defeat him.

I was breaking this news to my chiefs, when my mother, Basina, entered, ostensibly to bring food. She gave me what I call 'one of those looks' - with a slight nod and raised brows - I see you all know those looks!

I asked for silence so that my mother could speak.

'You all know that our forces are inadequate for this task. Yet I deem that the task must be completed. I suggest we remember that we are not alone in these Frankish territories. To our north, in Cambrai, is Ragnar's tribe.'

The mention of Ragnar caused a little muttering. He ruled a Frankish tribe, but they had had few friendly relations with our clans.

'And to our east is Caric...'

Now there were louder noises from the chiefs.

'Yes, Caric. I know he has been a pain in our side for many years, but he is still a Frank and it may be that with the promise of good fortune, he will join us. I think his forces are equivalent to Ragnar's and if put together they are equal to ours. Combined, we have enough to take on the high and mighty Duke of Suessionum.'

I looked around the circle of my chiefs, all were pondering, squinting upwards, hands to lips, brows furrowed, calculating in their heads the balance of forces.

My mother bustled out. I said nothing, but watched the faces. Gradually the brows cleared, the hands fell and the eyes came back to me with looks of reluctant assent.

'I know it is not what we would prefer, but what is your assessment? Can we do it? Shall we send to Ragnar and Caric?'

All heads slowly nodded.

'I will plan and then I will call another meeting.'

Only six days later, I called my men together again.

Ragnar and Caric joined us.

I commenced. 'Welcome my Lords Ragnar and Caric, I introduce to you my clan chiefs. We have sent to you our plans, would you now address us as to your thoughts?'

'I will only help you if Ragnar does as well!' Caric almost shouted, breaking in on the meeting as if he were a displeased child.

Everyone looked at Ragnar, but Caric had not finished. 'And I want one third of the spoils, and I want to count them out myself, and I don't care how long it takes!'

Sound of breath escaping through teeth.

Ragnar at last spoke. 'I have reviewed my resources, as I am sure you both have, and I judge that if we are combined, with a good battle plan... ', here he looked hard at me, 'we have a good chance of succeeding.'

'Thank you - both.' I said, carefully, 'Here is what I have arranged so far.'

I only have hearsay about the response of Syagrius when he received our challenge. Defiantly, I notified him not only about our threat, but also the place of the battle, the day and time. Apparently he was heard screaming and shouting at his officials until nightfall.

You may think it ill advised to give away our intentions in such detail, but I wanted to choose the exact battle design myself. The only way Syagrius could avert that would be to try to strike us first, which would put him in a weak position.

I had chosen a battle site, not too far from his own capital city of Suessonium, where there was a long valley sloping up to a summit.

We met on the appointed day. As I expected, Syagrius had taken the high point of the hill. Our troops were to advance directly up the centre of the valley. Then we would split into three groups, moving out sideways, each group with a pointed vertex towards the enemy, which would encourage the enemy to run down the hill between us.

We could see their swords, shields and spears, glinting in the sun. We advanced slowly. I gave a small wave, and loud trumpet blast sounded from our ranks.

Ragnar's men separated from our left flank, and Caric's from our right, moving out towards each ridge of the valley. Ragnar's group was forming a vertex to funnel the enemy, as was ours, but I suddenly noticed Caric's men running loosely towards their side of the valley, up the ridge, and disappearing over! They had fled!

I was tempted to let anger overtake me, but we had more serious matters to deal with. I waved again, twice, and the trumpet blew two blasts. Two blasts identified Ragnar's group. Then two long blasts sounded at my signal. This signified that they were to move right. Ragnar gradually moved his men closer.

One blast - our group, two long blasts - we move right, taking some of the position Caric had deserted.

While all this was happening, the enemy was obviously split. Some on the left had broken ranks and started to run at us down the valley. But I could see on the hilltop that there was indecision in the centre; men were milling about, some were moving out to our right to see what was happening on Caric's side of the hill.

I guessed that the confusion came because, despite the desertion on our right, Ragnar's forces were suspecting Caric had moved out to trap them.

Then the men who had broken rank from the left and run down the hill arrived. Our two groups funnelled them between us. They arrived out of breath and were easy to despatch. Once we were free of them, three short blasts sent both of our groups up the hill. My group retained its vertex and penetrated the enemy line where they were already splitting between centre and right. Ragnar's group slid round their line on the left and brought an attack from behind.

The right hand part of their line was now squeezed further out and down the hill to our right. Their whole force was in utter disarray. Suddenly repeated short blasts and a flag raised and waved. Syagrius had been found and captured!

Most of the opposing force had scattered, so there was little mopping up to do. We left some men investigating the disappearance of Caric, with instructions to report what had gone on as soon as they knew.

We made our way down to Noviodunum, shouting and trumpets blowing, to find the whole place almost deserted. We had 'encouraged' Syagrius to reveal where his storehouses were, and discovered the ill-gotten gains of more than a decade.

We set a large guard over the plunder. It would take us weeks to remove and divide it. Some probably needed to be returned to his victims, the rest for us.

Then the men arrived who had investigated Caric's disappearance. They had discharged all his men but had brought him with them. He looked a sorry sight.

'So, you cockroach Caric! Why did you run?'

He said not a word, but a defiant look came over his face.

'His men say that he wanted to see which way the battle was going before he would fight', explained one of my clan chiefs. 'So he had them move over the ridge, leaving a lookout on the top to find who was winning.'

'Well you'd better be glad we had such an easy win', I said, 'or you wouldn't see another day. Tie him up, I'll invent some sort of retribution for his cowardice.'

Over the next few weeks, I made sure Ragnar had more than half of the plunder.

So I am still a warrior at heart, from a people who have been raiders as long as Franks have existed. I love nothing more than exploits such as this. Who knows what might result from the rescue of a princess from a tower?

Chapter Fifty-Seven

Peace and Plenty

They all sat quietly for some moments after Clovis had completed his story. Then the silence was broken by laughter. Every head turned to look at Claennis. 'I'm so sorry', she said, 'Please take no offence, I am just amazed how wrong I was.'

'Wrong about what?' Clovis's brow was furrowed, but he did not look angry.

'Since the day we met, my Lord, many weeks ago, I have remarked in my mind that you are a great man of action, but you are sparing with words. So much so, that it has been difficult to get to know you. It has been a delight to hear you speak so freely, and when you allow yourself, you do it well. I have very much enjoyed listening to you.'

'And I agree with the lady Claennis', bellowed Dormian. 'A story worthy of telling many times over. I can imagine what fate befell Syagrius, but there is still one thing I'd like to know, my Lord, what punishment did you devise for Caric?'

Clovis smiled. 'I made him a monk, good Dormian, complete with tonsure, then put him under the authority of a very strict Abbot I am familiar with. He will not have an easy life. His tribe is now under the leadership of my uncle, Basina's brother, so I am able to watch over them.'

He smiles well, thought Claennis, and he looked more relaxed than she had ever seen him.

Then Clovis turned to Denua, 'If we are telling stories, good Queen Denua, there is something which has puzzled me. I understand that Prince Lufian was seeking you when he fell foul of my men, and that you had been asked to resume your duties as Queen of the Parisii for a short time while they selected a new monarch. But we found you in Alsiodorum, where your children study. Can you tell us why it was that you went there from Lutetia?'

'It is quite simple, King Clovis, I spent two months in Lutetia. I found that they did not really need a Queen so much as an arbiter and judge. Licnos had left the kingdom in complete disarray. The people had not had sound judgments delivered for so many years that they had forgotten what justice was. There was no public money; Licnos had spent what there was on self-indulgence. The few who had assets quickly hid them when they realised how their money would be wasted. When Licnos was alive, the family leaders fell out with each other about what should be done about him. Now he was dead, they were falling out about who would deal with the mess he had left.'

'Just as I had heard', said Clovis, 'but what did you do?'

'I gave them a choice. They could decide there and then on a monarch and I would act as a mediator, or I could appoint a council.'

'Er, a council? Without a king? What sort of council?'

'Every family would be represented by one person. They would elect a council leader to preside over their discussions. They would arrange between themselves to render justice, to raise finances and administer the land. They could discuss later what they wished to do about a monarch, or even whether a monarch was necessary.'

Clovis and Gisel simultaneously roared 'What?'

'My Lords, I know that you have a special interest, but if the council were effective in administering justice and financing public life, the need for a monarch would decrease, surely?'

'A recipe for disaster!' said Clovis, loudly.

'Sure to provoke civil war!' said Gisel.

'Well, in the end, it didn't quite come to that. They decided to have a council, but the first business would obviously be to appoint a king. However, they wanted to put off dealing with Licnos's legacy. I told them that they needed to help the ordinary people to get back on their feet, but they wouldn't listen. So I said I would spend two months in Alsiodorum, then return to see what they had accomplished.'

'And do you have any confidence that they will accomplish anything at all?'

'I'm sorry to say I don't have much confidence. But they are a tribe in their own right, despite the troubles Licnos has brought on them. They have the right to decide their own fate.'

'Do they indeed?' said Clovis, 'That is indeed a novel concept. I will have to give it some thought.'

There followed one of the most delightful times that Claennis had known. For two weeks the comfortable palace became their home. They took walks along the banks of the beautiful lake and made visits into the bustling centre of Geneva. Each night they feasted at Gisel's table.

Once away from the palace, Clovis and Clotilde were inseparable, though they maintained a decorous distance when in the presence of Gisel.

Claennis watched their growing relationship and found strange feelings returning, just as when Lufian kissed her. The fifth day, on a morning walk to the lake, she took his sleeve and pulled him away from the rest of the party.

'Lufian, my dear cousin.' She stopped, not knowing what else to say. He looked at her, waiting for her to speak. They walked slowly, looking at one another, each unable to speak, until Claennis burst out laughing. 'Cousin, it's so silly!'

'Why don't you explain what it is that is silly, then we can talk about it', said Lufian, gently.

'All this, this...' Claennis moved her hand to and fro between them, trying to express by gesture that which she found herself unable to say in words.

'Do you think things have changed between you and me?' said Lufian, making an effort to help Claennis to explain herself.

'Well, yes, and you have told me how you feel, and...'

'And?'

'And I think I have started to feel the same way!' The words, which were more than she really intended to say, came out in a rush.

Her mind raced. But the words were said. There was no going back. And now that she had admitted to Lufian - more than that, she had admitted to herself - how she felt, suddenly she realised she had been suppressing a passion within her. And the passion was growing by the second. Why had she not seen it? Why had she left it so long? Why had she not responded to Lufian's first kiss? Why had he not told her how he felt, back in Éire? Why had he waited till they were on this journey to tell her? It was his fault she was in this mess!

'You...!' She gave him her customary playful punch on his shoulder, But he grabbed her hands, pulled her close and kissed her, full on the lips. She started to pull back, then gave in, abandoning herself to him in a long embrace. She wanted it never to stop.

'Whooa!' came the cry from several voices. Claennis opened her eyes to find all the others looking on. 'At last!' said Ardith, who was nearest. 'We"ve been wondering whether you'd actually get on with it since we found Lufian!'

Chapter Fifty-Eight
Alliance is Proposed

*I*t was on the afternoon of the next day that Clovis approached Gisel. 'My Lord Gisel, I seek to have private conversation with you on matters which may be in our mutual interest.'

Gisel welcomed Clovis to his private quarters, and they sat in comfortable luxury.

'Now, my Lord Clovis, tell me what you have in mind.'

'You know that the lands I rule are well to the north. Between your lands and mine are kingdoms which I have assessed. I can tell you, between ourselves, that these kingdoms are due to fail and will fall. I am the only ruler, and my people are the only people, with the strength and purpose to exert authority over those lands.'

'You speak of the kingdom of the Parisii and the kingdom of my dead brother in Vesontio?'

'Yes, my Lord Gisel. We have already heard of the indecision of the Parisii over choosing a leader to replace Licnos. A threat from the eastern tribes of the Alemanni is growing. It does not allow for dithering. If the Franks do not take authority in Lutetia, I judge that those lands will fall prey to invaders, or descend into chaos and civil war.'

Gisel frowned, 'Either of those outcomes will make our separate kingdoms more vulnerable.'

'That is true. The Franks need to have secure borders, as do you. But if we do take authority in those two areas, your lands and my lands will share a common border. Now allow me to reassure you immediately that

I have no designs on your land. I judge that you have a stable, strong kingdom. But, to me, that means that it is fitting that you and I form a mutual agreement. An alliance.'

Gisel was silent for some time. 'And my brother Gundric?'

'I think that he might respect strong neighbours. His inroads so far have been against his brothers. I think he perceived them as weak, and not worthy of their quarter when your father's kingdom was divided between you. He has made no act of aggression against your kingdom, though I am sure that he would have no scruples in doing so if the opportunity arose. I do not think that we ought to give him that opportunity.'

Gisel again sat quietly, his fingers steepled against his lips. 'And if I agree to your proposal?'

'Then in the next few months, Elico will visit you, and discuss with your lawyers to arrange mutually desirable terms. I will abide by their decision.' Clovis hesitated. 'There is one more thing...'

'Yes?'

'I will try to put this gently, you may need to hear me out before you make your decision. I wish to ask for the hand of your niece, Clotilde, in marriage.'

Gisel visibly started, but Clovis continued quickly. 'Think of the benefits to you. The kingdom bordering on yours would be ruled by the husband of your own niece. Her children will inherit that kingdom when I die. That relationship will make your kingdom more secure in that day. It will be good for Clotilde too, you might find it difficult to find a husband for someone who has - how can I put it? - been through so much. But now she will be Queen of all the Franks, with riches to spare.'

Gisel sat there, mute, so Clovis plunged on, 'And, I hope I am not being too forward, my Lord, but your kingdom must be very expensive to administer. I wonder if the possibility of a large marriage settlement, in Gothic gold, might help you somewhat?'

Gisel looked black, 'I have just had my niece restored to me, and you now wish to remove her. I must tell you that my heart is against this. I will, nevertheless, think on what you say, and I will converse with my niece.'

As their time in the beautiful surroundings of Gisel's palace came to an end, they found themselves one morning, packing their fine clothes onto Rodor's old cart. As Clovis had said, 'We do not want to start attracting attention between safety here and safety back in our own land.'

They dressed as travelling traders once more. Then Clovis said, 'I will explain this instruction later, but for now, you will have to trust me. Do not put anything valuable onto the cart. Pack anything important with you on your mount.'

They secreted weapons in their tunics and all their gold in their saddle packs. They moved out along a road to the north, hoping to avoid Gundric's forces which lay to the west. They rode for half the morning, then became aware of hoofbeats behind them. Clovis had chosen, for a reason they knew not, to ride at the back of the group. He shouted, 'Rider approaching - do not attack!'

They had all turned to see who was nearing them, but saw only a cloud of dust. Then a figure came out of the dust, not heavily built, but wearing some sort of headcloth which hid the face.

The rider came right up to Clovis, and removed the cloth. They gaped to see Clotilde! She went close to Clovis and spoke. Her manner seemed urgent, but they could not hear what she said. Clovis spurred his horse to the centre of the group, Clotilde following.

'I will explain everything later', he said, 'But we need to act fast. Rodor, I need your cart. I am very sorry you will not get it back. But I will give you a cart three times as good when we arrive home.'

Clovis turned the cart to face a side-road which led down a hill. He then took a jar from the cart, one that Rodor had used for Greek fire, and opened it. He poured the contents onto the clothing in the cart and struck his flint. Flame soared from the cart. He slapped the rump of the horse, but it needed no encouragement to flee from the roaring flames.

As the cart careered down the hill, Clovis turned to the group. 'We are pursued by Gisel's men. Look! The dust on the horizon!'

Sure enough a cloud of dust rose. It rapidly grew bigger.

'Let us leave! We head for the residence of Vortrix!'

Chapter Fifty-Nine
Flight!

Two days of hard riding took them to the top of a hill. Behind them they looked down on their pursuers. There were about twenty of them. Gisel's men had been diverted down the side road to the flaming cart for only a short time, but the ruse had allowed the group to ride out of sight, so the pursuers had to use tracking to follow them. Unfortunately, they seemed good at it.

'Curse these Burgundians! They must have the tracking skills of a hound! We must be near Vortrix soon, surely!' grumbled Clovis.

They started down the other side of the hill and into a wide river valley. Clovis, who was now riding at the front with Clotilde and Elico, turned to the group, 'We must be careful! We must not get trapped against the river. We need to head at an angle to the bank to find a crossing place. But which way, Elico, east or west?'

'I am not sure my Lord. We need to head upstream, to shallower waters, but I am unfamiliar with this river and do not know the direction of flow.'

At that moment they heard distant shouting. Ahead of them, on their side of the river, was a band of warriors, gesticulating wildly at them. 'We are lost!' said Elico, 'They have circled round and cut off our escape!'

'Not so, Elico!' said Clovis, 'That is not the same group we saw from the hill! Unless I am mistaken, those are Vortrix's men!'

And so it proved to be. 'Trymian!' they all shouted when they drew close enough to recognise him.

'Yes, I am now with Vortrix's men', he said, 'I kept conducting travellers to his villa, never realising that I could also enjoy their privileges, if only I would bestir myself and join him. It is more pleasant than Lutetia by far.'

'But how did you know we were coming?' Denua's deep voice came from the back.

'We did not know when you would come, but we knew that you would approach from this sort of direction and that you would need to cross this river, so we have maintained a patrol along the banks since you left.'

'Is that Parisii land?' called Lufian.

'Yes it is.'

'Then we had better be moving onto it! Look!'

Heads turned, yet again. They saw a large group of horsemen (could it be more than before?) thundering toward them, only about three bowshots distance.

'Quickly, this way!' yelled Trymian, wheeling his men towards the river.

Claennis found herself gripped with panic. Most unusual, for me, she thought. Was this to be the end? So near their destination, yet there was no way across that flood of a river. Drown or die by the sword.

Then she came to herself. Trymian's men had divided, some behind them, some in front. They dropped down the river bank. It was closer than she had thought. The river was wider at this point! Before she knew it, she had plunged down the bank and her horse had entered the water. It only came just past the horse's fetlocks! This was a ford!

Within a few moments she was at the other side, but their pursuers thundered on.

'Behind us!' shouted Trymian as he wheeled his men between them and the river they had crossed.

Gisel's men entered the water behind them. It would not be long now. They would give as good as they got.

Then, suddenly, there was a huge thundering noise. Gisel's men turned and fled back across the ford.

The fugitives were surrounded by horsemen - and there was Vortrix!

After things had calmed down, Clovis said, 'Trymian, how in the name of the gods did you arrange that?'

'As soon as we saw you approaching us from those hills, we sent a rider to Vortrix requesting his presence to, er, "welcome" you', said Trymian. 'They arrived in good time.'

Back in Vortrix's villa, they removed stale garments and bathed in the warm water of the Roman baths, soaking tired and aching muscles.

A servant came round after some time to inform them that a meal awaited them. Still in the warm water, Claennis said to Ardith, 'There were times on this journey when I thought I would never want to eat any more, but, I have to admit, just now, I am ravenously hungry.'

They gathered around the table in the great hall, in front of a roaring fire. Clovis spoke as they were being served, 'I owe all of you an explanation. But may we leave the talking until we have eaten?'

This met with general consent and they fell to dealing with the mountain of food which Vortrix had laid on.

Chapter Sixty
Clovis Explains

'(T)wo days before we left, I asked Gisel for the hand of Clotilde in marriage', said Clovis, when they were quieter. 'I promised him a good marriage settlement in Frankish gold, an alliance between his kingdom and mine, and security and wealth for his niece and her offspring. He was displeased at the thought of the union, but conceded that it had many advantages. He spent some time talking with Princess Clotilde, and she was plain with him that she desired to marry me. You know that I am a pagan, but I promised her that I would respect her beliefs and support her in walking in the way that God - that is her God - called her. After some time, Gisel called me into his quarters and told me he was disposed to agree to my request for Clotilde's hand.'

Clovis paused for some time, then continued, 'Clotilde was summoned to Gisel's quarters, and in front of him, I gave her a gold ring to signify that we had been promised to each other. As we stood there a man burst in whom I did not know. Gisel introduced him as his advisor, Aredius, who had only then returned from Constantinople. Aredius gave his apologies, but said he must speak with the king privately and urgently. We left his presence, but were soon summoned back. Gisel told me that Clotilde was promised to a Byzantine ruler by the name of Diomedes, and our previous arrangement was withdrawn.'

Clovis took a deep breath, looked around the company and smiled, 'Apparently this man is more famous than I, rules more land than I, and, in particular, has more wealth than the Franks and Burgundians put together.'

He turned a soft gaze on Clotilde. 'Clotilde, would you continue with your part of the story?'

'I am not ashamed to say that my voice was cracking as I told Gisel that Diomedes had already visited my former home in Lugdunum. He had almost demanded my hand from my father Chilperic. Diomedes was an unpleasant and unkind man. He cared not that I found him repulsive, but remained insistent that Chilperic must give me away. But my father was a good man; he threw Diomedes out of the kingdom with his retinue. Even then, as Diomedes left, he vowed he would have me.'

Clovis resumed his account. 'When news of Clotilde's rescue reached Aredius, days before we arrived, Aredius did not tell Gisel, but left for Constantinople to notify Diomedes that Clotilde was free, hoping to receive a reward. Diomedes promised great riches to Aredius, and also to Gisel, if Aredius could persuade him to allow the union.'

'As far as Gisel was concerned, that was the end of the matter, but I planned with Clotilde for her escape. We made great play of packing without her, but I secretly had a horse prepared. We left, heading north, and Clotilde went on a walk to the south. That was where we had tethered her horse. She came around Geneva, and caught up with us easily, as we were going at the pace of the cart.'

Clovis turned to Rodor, 'Rodor, my friend, without you, I would not - we would not - be in this happy position. I promise you I meant what I said. You shall have the finest cart money can buy!' He looked around again. 'For those who have lost finery in the fire on the cart, I offer my humblest apologies, and I promise faithfully to restore all you have lost, and more.'

'Gisel soon found that Clotilde had gone', he continued, 'He had made sure that we were watched so that she did not leave with us, but he did not think of what Clotilde might do. When he found that she had gone, his men wasted a fruitless time searching southwards, as I had made sure they would be told that was the direction she had walked. But soon they realised their mistake and came after us. The rest you know.'

Clovis and Clotilde, along with Claennis and Lufian, were married in Autricum two weeks after they all arrived back. Word had been sent to Rodor's wife, Roveca. She and their daughter, Aia, travelled to Autricum and had a joyful reunion with Rodor.

Clovis proved a generous host, making his hot baths available for all, and this time Deogol did not have to be pressed to try the water. The lanky frame of Corbus bustled around attending to every need. Roveca, who was not used to such attention, was, by turns, overwhelmed by it and charmed by it. Their daughter Aia, by contrast, adapted instantly to the new environment. She rolled her eyes, 'I could live like this, mother, dear!'

Rodor's new cart arrived, with a pair of horses. Rodor's eyes popped when he saw it, it even had a covered portion made of thick cloth draped over semicircular hoops.

The Frankish clans gathered from all around, some had travelled for several days. Bishop Flavius performed the marriage ceremonies, though Clovis grumbled that he did not understand either the language or the process. Clotilde just smiled, 'One day, my Lord, one day you will understand.'

Then the feasting began. Lufian gave Claennis a merry glance, 'I will need to fast for a year to recover from all this eating.'

Chapter Sixty-One
The Ways Part

*T*hree days later, amid tearful farewells, Rodor and Roveca left for Sulis on their new cart. Galba travelled with them, having been promised his own room in their house.

Denua approached Clovis in the eating hall. 'My Lord, your hospitality is beyond compare, but the time has come that my party must also depart.'

'My Lady, it has been a delight to meet you, your kin and your friends. I already miss our time as fellow warriors.'

Clotilde came across the hall. She had lost the distressing thinness of her captivity and now walked with poise and confidence, her black hair falling in gentle curls to her shoulders.

'My love', said Clovis, 'our guests will soon be departing.'

A look of distress passed across Clotilde's face. 'So soon? I cannot hope to see you again once you go back to Éire.'

'Ah, well, that is the thing.' Denua turned to Clovis, 'You see, my Lord, I do not wish to depart for Éire at this time. I wish to ask two indulgences of you. The first is that you allow me to travel eastwards out of your lands to Lutetia. I need to find what the Parisii have done with my good advice.'

'That is as it should be; a Queen has duties which she must fulfil - and the second desire?'

'We will travel this way when we go back to Éire. I wonder if for a short time we may impose upon your hospitality once more?'

Clotilde's face, which had carried a trace of sadness, now brightened up dramatically. 'Oh good! We shall spend more time with you soon!'

Denua thought to herself, as she watched, what a transformation of beauty was made by a smile.

'It will be a pleasure to host you again', said Clovis, 'and perhaps you and I can then spend some time discussing the affairs of the tribes and clans. I hear the Alemanni are now moving west and taking territory. It seems only yesterday that we pushed the threat from the Goths to the south, and now another tribe is heading our way. I wonder if you would listen out for news when you are in Lutetia?'

'Of course, my Lord. Thank you for the warning.'

Early the next day, Claennis, Lufian, Denua, Deogol and Ardith took the road east from Autricum towards Lutetia, escorted to the border by a group of Frankish warriors.

Clovis was suddenly surprised as Clotilde laid her head on his shoulder and sobbed. He had known her for only a short time, but she had never shown this kind of - what was it? He would naturally think it was weakness, but he was not aware that she had shown weakness in any of her past trials. He was puzzled.

'What is it my love? Are you distressed by the parting of our friends? It will not be long till they return.'

'I can't imagine being without them. They had started to become like a family to me.'

'How stupid I am. You have recovered so well, it is hard to remember that the wounds from the loss of your family are still raw. I know I can never replace your mother and father, but I will do my best to be family to you.'

Clotilde squeezed closer to him, and he felt desire rise within. 'Let us go inside and be together, my dear one. It may be that I can help you to leave some of your suffering behind.'

It was late morning, three weeks later, when Denua's group arrived back in Autricum. They were spotted by Clovis's watchmen and escorted into the town. Clotilde ran to meet them and embraced them as they dismounted.

Then Clovis arrived and bustled over to Clotilde, 'My love', he said. Lufian smiled at Claennis with a look which said, 'so, it remains real.' 'Let us welcome our friends with a meal, then I must spend some time in discussion with Queen Denua.'

After they had enjoyed their midday meal, Clovis said, 'Queen Denua, allow me to introduce you to my planning room, where we can discuss what news you have.'

Clovis took Denua into a large room. She was astonished to find that the centre of the room was taken over by a wide table which had markings all over it. 'Do you recognise these marks?' he said.

Denua walked to the table, 'Not really, they"re just random marks, aren't they - unless - is that Lutetia?'

Clovis smiled. 'And if that is Lutetia, then this is -?'

'This must be where we are - Autricum! So this direction is north, east is over there, and south and west!'

'And do you recognise this line I have marked?'

'It starts here, travels, um, southeast, then south, then east to - Geneva! That says Geneva! This is the course of your journey! You must have picked me up in Alsiodorum - just - there!'

'Excellent! Now, what is that label over there?'

'That is well to the east of Lutetia, it says - "Alemanni". That is the tribe you asked me to find out about. Ah, I see. You have produced this drawing of these lands in order to trace where tribes are.'

'And, more importantly, where they are trying to go.'

'Well, on that subject, I have some information for you. Lutetia is abuzz with rumour and much fear about the movements of the Alemanni. Travellers from the east report that they are moving slowly, but, it seems unstoppably. They have already conquered much of Germania.'

'Can you show me on my drawing where you think they are, and also where you think they might be heading?'

Denua leant over the east side of the plan and pointed to an area of Germania. 'They have been based - here - for some years, but seem to be mainly raiding to their northwest, around - here, on either side of this river - this label says "The Rhenus". '

'That fits exactly with news I recently received from there. My Frankish cousin Sigebert, king of my mother's clan, rules the land beside the river Rhenus. He has notified me of Alemanni advances onto his land. It may not be long before I receive a call to go to his aid. So how are the Parisii dealing with the threat?'

'The Parisii are worried that the Alemanni may turn their attention more directly west. In their leaderless condition they do not think they can resist an attack, yet no man wishes to take the responsibility of leading them out of the mire they find themselves in.'

'So, tell me, what does your god think of war?'

Denua was taken aback at this abrupt demand. 'That is a very large question, my Lord.'

'It certainly is, would you like to sit comfortably with a glass of wine and answer it?'

'It seems to me that there are two sorts of war', commenced Denua, glass of wine in hand. 'One sort is where there is a threat to your very existence, and you have to oppose your own obliteration. The same if you saw a similar threat to others. The second sort is where, through greed for land, plunder or power, evil people wage war in order to take those things from others. The first I think is legitimate, even if you have to use force to pursue it.'

'Aha! Force!' Clovis triumphantly leapt on Denua's words. 'But the one you follow said that you should - how did he put it? - something about the side of your face!'

'He said that if we were to be hit on one side of our face, we should turn the other side to be hit there also.'

'There! That proves my point! And did he not die rather than fight the Romans?'

'Well...'

'So why should a warrior like me follow such a man? He does not teach me to fight, he teaches me peace! I only want peace when I have silenced all those who are threatening me and my people! And just at the moment, it seems as if they are the Alemanni!'

Denua decided that nothing was to be gained by arguing with Clovis. 'My Lord, I think that you are right on several counts: the main threat to you is the Alemanni, and you are right that Yeshua was a man of peace and he did give up his life rather than take up arms. Yet he did insist that the kingdom he was fighting for was not an earthly one.'

'Not an earthly one? What sort of kingdom would it be if not an earthly one?'

'Yeshua spoke about the rule, the kingship, of God over our human hearts. His people belong to a heavenly nation where he is king forever.'

'But I do not want my people belonging to another king!'

'My Lord Clovis, may I say this gently; your people will truly serve you as king, and you will be truly king over them, only if you surrender your own lives to the one who created you.'

'Is this also what my lady Clotilde believes?'

'Have you not discussed these things with your own wife?'

'When we pledged ourselves to be married, I gave her my word that I would respect her faith and not impede her practice or try to influence her in any way. I have therefore avoided questioning her on these things.'

'I understand, though I think you might be too reticent. I am sure that if you ask gently, she will explain to you the things of God that she has in her heart. As for these matters, I cannot say for sure what she thinks, but I do know we both follow the same Lord.'

'I will think on your advice. I am sure you speak sound good sense. And I am grateful for the information you have supplied. I will spend tomorrow planning with my advisors, but may I advise you that I will need to consult you again on my plans, probably later in the day?'

'I will await your call, my Lord.'

It was late in the afternoon of the next day when a servant called Denua to attend Clovis. He stood at his map-table with Corbus and Elico.

'Welcome Queen Denua, please come and see what we have been working on. You will observe that we have now put on the drawing the position of the Alemanni, and plotted their raids to the northwest. Our first concern is to protect our lands and people, should they turn their attention directly west. If there had been a strong kingdom of Lutetia between us and them, we would have some protection, but your information leads us to suppose that if Lutetia were attacked it is currently too weak to survive. What do you think so far?'

'I think you have made a correct assessment, though I am sorry that it is so.'

'The sensible option for us is to assume the protection of Lutetia ourselves. Of course we can best do so with the consent of the people, or we could have another war on our hands. So, we have to ask ourselves, what asset do we have which we could use to encourage the Parisii to comply with what we need for our own security?'

'And the answer is...?'

'You, my Lady.'

Denua had already guessed what Clovis would want; it was obvious, really, but she still needed him to put his own case so she could be sure she had not erred. 'What is it you wish me to do, my Lord?'

'We would like you to visit the Parisii, yet again. Explain to them that they are vulnerable if the Alemanni turn west. Tell them that the Franks are prepared to protect them against attack, and maintain peace in their lands.'

'But what if they do not wish it, my Lord?'

'Tell them that Clovis, the King of the Franks, will make their city the most important and prosperous in all Gaul. Traders from across the world will bring their wares, to buy and sell. Whatever trade and riches they have now will be as nothing compared with then.'

'And may I reveal to them how you intend to accomplish that?'

'You may. I intend to make Lutetia my capital and rule over all Frankish lands from there. I will insist that all trade in my lands is registered there. I also intend to rename Lutetia in their honour - if they accept my plans. It shall be known in all the world as "Paris". '

'That does sound very tempting, my Lord, but I am sorry that I must make one more enquiry; what if they continue to refuse your aid?'

'My Lady, it pains me to speak in this manner. My primary concern is the land and people for which I am responsible. If anyone stands in the way of this duty and will not move, then I must move them myself. Along our border with Lutetia, there currently stand eight thousand

Frankish warriors, awaiting my command. I want the Parisii to share in the prosperity I will bring, so I would rather have their cooperation, but I will move into their lands whatever they say.'

Chapter Sixty-Two
Back to Éire

*T*wo months later, as they sailed into port on the south coast of Éire, Denua reflected on what she had done. She still did not know how, or even whether, it would work out well for the Parisii, but she had asked for the spirit of El Elyon, and advised as best she knew how.

Elico had drawn up a treaty as formal and binding as she could make it. She had passed on Clovis's intentions to the Parisii. She told them that they had no real choice and reminded them that they might not be in this situation if they had agreed on a leader as she had advised. On the other side, she had threatened Clovis with a long campaign of unrest if he did not keep to his promises to rename the city Paris, and make it the first city of the Frankish lands.

Would he keep his word? That was the question which kept her awake at night. Clovis had treated her and her companions benignly, but she knew you did not get to be king of the Franks unless you put Frankish desires first. She knew that if he decided to rule the Parisii with an iron rod, no mere document could stop him.

As they neared their settlement, a shout went up and all the community came out to them. Beorn, despite his age, easily outpaced the rest. He threw his huge arms around each one in turn, jumping up and down when he hugged Deogol. They looked like a moving mountain.

'You better come in and eat! We have much to discuss!'

'What?' enquired Lufian.

'Let us tell you over a good meal.'

Claennis sighed, 'Oh not another one!'

During the meal, Beorn and Cwen plied them incessantly with questions about what had happened on their journey, but Denua finally spoke in mock exasperation, 'Beorn. You and Cwen have been exchanging glances, with poorly-hidden smiles, all the meal. Now. Will you please tell us what is going on!'

'Beorn, let me tell', said Cwen. 'Lufian, a messenger arrived here just over a week ago. He came from from the Ingwi families who settled in the land to the north of Ceint, across the river Tamesis. Their pronunciation is slightly different, they always said Angli instead of Ingwi. They now call themselves the East Angli.'

'Those are our cousins, aren't they?' said Lufian.

'Yes they are. You remember, after Hengest had died, Octha had become king of Ceint? And all the Ingwi-Seaxe in Ceint had been disappointed with him?'

'Yes, he was hardly able to rule his own mind, let alone the Ceintish people.'

'Well, it has reached the point where the people of Ceint are ignoring him and ruling themselves. That is fine for them, but it is spilling over into border disputes with the East Angli. It has got to the point that they desire their own king. As the son of Hengest is incapable, they are seeking the son of Kursa.'

'Me?'

'But how do they know Kursa had a son?' said Claennis, looking at Denua. 'Kursa was supposed to have died in the battle with Wyrtgeorn's sons, wasn't that what you told everyone? How do they know about Lufian?'

'It was my Parisii guard', said Denua. 'On my instruction they told everyone that Kursa was dead, to avoid enemies seeking him out here in Éire. But amongst themselves, they knew. They mostly moved and settled north of the Tamesis, with the East Angli, and gradually the story came out. As it had been many years, and the only ones who knew the story were our own Angli cousins, nobody was concerned.'

Claennis pulled a face. 'But as soon as they were raided by Octha's people and they needed someone to lead them, they settled on our Lufian. What a cheek!'

A hubbub broke out, with everyone talking at once, each with an opinion.

A low, calm voice broke through. 'I think it is an honour. And I think the honour comes, not just from the East Angli, but really from El Elyon.'

Everyone turned to look at Lufian. 'Claennis, do you remember what Padraig said to us the moment he met us?'

'Something about justice, wasn't it?'

He said, 'You are destined to be Royal servants of the Most High God. From you will come one who will unite two Royal Houses. But you must remember this. Be you ever so high, higher than all you rule, yet you are still only a servant to Him. So you must keep your hearts humble, as a servant is humble. Keep this in mind when you administer justice.'

'How on earth did you remember that?' demanded Claennis. 'We were only small children!'

'I wrote it down for him on a piece of parchment', said Denua. 'I gave it to him when he learned to read.'

Lufian put his hand into his tunic and pulled out a tiny scrap of old brown parchment. 'This one', he said. 'The writing is nearly invisible now, but I have read it so often that I well know what it says.'

'But if you become King of the East Angli, that is only one royal house.'

'And before today, I was not even destined to be king of that one. Now it seems El Elyon has given us this. I think we can leave the other details to him?'

Claennis looked down. 'I'm sorry, you are right. I have been so settled in our little community here, it will be a like a tear in my heart to leave everyone.'

A deep voice came from the back, 'But what if you don't leave everyone? What if we all come with you? There are plenty of Padraig's disciples here, they are well taught in his ways, they can carry on growing this community. We can start another community of Padraig's disciples among the East Angli. What do you think, Cwen?'

Cwen smiled at Beorn, 'Nothing would please me more than to spread the pleasure we have found here.'

'And they say less wet the weather is there!' Deogol observed.

Everyone laughed.

'So', boomed Beorn, 'If Lufian decides to take up the invitation, who would like to go with him?'

Chapter Sixty-Three
A Letter Arrives

*T*hree years passed.

Denua, Cwen and Beorn were sitting in a warm eating hall. They had used their gold to buy a large Roman villa near a small town called Camulodunum. It had once been the main house of a large Roman army camp. It now lay in the south of the East Angli lands. Denua was delighted when she found that the house had a hypocaust. 'Warm!' she had shouted, 'I am going to be warm in my old age!' Nevertheless, the weather was so cold they had lit a fire in addition.

'Brecc! Keep away from the fire!' Cwen spoke loudly to a small boy on the floor. The noise woke up a tiny baby in a cot by the table, who started to howl.

In bustled Claennis. Brecc ran to her, 'Mummy! Firman is awake!' 'Thank you, Brecc. It is time for his feed.' She sat, undid her tunic and put the boy to her breast. Quietness and peace descended on the warm room.

'Where is Lufian?' asked Cwen.

'Out visiting some villagers. They have had a dispute over land. He should be arriving back soon. He will be hungry when he arrives.'

The door opened with an icy blast and Lufian stumped in. He was muffled up to the eyebrows against the cold, but nevertheless was frozen. He crossed the room and stood in front of the fire.

'I will get some meat', said Beorn, 'and is it tonight that Deogol and Ardith are joining us?'

Deogol and Ardith lived in separate rooms on one side of the villa. Deogol had asked Ardith to marry him on their return from Gaul in his characteristic way. 'Ardith. People other married getting are. You think, do you, that married we also should get?'

Ardith often told the story, demonstrating how she was laughing almost too much to say 'yes'.

The latch lifted and heads turned to greet them. But through the door came a man with a mask across his face and some sort of weapon in his hand.

Beorn and Lufian jumped from the table, reaching for sticks to defend themselves. But the intruder cried, 'Peace! Peace! I am but a messenger!'

He held out the cylindrical object he carried, 'I serve Clovis, King of the Franks, and am tasked with delivering this letter to Queen Denua and her family. Have I come to the right house? I expected a great hall and many servants.'

'I am Queen Denua. You have found the correct place. Here we live simply with our community. You must be frozen. We will warm you up and ensure you have a comfortable bed. May I see the letter?'

Denua laid the vellum scroll on the table and broke the seal. 'Oh dear! It is in Frankish. Lufian, you have a better memory for Frankish. Would you read it?'

Cwen went to fetch meat and drink for the messenger, then Deogol and Ardith arrived.

'You arrived just in time', said Lufian, 'This is apparently a letter to us from Clovis.'

He looked at the scroll and started to read in Brittonic.

Chapter Sixty-Four

Clovis's Letter

lovis, King of the Franks, Paris.

  To: Queen Denua, King Lufian, Queen Claennis, their family and friends in the land of the East Angli.

Seven years have elapsed since we were privileged to welcome you to our lands. Rarely a day passes without my thoughts turning back to that blessed expedition where, largely thanks to you, my wife was rescued.

I write to let you know of our experiences since we last met. I expect you have heard news of the movements of nations, but little, I anticipate, of our private circumstances.

My wife continues to light up my life with her constant support, love and good humour. But there have been times when I have found it difficult to agree with her. Our first son was born sickly. As we had agreed, I did not interfere when she proposed that the child should be baptised. The ceremony took place, but almost immediately Ingomer died.

I found myself very angry with her god. I shouted at her, demanding to know why she believed her god would give her a child, then take it away again. She could give me no answer which satisfied me, simply saying that she 'trusted' her god, and that Ingomer was now safe in his presence.

It was just over one year later when our second son, Chlodomer, was born. Clotilde wanted him to be baptised also. To my shame, I became very angry again. I could see only that, as Ingomer's death had followed his baptism, Clotilde's god did not care one whit about us. I ranted and raved at Clotilde, but she responded only by kissing me till I regained my composure, then gently reminding me that both kings and lovers keep their word.

I thought I had been proved right about her god when, two days after his baptism, Chlodomer, who had been healthy, fell ill. I took to walking around with a superior smile on my face, while inside, my heart was breaking. I now realise this was only partly for the expected loss of our second son, my distress was also for the loss of my wife's god. For surely, she could not continue to follow him after this? Yet I also admitted, within myself, that her god had brought her much comfort and strength, and I did not know how she would manage without him.

She spent all day beside Chlodomer's bed, praying to her god for him, though the physicians gave him no chance of survival. Then, to my surprise, one week later, he suddenly rallied and became as healthy as he had been before. I went to her room as soon as I heard the news. Clotilde looked at me triumphantly. 'My prayers have been answered!'

'Coincidence!' I cried.

Clotilde smiled, the first I had seen since Chlodomer's illness, 'All I know, my Lord, is that when I stop praying, the coincidences stop happening.'

'But not all of your prayers are answered', I replied. I could not see that I was wrong.

'But if I did not pray, there would have been no answers at all. Do you not see, my Lord, that you yourself are an answer to my prayer? In the depths of my despair, I called out to my God. I asked for freedom. He answered my prayer with much more than I had asked. You came and rescued me from Gundric's clutches, took me to safety, then elevated me to be the queen of the Franks. You yourself are God's answer, my Lord!'

I now recognise that what happened then was significant, though I thought little of it at the time. I found myself - my heart - suddenly swayed by her words. Tears - which I knew little of - sprang to my eyes, though I immediately blinked them away. I regained my composure almost immediately, and quickly forgot the incident.

What we had all been fearing started only a few months after Chlodomer was born. We received a messenger from the east Franks, from my cousin Sigebert. He told us that that a few Alemanni had been moving north into their lands. Sigebert had been holding them back quite well with his own men, but then the trickle became a flood; the whole Alemanni nation seemed to be on the move.

Sigebert decided to meet them in the south of his lands, at Tolbiac, but even as his men moved into place his scouts told him that they would be outnumbered.

Fortunately, I had taken the precaution of stationing a sizeable army northeast of Paris, a short march from the Rhenus. When I received Sigebert's call, I joined my men. I said some prayers to my pagan gods, and we set off.

It was but a little distance directly east to Tolbiac, but I judged that we should come down on the battle from the north, so we swept round to approach the fighting from that direction.

What a sight met our eyes! As we looked south, we saw Sigebert's men were in full flight, leaving many dead on the field. A vast multitude of Alemanni warriors covered the field like a plague of locusts.

They swayed back as we fell on them, obviously startled to be attacked by fresh men when they had thought the battle was finished.

I judged them to be but hordes of farmers, armed with swords and pikes, but little else. I thought, despite their numbers, we had the advantage. How wrong I was!

Their front line fell beneath our attack, then the men behind them, then the next rank. We hardly lost any men. I began to breathe easier. But as time passed, their numbers seemed not to have diminished at all. Then our men started to tire, and we lost one or two, here and there along our line. Each man we lost seemed to spur the Alemanni on more. Their onslaught seemed relentless.

Suddenly my heart was gripped by a fear I had never known. We would lose the battle!

I had never led my men into a battle that was lost; I had always felt supremely confident of victory, only requiring to keep a level head, and follow my plans. It had always gone my way. And now it was not.

I wildly searched in my mind for a correct course of action. I found no answer there. I considered retreat, but knew we would be followed and destroyed, even as Sigebert's men had been.

My mind turned to my beautiful wife. I would not return to her, not see her again, never know once more the gentle touch of her hand on my flesh.

As I thought of her, my mind reflected on her god. I found myself astonished that, this time, I did not feel angry against him. I knew not why, but it seemed strange. I felt almost as if - he knew my distress.

In this strange state of mind - part of the battle, yet somehow detached from it - I wondered on the way Clotilde seemed to talk to her god - as if he were really there!

Then - something crushed me. It was not physical, it was in my inner being. My soul was suddenly overcome by the realisation that my wife had been right, and I, all this time, had been wrong.

I shouted out to her god - out loud, caring not for the opinions of my men, 'God!' I cried, 'Clotilde's God! Can you not see how we fare? How we are overcome by our enemy - by your enemy? If you exist, come to our aid! Clotilde calls you the Living God! If you live, show yourself! Come to the aid of my men - my land - and I will devote my life to following you!'

The words had not fallen from my lips when there was a commotion to our right, to the west. Flames erupted from the western side of the battle. The eruption of fire sped towards the centre. Suddenly there was a shout of dismay from the Alemanni. They melted back before our eyes. I was perplexed as to what had befallen them. It reminded me of the way men behave when they lose their leader.

As they fell further back, the source of the fire became clearer. It was a cart, drawn by four horses. It had a strange apparatus mounted on it, and two men who seemed familiar.

'Rodor and Galba!' I urged my men forward. They took heart and we swept forward, against no resistance.

We reached the cart, and found the Alemanni king, blackened and burnt, beneath the wheels. 'Onwards!' I screamed at my men, 'Realise our victory! We have beheaded the Alemanni - make our victory secure!'

They swept past me, leaving me at the cart - the same that I had presented to Rodor. He was bent over Galba, who lay to one side. I leapt up onto the cart, but could see from his wounds that Galba had already left us, gone to his God - and I supposed, now, mine.

Rodor lay on his brother and wept great heaving sobs. I embraced them both and wept with him.

The Alemanni collapsed before my men, so far that we overran them. In the next few weeks, we established Frankish rule in their lands, and ensured payment of tribute and promises of allegiance.

After the battle I returned to Paris with Rodor and Galba's body, where he was buried that same day with great honour.

After the ceremony, I asked Rodor to join my wife and me in our private chambers.

'Rodor, would you explain to Queen Clotilde what brought you to the battle at Tolbiac?'

'Certainly, my Lord, my Lady. Twelve days ago I received a letter from Lufian. He is now King of the East Angli. I have it here.'

'Please, read it.'

Rodor, from Lufian.

You should know that I recently had a visitation from God. I know not whether I slept, or was awake, but I saw a man standing with a battle raging behind him. The man spoke to me 'Rodor - this battle is your battle. You need Greek fire. Tolbiac is the place. Go, now!'

I protested that my name was not Rodor, it was Lufian, then realised the message was not for me, but you. I pray that God will use you. May his blessing be upon you. Lufian.

Rodor continued. 'It took a day to acquire the needs for the journey, and to ascertain the location of Tolbiac, the other side of Paris. As soon as I told Galba, he was eager to accompany me. We equipped our cart to pump out Greek fire, and hitched four horses for speed, then came to Tolbiac with all the haste we could. The battle was before us. We could see the Franks being beaten back to our left. We decided to turn on the Greek Fire and head for the centre of the Alemanni, caring nothing for our own lives. We did not know we had killed their king until they suddenly fell back. By that time, my dear brother had been run through with a pike.'

'We are so sorry for your loss', said Clotilde. Silence reigned for a few moments, then she continued, 'but tell me again, when did you receive the letter from Lufian?'

'It would be twelve days ago, my Lady.'

'And the letter would have taken - how long - to reach you?'

'From Lufian, by boat, then across Armorica, about one or two weeks, my Lady.'

'And when did you receive the call for help from Sigebert?' This time her question was directed towards me. I could feel the sharpness of its direction.

'Ten days ago, my love.'

'So', her voice was slow and determined, 'these good people say that God spoke to them about your need', she fixed a steely eye upon me, 'weeks before you knew anything of it yourself!'

That night, as we embraced, an embrace I had not long ago considered lost to me, she lifted herself up on one elbow and stared into my face. 'Tell me what has happened to you.'

I told her about the battle, how it turned against us till all seemed lost, how I cried out to her God, and the sudden answer to my cry.

'That I knew, gossip has told me that, I want to know what has happened inside you! You are a different man! I knew as soon as you returned!'

Suddenly I felt very ashamed, and un-manly. 'You will think me weak, but when I asked for the help of your God, I vowed that I would follow him if he rescued us.'

'Weak? Weak?' She sat up and looked at me. I had never seen her so angry. 'It is not weak to follow the Living God!' She looked at me even more intently; I felt as if her eyes pierced my flesh, 'And will you keep your vow?'

I said nothing, but tears came unbidden to my eyes. I decided, in the privacy of our room, to let them flow. I put my face on her shoulder and sobbed. I sobbed for Galba, for the men I had lost, for Sigebert's men, but most of all for myself, a poor lost soul, who had thought himself so grand, but who had been sought out, pursued and captured by a God who had been following me for years.

Two days later, I called the Frankish clan chiefs together, with their families and friends, in my great hall in Paris. When the hubbub had died down a little, I called them to quietness. 'Listen carefully to me. You know that I have always followed Frankish gods, whereas my wife has followed a man. They call him God's son, and claim that he died and lived again. This God-man came to our aid at Tolbiac. We had no hope of victory. We were being wiped off the face of the earth by the Alemanni. It was then, in desperation, I called on him to help us. His answer was immediate, and you will have heard of our great victory, which has now brought us lands and tribute which we did not seek. I wish to tell you that I will now follow this man as my God.'

The hubbub started again. I banged on the table with my tankard, 'Quiet! In the custom of my new faith, I have asked Bishop Remi to baptise me in his church at Reims. All who wish to attend will be welcome.'

When I arrived at the church, early on that same winter's day that believers celebrate the birth of Yeshua, I was astonished to find around three thousand Franks had gathered. I remarked to Corbus that I was humbled because they had come to see me baptised. His reply staggered me. They had not come to see me baptised, he said, they had come to be baptised themselves.

The baptisms started with mine, in the early morning, and went on well past nightfall.

That night I returned to Paris, not just as king, but the head of a large community of believers.

Chapter Sixty-Five

The Old Woman

'Well, there it is, Ardith; that is my story - it started with Claennis and Lufian but ended with the beginning of Clovis's life as a believing King. I always pray for him that El Elyon will bless him and his rule, as He has blessed me. I have heard rumours, in the years since we had that letter from him, that Clovis has taken control of all the old Roman forts throughout Gaul, and that his Empire is now being called Francia. Is that not utterly too big to comprehend?'

It was now many weeks since Denua had started to tell me this history that was on her heart. I had settled in very well to her comfortable life. Spring had come upon us and a bright sun shone as we sat out in her garden.

I put down my stylus. 'And to think that would not have happened without one person, and I am sitting in her garden! How blessed am I!'

Chapter Sixty-Six
Epilogue

*D*enua opened her eyes. She had slept so well! The light was - odd. It was too bright, yet it seemed pleasant. The sound was odd too. Water. A lot of it. There was some sort of waterfall? No, the sound was too loud - very loud. Yet somehow, pleasantly loud.

A shadow fell across her vision. 'Hello, old friend.'

'Kursa! How long have you been - here?' Realisation slowly dawned. 'This is not our house! Where are we?'

Kursa laughed - a very loud laugh. Yet it was not deafening - a sound like honey would make - if something so sweet could make a sound.

'This is very strange! Kursa, what is happening?'

Kursa gave another guffaw. It sounded so - healthy. 'You'd better get up and come and see.' He put out his hand. His right hand!

'Not that hand... Kursa! Your hand - your arm!'

Kursa grabbed Denua - with his right arm - and lifted her to her feet. Denua noticed that her body felt different. It was an odd feeling; the pain in her left hip - she'd had it for the last few years - had gone!"

'Time for you to meet someone.' Kursa pointed up into the sky above them - the sky was too blue.

Denua caught her breath. There, towering above them, was an immense seated figure - they hardly reached his ankles. The figure was white - and glowing with colours, like a rainbow, but still white. Looking up, Denua thought she recognised the shining face, but couldn't place it.

The face slowly turned downwards to look at her.

As she remembered familiar words, she realised.

'May the Lord bless you and keep you.

May the Lord make his face shine upon you

and be gracious to you,

May the Lord turn his face toward you

and give you peace.'

She tried to speak again to Kursa, but she could not.

The face somehow seemed closer - approaching her - her own height. She looked into the sky. The figure was still there, yet - he was also here, with her, standing right beside her. Yeshua - for it was he - threw his huge arms around her and hugged her close. A whisper sounded in her ear. 'Well done, good and faithful servant!'

Appendix

Historical Events

Many of the individual events in the story are fictitious, but the whole is based upon historical accounts. Let me say straightaway that I am no accomplished historian, simply a researcher of histories of a time which attracts and intrigues me.

Most accounts of this time were written many years, even centuries, after the events. Legend and Chinese whispers may play a large part in their lack of concrete reliability. This means that often 'historical' accounts disagree among themselves. I have often had to choose between differing accounts to piece together my backdrop to the story.

My principles were to try to represent actual events, but where there was uncertainty, I have unashamedly chosen to tell a good story first, and let others argue over the 'facts'.

Names

I have chosen to represent, as closely as I can, what might have been the pronunciation of names at the time. For example, the Roman historian Tacitus referred to the Angles as 'Ingvaeones'. Other accounts shorten this to 'Ingvi', but in those days, the 'v' may have been pronounced 'w' so I have deliberately chosen to render the spelling as 'Ingwi' to give my readers the sound. Ironically, the pronunciation of the first syllable of 'England' has gone through 'Angle'-land, 'Aeng'-land, and has now returned to Tacitus's original 'Ing'-land. I have allowed this and other pronunciations to swing gently towards more modern versions as the story progresses.

You may also find that I have taken liberties with some names; in the interests of not distracting you with oddities, I have allowed myself the luxury of shortening some of the more difficult names so they are easier to read, so: 'Ragnar' for 'Ragnachar', and 'Caric' for 'Chararic' and so on. The originals are denoted in the list of names by an equals sign.

You may also think I've got some names wrong. That may be so. This sort of 'history' is disagreed on by nearly everybody. Do join in!

Major Themes

I have portrayed two major international events: The coming of the Angles and Saxons to Britain, which set the stage for the emergence of modern England, and the love story of Clovis and Clotilde, which set the stage for the emergence of modern France.

The Story of England

There really was a Vortigern and he was King of Rhegin, a land in the south of Britain with its capital at modern Chichester. The Romans had departed Britain in 410AD, leaving space for local leaders and regional kings to rise up in their place.

We know that Vortigern invited two brothers, Hengist and Horsa, to help fight off attacks from the raiding bands of the Picts. Hengist and Horsa were successful, and there was consequent friction as Vortigern tried to wriggle out of their agreement as the threat receded, and more Angles, Saxons and Jutes decided to settle in Eastern Britain. I have deliberately portrayed Hengist and Horsa as Angles, rather than Saxons, because different sources vary, and in any case, I wanted to tell the story of 'Angle-land'.

Vortigern did marry Rowena. She was many years his junior, and was somehow related to Hengist and Horsa. I have invented how.

Hengist did have a son, Octha, who apparently ruled after him. The accounts of Horsa indicate that he died in a battle in Kent. I have allowed him to reproduce!

(Saint) Patrick, of course, was also a real person, he originated from the west coast of Britain, was taken to Ireland as a slave, escaped, studied to be a priest in Auxerre (Alsiodorum) and other places in Gaul, and eventually went back to Ireland, where he worked with friends as a travelling evangelist.

The Story of France

France came from the lands ruled by the Franks, who were a warlike tribe, with several squabbling clans, either side of the banks of the Rhine (Latin: Rhenus). The Franks came into conflict with the Visigoths (West Goths) who were sweeping west through Europe, and the Alemanni, a Germanic tribe to the south east of the Franks, who also wanted

Frankish lands. Merovech (Marvig) became a Frankish tribal leader and his son Childeric followed him. His grandson, Clovis, united all the Franks on the west of the Rhine to face the threat from the invaders. He became the first proper 'King' of the Franks, and so, as his rule swept south, by the brilliant tactic of taking all the Roman forts, 'King of France'.

The name Clovis gradually became pronounced as 'Louis', becoming the popular name of many French rulers, and gives us 'Ludwig' and 'Lewis'.

Intriguing Mystery

A mystery I have tackled is how did this Frankish king Clovis come into contact with a captured and ill-treated Burgundian girl, Clotilde? As Saint Clotilde (sometimes Clotilda) she is well known in the early church records. But she was an ill-treated captive well to the south, whereas Clovis ruled lands far to the north. Yet they somehow met, and had a long marriage, and several children. The stories of their marriage bear the hallmarks of a love-match, rather than an arrangement. How puzzling!

About the Author

Philip Gregge

Philip Gregge became a Christian at university in Birmingham, UK, where he studied Optometry. He went on to study Theology at Birmingham Bible Institute and joined the leadership team of a charismatic church in Rugby, UK.

Philip enjoys teaching Theology and is the author of a Systematic Theology training manual which has been used successfully in study groups. He has a website called 'Let's Ask Phil', in which he answers a range of theological questions.

Regarding his writing journey, Philip describes waking up after a back operation with the germ of a plot in his head. He wrote an unpublished novelette about a murder mystery in Anglo-Saxon times. This whetted the fascination he already had for this historical period, and his research led him to write and publish this book, as he puts it, 'based upon history, but with some of the intriguing blanks filled in'.

Philip has been married to Anji for forty-seven years and they have three adult sons. In his spare time he plays dance music on the banjo in a small Irish Music band.